"Hope? It's really you? Ah...hi. What are you doing here?"

Luke reached out. With the utmost care, he clasped Hope's elbow to help her up.

Hope mumbled a thank-you, and became absorbed in brushing off her legs and her clothes. Drops of blood welled on her knees. When Luke pulled a blue-checked bandanna out of his back pocket and held it out to her, Hope's eyes shifted from the bandanna to Luke's hand...free of a wedding ring. Appalled by her own thoughts, she frowned.

"It's clean," he assured her. "Go ahead. Use it."

Her look had nothing to do with the bandanna and everything to do with bumping—literally—into the one person she was least prepared to see.

She didn't move, so Luke bent down and, placing one hand behind her knee, gently dabbed at the abrasions.

That simple, impersonal touch made her feel as if a two-hundred-and-twenty-volt electric current surged through her body.

Dear Reader,

My heroine, Hope, and I have a number of things in common, most notably our love of animals. Veterinarians have worked miracles for our furry, four-legged family members. They restored our Malamute's sight after a congenital disease rendered him nearly blind when he was barely a year old, saved our yellow Lab following a horrific adverse reaction to a vaccination, and years later cured his cancer.

When my husband and I had to say goodbye to our last three dogs, we were heartbroken. Then by happenstance we met Harley and Logan—both black Labs. They were eighteen and fourteen months old respectively at the time, didn't know each other and had only lived in kennels up to that point in their lives. Whether we thought ourselves ready for more dogs or not, they stole our hearts, adopted us and have enriched our lives in so many ways.

I offer sincere thanks to Hope's real-life counterparts—people who care for, rehabilitate and locate forever homes for the animals that find their way into shelters.

Thank you for choosing to read Hope's story. Whether by email, a letter, a comment through my website or a Tweet—I would love to hear from you.

Happy reading!

Kate

Email: readers@kate-james.com

Website: kate-james.com

Mail: PO Box 446, Schomberg, Ontario, L0G 1T0, Canada

HEARTWARMING

The Truth About Hope

Kate James

Recycling programs for this product may not exist in your area.

ISBN-13: 978-0-373-36724-5

The Truth About Hope

This edition published by arrangement with Harlequin Books S.A.

For questions and comments about the quality of this book, please contact us at CustomerService@Harlequin.com.

Printed in U.S.A.

Kate James spent much of her childhood abroad before attending university in Canada. She built a successful business career, but her passion has always been literature. As a result, Kate turned her energy to her love of the written word. Kate's goal is to entertain her readers with engaging stories featuring strong, likable characters. Kate has been honored with numerous awards for her writing. She and her husband, Ken, enjoy traveling and the outdoors with their beloved Labrador retrievers. Watch for her upcoming trilogy featuring a K-9 unit.

Books by Kate James

Harlequin Heartwarming

A Child's Christmas

To my parents.

Acknowledgments

I am privileged to have Paula Eykelhof as my editor.
Her brilliance, industry expertise and generosity
of spirit never cease to amaze me.
I can't thank her enough for both teaching me
and challenging me as I strive to perfect my craft.

I am also grateful to senior editor Victoria Curran
and the entire team at Harlequin.
They are a dream to work with!

CHAPTER ONE

Canyon Creek, Texas
August 2001

"I AM *NOT* moving to San Jose!" Hope Wilson surged out of her chair and sent it toppling.

Arthur Burrows raised a hand. "Calm down, please. I know this isn't easy for you."

Hope leaned forward, bracing her hands on the lawyer's desk. "Isn't *easy* for me?" Her eyes stung and she felt the familiar tightening in her chest, but she refused to let the tears come. The anger somehow made her feel alive again. "My mother's funeral was yesterday, now you tell me this, and you say it's not *easy*?"

"I know this is all very difficult. No one could've foreseen your mother passing away so suddenly. Why don't you sit down?" he encouraged her. "Let's finish going over your mother's will."

Instead, Hope spun around and moved to the window. Outside, the brilliant sunshine filtered through the high canopy of ash and oak trees. Wicker baskets hung from decorative lampposts, their profusion of flowers spilling over in bold sweeps of color. People strolled along the wide, cobblestoned sidewalks of Center Street, as if they didn't have a care in the world.

How could everything look so *normal* when her life was over?

"Hope, please sit down," Arthur repeated.

She was on the verge of another tirade but stopped herself. She couldn't blame Mr. Burrows. He hadn't caused her problems. He was her mother's lawyer, and if anybody could help her find a way out of this predicament, it would be him. It certainly wouldn't serve her purposes to antagonize him.

She turned from the window and strode to the chair, righted it and flopped down. Continuing to fight a battle with her temper, she could almost hear her mother's admonition about being polite and respectful. It made her want to cry again. "Sorry about the way I behaved just now," she said in a subdued voice. "But I'm *not* moving to San Jose."

"Now, Hope." Arthur sat back. "I'm afraid you don't have much choice."

"But my mother wanted Aunt Clarissa to take care of me. You said it's in her will."

"That's true," Arthur agreed patiently. "However, your father's rights override your mother's wishes in this case."

Hope's fury began to simmer once more, but it was overshadowed by a debilitating sense of anguish and fear, of being alone. "You can't make me leave Canyon Creek. I'm not a child anymore," she cried, but suddenly felt very much like one. Even to her own ears she sounded like one. She blinked furiously to stave off the tears.

"Look, Hope. I understand how upsetting this is for you, but you really *don't* have a say in the matter. According to Texas law, at seventeen you're still a minor. When I notified your father that Rebecca had passed away, his lawyer contacted me immediately. He was unequivocal about the fact that your father wants you to live with him." Arthur's voice turned conciliatory. "He's your *father*. He's *family*. Where better for you to be, with your mother gone?"

"He is *not* my family!" Hope raised her eyes to the ceiling and took three deep breaths. "He stopped being my father when he walked out on Mom and me, when I was two. I don't even remember him. Don't make me go," she pleaded. "Mom had some money saved, and I have our house. I can work part-time while I finish school."

"Hope, you don't have to do that. Your father is a very wealthy man. Financially, he's prepared to give you a lot more than the allowance your mother was receiving from him. He's willing to take you in, pay for your education. You can't imagine how hard that would be for you on your own, even if it was a possibility."

"What about what he did when he left? Closing down his business and hurting all the people who depended on those jobs? He and my mother grew up with the people who worked for him. What kind of man does that to his friends? How guilty do you think that's always made me feel? And you want me to go live with a man like that?"

"It's not a matter of *me* wanting you to live with him. It's what *he* wants."

Hope swiped a hand under her nose. "I don't want to leave. I want to stay here. Aunt Clarissa said she'd move to Canyon Creek to be with me. You're a lawyer. Can't you figure something out?" she beseeched. "Other kids my age are allowed to live on their own."

"It's called *emancipation* and it's rare. There has to be a reason for a court to grant that. I'm afraid there's no compelling argument in your case. Take some time, Hope. Get used to the idea. I'm sure it'll turn out just fine."

LUKE CARTER PUSHED away from the bicycle rack he'd been leaning against as soon as Hope came out of the building. With his long strides, he was next to her almost instantly. "How did it go?"

"Okay," she mumbled, walking past him.

"Hey. *Hey!*" He hurried after her and reached for her hand. "You don't look like it went okay."

She yanked free and stuffed both hands in her pockets to keep Luke from grabbing one again. Her head bent, she moved forward at a brisk pace.

"Hey!" He passed her and stopped directly in her path, grasping her shoulders. She kept her head lowered, her long mahogany hair hiding her face. Luke shook her gently and bent down to study her face. "It's me. You can't lie to me."

When Hope remained silent, he gave her another light shake. "It's *me*," he said again. "You can tell me anything."

On top of the pain and fear, Hope was now livid with herself. What was she doing, shutting him out? This was *Luke*. Her best friend since they were in grade school. Her *boyfriend* since last year. Luke had been there for her all her life. She knew firsthand how hard it was when people you cared about left you—as her father had and now in a different way her mother, too. How could she tell Luke that she was leaving Canyon Creek? That she was leaving *him*.

Hope let out a ragged breath. Through lowered lashes, she studied Luke's perfect face, the thick mop of chestnut-brown hair and those expressive gold-flecked amber eyes that made her think of a lion. How was she going to do it? How was she going to break the news to Luke, explain to all their friends that she was going to live with the man who'd caused so much harm to their town and to many of their families?

She pulled one hand out of her pocket and placed it gently in the crook of Luke's arm. "I just need a little time." She saw the flicker of frustration on his face before compassion eclipsed it. He took a step back and to the side. "Yeah, okay. But remember I'm here. Whatever you need. We've always been there for each other."

"I know." She rose up on her toes to kiss his cheek. "I appreciate it."

Hope walked home alone to the little brick

bungalow she and her mother had shared since they'd been on their own and let herself in.

Once inside, she stood very still. Everything was the same, but everything had changed.

She knew Aunt Clarissa was there because her Camry was parked in the driveway.

Aunt Clarissa, who lived in San Antonio about two-and-a-half hours southwest, had hurried to Canyon Creek to be with Hope when Hope's mother had collapsed from a burst brain aneurysm a week ago, killing her without any symptoms or warning. Fortunately, as a survey associate for a market research company, Clarissa was able to work anywhere there was a telephone and an internet connection. They'd talked about Clarissa's moving to Canyon Creek and becoming Hope's legal guardian, as her mother's will specified. With the lawyer's bombshell, that was no longer an option.

Maybe if Clarissa was truly her aunt it would've been possible. But just like Hope, her mother had been an only child. Rebecca and Clarissa had become best friends as teenagers, and Clarissa was the closest thing to family that Hope had. She'd called her aunt since she was a toddler and loved her as much as she could've loved any family member.

Clarissa had wanted to accompany her to

the meeting with the lawyer, but Hope knew Clarissa was in the middle of a project with a tight deadline. When a problem had arisen that morning, Hope had insisted she'd be fine on her own. Besides, Luke had offered to walk over to the lawyer's office with her, to keep her company and then wait for her outside. In the end, Clarissa had agreed to stay home. Now Hope had to tell her what the lawyer had said. Unlike the way she had with Luke, she wouldn't be able to forestall the inevitable with Clarissa.

Hope found Clarissa in the kitchen, bent over her laptop, fingers flying across the keys. Red-framed reading glasses perched on the bridge of her nose, and her hair looked as if she'd dragged her fingers through it more than once. Her foot tapped the tile floor to some silent beat. Clarissa always seemed to have limitless energy, yet just seeing her calmed Hope and eased her feeling of despair.

Clarissa had been there for her, as had Luke, in the long, dark days since her mother died. Now Hope would have to say goodbye to her, too. Canyon Creek and Clarissa's home in San Antonio were a world away from where she'd be living in California. Hope's throat clogged with unshed tears, and she tried to clear it with a little cough.

Clarissa's fingers stilled. Noticing Hope, she jumped up and rushed over, pulling her into a comforting hug. "You're back. How'd it go?"

"Not good" was Hope's muffled response.

With a final squeeze, Clarissa stepped away and searched Hope's face. The concern in her eyes was enough to make Hope lose control, and her body began to shake.

Clarissa slid an arm around Hope's waist and guided her to the kitchen table. "Here. Sit. I'll get you a cup of tea." She passed Hope a box of tissues, fixed two cups of tea and sat next to her. "I knew I should've gone with you. I just *knew* it. Tell me what happened."

Hope reached for a tissue and blew her nose. "The lawyer—Mr. Burrows—he says I have to live with my father. Move to San Jose," Hope said in a strangled voice.

"Your *father*?" Clarissa appeared shocked. "How is that possible?"

Hope's face crumpled, and another deluge of tears threatened. She managed to explain what the lawyer had told her. "He...he said I...I don't have a choice." Her voice sounded that of a much younger child rather than the adult she had so vehemently asserted she was to Arthur Burrows. "What am I going to *do*?"

Although they'd spoken about the possible scenarios, Clarissa had insisted she'd move to

Canyon Creek so Hope wouldn't have to leave her school and her friends. Now it seemed she'd be uprooted anyway, forced to live in a place she'd never seen, with a father who was a complete stranger to her. "This is so unfair," she wailed. "Mom was only forty-three. Why did she have to die?"

Hope's hands were busy shredding a damp tissue, and Clarissa enfolded them in her own. "There are no easy answers to your questions, honey. I'm not sure anyone knows what causes a brain aneurysm, and there's no telling when or if it will rupture. It was sudden, which means your mom didn't suffer. There should be some comfort in that."

Hope pulled her hands back and dropped her head into them as she continued to weep.

Clarissa wrapped her arms around Hope and rocked her gently. "Oh, Hope. I'm *so* sorry." When Hope's tears slowed and her breathing leveled, Clarissa eased back. She got another tissue and mopped the moisture streaming from Hope's eyes. "I should've gone with you."

"No. No, it's okay. It wouldn't have changed anything."

"Well, this isn't right." Clarissa rose. Riffling through the letters and notes in a basket on the kitchen counter, she located the lawyer's business card.

Hope felt a glimmer of optimism. She held her breath as Clarissa had a mostly one-sided conversation with Arthur Burrows, concluding the call with "I see. Yes, tomorrow's fine" and a curt "Thank you."

"What did Mr. Burrows say?" Hope asked as Clarissa sat back down.

She smoothed a few tendrils of Hope's hair from her forehead. "I'm going to see him tomorrow. We'll see what can be done."

HOPE WAS SITTING on the front steps of the house, a book on her lap, when Clarissa returned from her meeting with the lawyer. Clarissa lowered herself to the step and slid an arm around Hope's shoulders, drawing her close.

"I'm sorry, honey," Clarissa began. "I think Mr. Burrows is right. If your father wants you to live with him, there's not much we can do."

"But you said I could stay with you!"

"I did. But I never expected that we'd hear from your father—or that he'd insist on having you live with him."

"Can't we stop him? Can't we get him to change his mind?"

Clarissa ran a hand down the length of Hope's hair.

"I don't think so. Your father has the law on his side. Jock's lawyer made it clear to Mr.

Burrows that he's adamant. Mr. Burrows didn't get the feeling that it was negotiable."

"Can't we take some sort of legal action?"

"Your father has money, lots of it. Even if we wanted to fight him in court, we'd run out of money long before Jock felt the slightest ripple in his net worth. I'm sorry, but I can't see any way around it. It'll be okay, honey," Clarissa tried to reassure Hope.

"How *can* it be? I don't *know* my father. I've never been to California. You and Luke and all my friends are here. It's going to be *awful*."

"I'm sure it's not going to be that bad. We'll only be a phone call, Skype or email away. I'm certain your father will let you visit, too."

"That…that's not…the same." Hope could barely get the words out, she was sobbing so hard.

"Come here… Shh." Clarissa held Hope tighter. "You're going to be eighteen in less than a year. At eighteen, you'll legally be an adult. If things don't work out for you with your father, you can live with me then. But give it a chance first, okay?"

"It's almost a whole year. My friends will forget about me. And Luke…Luke will have a new girlfriend."

Hope thought about her father leaving her. Now her mother was gone, and it seemed that

Aunt Clarissa was abandoning her, too, despite her promise. If she moved, Hope faced losing everyone close to her. She'd be all alone.

CHAPTER TWO

SLEEP ELUDED HOPE that night. When she wasn't crying, she was either staring up at the ceiling or out the window at the black velvet sky with its myriad of diamond-bright stars. By morning, her eyes were so puffy she could hardly open them, and it felt as if there was a jackhammer pounding in her head.

Despite the sleepless night, she hadn't come up with a way to resolve her dilemma. Based on what the lawyer and Aunt Clarissa had told her, she had a week. In that time she'd have to pack whatever she was taking to California, leave everyone who mattered to her and prepare for her life to end.

Hope groaned when she saw her reflection in the bathroom mirror. She splashed cold water on her face, cleaned her teeth and ran a brush through her hair. She didn't look much better, but it would have to do.

The long, sleepless night had driven one

thing home: there was no alternative. This was her reality.

Aunt Clarissa had breakfast ready by the time Hope shuffled into the kitchen, although it was still shy of six. They ate in silence, neither of them knowing what to say.

While she played with the food on her plate, Hope tried to find the words to tell everyone, but didn't come up with anything workable. Worst of all, she had no idea how she was going to say goodbye to Luke. She had to see him first. She knew how quickly news spread in their small community, and she didn't want to risk having Luke hear it from someone other than her. Malcolm Rutledge, Luke's best friend and as close to her as a brother, would be next.

Then she'd figure out the rest.

After helping Clarissa with the dishes, she pulled her backpack out from the bottom of her closet. She stuffed in a bottle of water, a notepad and pen, her mobile phone and the book she was currently reading. She put on a pair of sunglasses and set out.

But she wasn't ready to face Luke. She followed the road until it intersected with McCullock Street. With no definite plan, she turned left and continued walking until the street started to rise. There she took a right onto Yardley Drive and walked all the way to the end. The road dead-ended on a promontory, which had been made into a park and observation area. It was the highest point in Canyon Creek, and it provided a panoramic view of the whole town, Gulch River snaking around its perimeter and, in the distance, the silvered surface of Stillhouse Hollow Lake.

It was early and the park was tranquil. It would be at least an hour before the chatter of preschoolers and the exuberance of dogs would shatter the quiet. For now, it was just her and a handful of joggers taking advantage of the relatively cool temperatures.

Hope flung her backpack on a wooden bench and sat beside it. The early-morning sun gilded homes, land, river and lake, giving it all an ethereal luminosity. She'd heard that Northern California was beautiful, but how could it compare to her hometown? She'd never been outside Texas. She'd never wanted to be.

A bubble of panic formed in her belly, and she pressed a hand over it. No, she wouldn't let herself fall apart again. It was too important to handle her discussions today with a level head. She kept her eyes on the vista before her. The town that was her home, the town that in one short week she might never see again.

She blinked back the tears.

No! That couldn't be. *Of course* she'd see the

town again. She'd be back to visit her friends and, as Clarissa had pointed out, in less than a year she'd be an adult and could do as she pleased. She could come home if she wanted, and she did. Everything she knew and cared about was here. She'd just have to get through the next year and—

"Well, you're up early."

Twisting on the bench, Hope saw Suzie Walbridge behind her. Suzie, obviously in the middle of a run, was bent at the waist, hands on her knees, head lowered. She wore cropped, black spandex pants and a hot-pink tank top. The color of her Nikes matched her top. Her long blond hair was tied in a ponytail that hung over her head, its ends skimming the blades of grass.

Hope and Suzie were classmates, but Suzie didn't like her. Hope suspected it might have had something to do with Luke. Suzie had never had a kind word to say to her in all the years they'd known each other. The last thing Hope wanted right now was a confrontation. She needed all her wits and energy for what lay ahead.

"Look, Suzie. It's a big park. Can't you find somewhere else to take a rest?"

Suzie lifted her head and flipped back her ponytail. Her vivid blue eyes drilled into Hope's.

"I could...but I don't want to." She straightened and tugged her water bottle out of its holster on her belt and took a long drink. "This is where I always take my break. I don't plan to change my routine for you."

Hope shrugged and tried to ignore her.

The sun had crept up in the sky. The gold sheen it had cast over land and buildings had faded. Focusing on the silver-blue surface of the lake in the distance, Hope willed herself to stay calm. She was doing a pretty good job until Suzie stepped into her line of vision.

"Go away, Suzie, and leave me alone."

Suzie placed her hands on her trim hips and bent backward from her waist, moving her torso in small circles. "You want to be alone, huh? Shouldn't be too hard. Who'd want to hang around with you anyway?"

Hope had just about had enough. She tried for calm one last time. "Can we not do this today?"

"Why not?" Suzie narrowed her eyes. "Hmm... you know, you don't look so good this morning. Did yummy Luke see you like this and tell you to get yourself together or he'd break up with you?"

Hope shot to her feet, clenching her fists at her sides. All the years of conflict with Suzie converged in that single moment, bound up with Hope's anguish at losing her mother and her fear of losing everything she knew. "This has *nothing* to do with Luke!" She bent over to lift up her pack, but Suzie pulled it out of her reach.

"I bet it does," Suzie taunted.

Hope felt the pressure build in her chest at the thought of leaving him. It was for only a year, she tried to convince herself, but her thin thread of control finally snapped. "Leave me alone," she repeated. "In a week, I'll have left Canyon Creek."

She unclenched her fists and went very still. Had she really said that? Had she blurted out to Suzie, of all people, that she was leaving?

"Where are you going?" Suzie asked. "Like a vacation?"

Hope's body remained rigid but her mind worked furiously. What should she say? How should she handle this so Suzie wouldn't see her as a helpless victim? She couldn't bear to let her think that. "It's not a vacation. I'm moving," she said. "I..." She was still searching desperately for a way out. It was bad enough that everyone already felt sorry for her because of her father and now her mother. She couldn't, *wouldn't*, let Suzie know the depth of her misery. "I'm going to live with my father."

"Your *father*?"

Hope nodded. "Yes. My father. In San Jose."

"You're going? Just like that?"

Hope had to save face. She couldn't bear the idea of explaining to Suzie that she didn't have a choice. "This is my big chance," she improvised. "You can't imagine how rich my father is. He could buy this whole town, if he wanted to!" Suzie's obvious glee was replaced by…what? Envy? It didn't matter. Hope was on a roll. "Me? I'm tired of just hanging around here." She made a sweeping motion with her arm toward the town spread out below the precipice. "I'm going to be rich, like my father. Do you realize how great San Jose is?" She'd checked it out on the internet; she'd been able to see her father's place on Google Earth. "My father has a huge house," she boasted.

Suzie stared at her, speechless.

Hope pushed her sunglasses higher on her nose and fixed what she considered a gloating smile on her face.

Suzie opened her mouth, then closed it again. Finally, she mumbled, "Good for you" and jogged away.

Well, she'd done it. This wasn't the way Hope had wanted to communicate things, but at least no one would feel sorry for her—and there wasn't much she could do about it now. Not only was Suzie unkind, she was an incorrigible gossip. Their conversation would be town fodder in no time.

Then the realization struck her. She hadn't told Luke yet! "Oh, my gosh," she exclaimed. She *had* to speak with Luke.

Hope grabbed her pack and raced across the field, down Yardley Drive and toward Luke's house. While she ran, she tried to figure out what to say. She didn't like being helpless. She didn't like not being in control. She didn't want him feeling sorry for her.

She came to a sudden stop and tried to catch her breath.

What if he wanted to go with her? They'd talked about where they'd go to college. Luke had insisted that he'd go wherever she did.

Would he do that? Go to San Jose with her? Her mood brightened. He was the one person who wouldn't desert her. Then she wouldn't be all alone.

But that was selfish. His family was struggling to make ends meet since his father had left them. That was a common bond they shared—the fact that they each had only a mother. But he had a younger brother, Travis. Luke worked after school, on weekends and all through the summer to help out. Travis wasn't old enough to have a job; he did his share by looking after the chickens and goats they raised. How would his family get by if Luke left? Besides, how could he afford to live in San Jose and finish school? No, it was out of the question.

Hope loved Mrs. Carter almost as much as her own mother. Yes, Luke would be going to college in another year, but Hope couldn't be responsible for his leaving before that, making life even harder for his mom and younger brother.

The more Hope thought about it, the more she realized how easy it had been to let Suzie think it was *her* own decision. That she wasn't a victim, and she needn't be pitied.

That would be her story. Now that she'd told Suzie, everyone would know what she'd said anyway. Why not just let them believe it?

Suzie had probably told lots of people by now. No longer having to race against the clock, Hope walked resolutely to Luke's house.

She found him outside, working in the chicken coop. He was hunched over, his back to her, collecting eggs. He was so tall, so strong, things that had attracted her when they'd already been best friends. "Hey," she called out.

Luke jerked upright, banging his head on the two-by-four beam at the top of the opening. He grunted loudly. Rubbing his head, he backed out of the coop and straightened. His look of mild irritation turned to pleasure when he saw her. "Hey to you, too, Sprite," he responded, using his nickname for her. He hurried over and brushed his lips lightly across hers. "Here, I'll take that." He reached for her backpack.

She moved the strap farther up her shoulder. "No. It's okay."

His eyes narrowed briefly, and then the smile was back on his face. He gently set the bucket of eggs down on the grass and slung an arm around her shoulders. Since his arm nestled her tightly against his side, it would've been awkward to resist, so she let him lead her. And it felt so good. She wished she could turn into his arms and he'd tell her everything would be okay. She resisted the temptation. It wasn't going to happen. Nothing was going to be okay ever again, she thought as they walked along.

Hope could guess where they were going. To the swimming pond on the Hawkins ranch abutting the Carter property. All the kids were welcome to use it. The large rock at the edge of the pond was one of their favorite spots. That was where they'd first kissed. Where they'd first said they loved each other. It was a special, magical place for her, and she knew it was for Luke, too.

She stopped abruptly. If that was where she told him, the magic would be gone. It didn't matter to her, or so she tried to convince herself. But was it fair to ruin it for Luke? On the other hand, maybe that was fitting. Maybe it had to happen there. Where it all started would be where it ended, too. Where she'd shatter their dreams.

They walked in silence, the only sounds the crunching of the dry grass beneath their feet, the whinny of a horse in the distance and the mournful cry of a dove gliding overhead.

When they reached the rock by the cattail-edged blue-brown water, Luke dropped his arm. As Hope slipped off her backpack and climbed up, Luke took a small bag of crumbled bread from his pocket, which he habitually kept there for the chickens, and held it out to her. She grabbed a handful and began tossing it into the pond. They watched the koi leap and dance as they fed.

Luke nudged Hope with his shoulder. "So, are you going to tell me what's on your mind?"

It was now or never. "I've been thinking… With Mom gone…it changes things."

"Oh, Hope…"

He reached for her, but she pulled away. There was no easy way to do it. She just had to get it out. "I'm leaving Canyon Creek."

"What?" The word exploded from Luke's mouth. "What do you mean you're leaving?"

She inched farther away from him. She couldn't go through with it if she could feel him next to her, touching her. His nearness made her resolve waver. Her heart was racing, and there was a terrible constriction in her chest that made breathing almost impossible, but she tried to keep her voice unaffected. "I'm going to live with my father in California."

Luke jumped off the rock. Bracing his arms on either side of her legs, he caged her in. "Your *father*? The man you can't remember? The man who practically destroyed this town?"

"He's still my father."

Luke shook his head, but kept his eyes, intense and angry, on hers. "What kind of sick joke is this?"

Hope broke eye contact, focusing on a spot over his left shoulder. She couldn't continue, if she had to keep looking into his furious gaze. "It's *not* a joke."

"You're not making sense. Why would you do that?"

"Because he asked."

Luke turned, picked up a large stone and heaved it into the water, where it landed with a splash. He watched the ripples spread before turning back. His voice was more controlled when he spoke again. "Hope, what's this all about? You don't want to live with your father."

He knew her too well. She nearly shrieked that, no, she didn't want to. She almost begged him to make it all go away. Instead, she nodded slowly. "Yes. It *is* what I want."

"It makes no sense. Why?"

She slid off the rock and threw up her arms. "I'm tired of living in a place that's so small everyone knows your business. I'm tired of not being able to buy a new pair of sneakers or go on a school trip because I can't afford it." More calmly now, and with full honesty, she added, "And I can't impose on Aunt Clarissa. I can't expect her to move here and give up her life to take care of me."

"She'd do it. She loves you. Or you can live with us. Mom won't mind. Travis would love it."

"No, Luke. I'm leaving," she said emphatically. And with finality.

CHAPTER THREE

IT WAS HOPE'S first time on a plane. With every passing minute, she was inexorably transported toward an uncertain and terrifying future. The distance between her and everything she knew and loved increased. Far below, the ranches formed a patchwork quilt of greens and browns. The occasional ribbon of blue water haphazardly transected the rectangles of varying textures and sizes. Gauzy white clouds drifted by.

Hope leaned her forehead against the cool window and thought about her mother as she watched the ground rush by. It still didn't seem possible that she wouldn't see her bright, vivacious, loving mother again. When reality did come crashing down on her, the weight of it seemed too much to bear. Her reflections turned to her father, what she'd known and what she'd learned over the past week.

Jock Wilson had left her and her mother

when Hope was barely two. She wasn't aware of the details because her mother never talked about it. Aunt Clarissa didn't know much either or, if she did, she wouldn't say. Her father had taken off to make a fortune with the internet. Hope had no idea if he'd wanted them to move with him and her mother had refused, or if he'd simply left without giving them a choice. Hope wondered if he'd enlighten her, but did it really matter?

Her father had owned and operated a computer components manufacturing plant in Canyon Creek. He was reputed to be one of the most successful businessmen in the area at that time. Evidently it hadn't been enough for him. She and her mother hadn't been enough.

Manufacturing was a huge contributor to the Texas economy, and a lot of people in Canyon Creek had earned their living at her father's plant. His company had been one of the largest employers in town. As a consequence, her father's leaving—or more accurately, the closing of his plant—had created considerable hardship. Nearly everyone in Canyon Creek had been negatively affected.

Hadn't Luke thrown it at her when he'd mentioned her father's having destroyed the town? Many people had lost their jobs, Luke's father among them. The impact on the local economy was still talked about fifteen years later.

Hope had heard, too, that her father's employees wanted to buy the business from him, but he'd refused their offer. Instead he'd closed the plant.

She would've thought he'd want the proceeds from the sale of his business, either to his employees or a competitor. Aunt Clarissa told her it had to do with some sort of financial advantage folding the company would create for him. Apparently he wanted to show he'd *lost* money on it. One thing she understood about her father was that he was a shrewd businessman. It must have made sense for him from a business perspective, if not a human one.

The building had sat empty for years until it was finally torn down. Now there was a Taco Bell and a gas station where the plant had been.

After Jock Wilson left Canyon Creek, no one heard from him again, as far as Hope knew. If he'd had any contact with her mother, Hope was unaware of it. Her mother had received some sort of financial support, but again the details were sketchy, and it couldn't have been much. Hope speculated that might be part of the reason her father had wanted to show a business loss, to decrease the amount of support he'd have to pay.

Whatever the circumstances behind her parents' split, it had obviously been acrimonious. There hadn't been a single picture of her father in their home. The only images Hope had of him were those she'd found on the internet.

He was a tall, distinguished-looking man, slender, with short, slicked-back hair. She guessed the color of his hair would've been close to hers at one time, but now it was streaked with gray. His eyes weren't anything like her deep brown ones, though. They were a piercing slate gray. There was no warmth in them, judging by what she could see in the pictures. Even when he smiled, it never touched his eyes. She pulled a picture from the side pocket of her backpack to refresh her memory of the man who was her father.

Examining the picture, Hope resented the guilt she felt every time she remembered what her father had done. But was she any better? Here she was, leaving Canyon Creek, too. As far as everyone was concerned, her reasons weren't very different from her father's—and she was the one who'd convinced them of that.

A few days after her run-in with Suzie, Hope had come to appreciate the significance of her impulsive actions. She'd been prepared to endure the move to San Jose, with the expectation that when she turned eighteen, she'd come home again. But what she'd done—what she'd *said*—made that impossible.

With the pretense she'd created, there was no way she could return. The dynamics had already shifted during the week since her "revelation." People treated her differently.

What she had done weighed heavily on her. Aunt Clarissa had urged her to tell everyone the truth, but Hope couldn't bring herself to do it. She just didn't have the strength or the energy to set things right. Still believing that moving to San Jose was her decision, Luke had tried to change her mind until the very end. She couldn't forget the look of hurt and anger—and astonishment—on his face when she'd seen him that last time. When she'd told him there was nothing left in Canyon Creek for her. In some respects that was true. Her father had made all the arrangements to settle her mother's estate, what there was of it, and sell their small house and its contents. She was on her way to her father's with nothing more than a few suitcases and no idea what lay ahead.

Usually she looked forward to summer. Being out of school, working with her mother at the garden center where she was a manager and being with Luke. But now the months without classes stretched unnervingly ahead of her.

The plane was soaring higher, shrouded in dense white clouds. She put in earplugs, laid her head back against the seat and closed her eyes—until she suddenly jolted awake. Confused, she glanced outside and saw that they were on the ground and the tarmac was rushing past at an alarming speed. She clasped the armrests to steady herself and wondered where they were. Hadn't they just taken off? Checking her watch, she was surprised to find that she'd been asleep for over three hours.

The plane slowed and pivoted, and the terminal building came into view; they were at the gate in minutes.

As soon as the flight attendant announced that it was safe to do so, Hope gathered her belongings. Having been seated in business class, she was among the first passengers to deplane. She made her way to the baggage carousel, searching for her father.

There was no tall, slender, silver-haired man that she could see. A hint of panic shot through her. Then she noticed a man in a dark blue suit walking toward her. Surely this wasn't her father. He couldn't be. He was shorter than she'd imagined, had a stockier build, and his hair was thick and black. Most significantly, he couldn't have been much older than thirty.

But he was definitely headed in her direction. She took an involuntary step back as he reached her.

He swept his gaze over her. "Are you Ms. Hope Wilson?"

She wanted to take another step back but resisted. "Yes."

He nodded. "I'm Mr. Wilson's chauffeur, Morris. I'll take you to his home."

"Oh" was all she could say. It came out as a squeal. Here she was, leaving her *life* behind, and her *father* couldn't meet her himself? She didn't think she could've been more disappointed, but she'd been wrong. And the chauffeur hadn't said "your father." Or "your home." She hadn't realized that she'd nurtured some small kernel of hope that maybe—just maybe—her father wouldn't be as bad as she dreaded. That he'd welcome her and they'd be able to find some common ground.

Instead, he'd sent his chauffeur. Hope had an overwhelming urge to run back up the bridge, back on the plane. But that wouldn't have accomplished anything.

With a sinking heart, she knew her only option was to go with this Mr. Morris, to a house that wouldn't be her home, to a man who'd be a father to her in name only.

She wouldn't let them see her pain and disappointment. She straightened her spine. "Thank you, Mr. Morris," she said with as much dignity as she could muster.

"It's just Morris, miss," he clarified, as he took her backpack and arranged for a porter to carry the rest of her luggage to the sleek, silver limousine waiting at the curb.

Soon they were driving through a residential area with gated properties, pristine lawns, tall hedges and sprawling gardens. As Morris signaled a turn into one of the entrances, Hope shifted forward to get a better look. Black wrought-iron gates opened smoothly to let them pass and they drove along a textured concrete surface intersecting areas of brilliant green, perfectly trimmed turf. Rows of towering palm trees marched along on either side. As they rounded a curve and the house came into view, Hope sucked in a breath. It wasn't a house. It was a *mansion*.

Grand and imposing, it had turrets and balconies and iron railings. The walls were warm, butternut-yellow stucco, the roof deep-red clay tile and the wood of the doors, shutters and trim a rich coffee brown. Flowering shrubs abounded. Although it was just early evening, lights glowed cheerful and inviting.

Morris pulled up adjacent to a set of wide stone stairs leading to the front portico and ornately carved double doors.

Hope was so stunned by the magnificent mansion her father called home that she sat motionless, even when Morris held the car door for her.

"Miss," he prompted, and she glanced up, having almost forgotten he was there.

She exited the car, grateful for the hand he offered. She moved toward the trunk, but Morris forestalled her. "I'll take care of your luggage. You go on in."

Hope climbed the steps, and before she reached the landing, the door opened. A woman in her early thirties, with a pleasant, serene face, shoulder-length brown hair and wearing a pale blue uniform, stood in the entryway. A small smile curved her lips and she seemed to curtsy, more a bob of her head. "Welcome to Glencastle, Miss Hope. I'm Priscilla. We're happy to have you here."

Those simple words pierced Hope's heart. If only her father *was* glad to have her, things might've been tolerable. But she didn't believe it for a moment. If he'd been happy, why wouldn't he have met her at the airport or at least greeted her here?

She forced herself to be more positive. Maybe there was a good reason for his absence. He was an important businessman. Maybe he had an unavoidable meeting. "When will my father be home?" she asked timidly.

"He *is* home, miss. Come in, please." Priscilla gestured for Hope to enter the vestibule and left the door open for Morris, who was right behind them with some of Hope's luggage.

Hope's heart sank further. Her father *was* home and didn't consider it important enough to meet her? "Will you take me to him?" she asked, unsure of herself.

"That's not possible. He's busy right now. You'll see him later, as he made sure he'd be dining at home, since this is your first night here. Well, come with me. I'll take you to your rooms."

Hope followed Priscilla up an elaborate circular staircase. An enormous chandelier hung overhead, dripping with sparkling crystals, and paintings with bold slashes of color decorated the curved walls. Priscilla led her down a hall and through a doorway.

"These will be your rooms," Priscilla announced. "If there is anything that's not to your liking, please let me know and I'll take care of it."

Hope hugged her backpack tightly to her chest and entered the enormous room. Or rather, suite of rooms. There was a sitting area with a large flat-screen TV and sound system, an alcove with a desk, and a large bedroom, with an adjoining bathroom. Morris must have taken another stairway, as two of her suitcases were already inside, next to the corridor leading to the bedroom.

"Would you like me to unpack for you?" Priscilla offered.

"Oh, no, thank you." Hope managed a smile, grateful for this small offer of kindness. "If you don't mind, I'd like to rest for a while."

Priscilla nodded. "I should've realized you'd be tired. You've been traveling, and it must all be very difficult for you. Can I get you anything?"

"A cold drink would be nice, thank you."

"Of course. I'll be right back." Priscilla executed another little head-bob as she backed out of the room. No sooner was she gone than Morris appeared with her other suitcases.

Hope had barely had time to open her first bag before Priscilla was back with a silver tray holding a pitcher of iced tea, a glass and a plate of sugar cookies. She placed it on the coffee table in the sitting area. Pulling a small cell phone from her pocket, she set it next to the tray. "I'll leave this for you. I've put my number in it. If you need anything, just call."

"Thank you," Hope murmured. She imagined she looked as forlorn and miserable as she felt, because Priscilla gave her a reassuring smile. "You'll get used to it here. Take all the time you need to settle in."

Rather than easing Hope's trepidation, Priscilla's compassion threatened to destroy what was left of her composure. "I…I…" To her horror, tears welled in her eyes. She dropped her backpack and covered her face with her hands.

Seconds later, Hope felt Priscilla's arms around her. The woman smelled of lavender and cinnamon. She rubbed Hope's back reassuringly. "Shh. Shh," she soothed. "You've been through a lot. Take a rest or a bath. Leave the unpacking. I'll take care of that for you later. Just relax for now."

Hope accepted her comfort for a minute before stepping back and brushing at the moisture on her cheeks. "So I get to meet my father at dinner?"

Priscilla reached forward, then seemed to reconsider and dropped her hand. "Yes. It's at eight, as it is every night Mr. Wilson dines at home. I'm supposed to finish work at five, but I often don't leave until well after. I've made arrangements to stay late this evening. I'll come and get you shortly before eight to escort you to the dining room."

Priscilla's gaze skimmed over Hope's T-shirt, jeans and sneakers. "You might want to wear something else. A dress, maybe. Your father believes in dressing for dinner." Priscilla's face softened. She motioned toward the cell phone. "Please call if there's anything I can do."

HOPE WAS WEARING her best dress, a pretty floral print her mother had bought for her seventeenth birthday. Simply seeing the dress made her long for her mother, but she'd managed to contain her grief by the time Priscilla came to fetch her shortly before eight. Walking into the spacious, formal dining room, Hope noted that everything appeared old and staid, in stark contrast to the modern feel of what she'd seen of the rest of the house. There was a well-worn carpet on the floor, an imposing wooden table with matching chairs upholstered in rich brocade, and deep-rose velvet drapes edging the tall windows.

Soft music, something classical, was playing in the background.

Seated at the head of the long table was

her father. He had a narrow, chiseled face and short-cropped gray hair. He wore a charcoal suit, white shirt and a yellow-and-blue paisley tie. There was a stack of papers in front of him and he held a multifaceted crystal tumbler filled with a rich gold liquid. A man, formally attired in a black suit and tie and wearing white gloves, was standing behind her father. For some reason Hope wanted to giggle. Instead, she said a silent thanks to Priscilla for her advice about what to wear. In her jeans, she would've been seriously underdressed and would've felt at an even greater disadvantage. Self-consciously she smoothed her hands down her skirt.

Her father's eyes shot up, a pale gray, no warmer than they'd been in the photographs she'd seen of him.

"Well, don't just stand there." Her father's voice boomed across the great expanse of the room. "Come, come." He gestured toward the place setting to his right without rising. "Have a seat."

Priscilla pushed Hope gently from behind. "Go ahead. It'll be fine," she murmured in her ear. "He won't respect you if he thinks you're afraid of him," she added in a whisper.

Hope felt her knees wobble and was relieved that they weren't actually knocking together so that her father would notice. When she reached the chair, the black-suited man pulled it out for her. She mumbled a thank-you and began to sit—only to spring up again as she felt the chair hit the backs of her legs, presumably because the man had pushed it in for her.

She squirmed a little and had just settled in her chair, when Black Suit draped a napkin across her lap.

Her father set his papers aside, finished his drink, and the butler, or whatever he was, removed the empty tumbler and replaced it with a crystal goblet into which he poured a small amount of deep-red wine. Her father tasted the wine, and at his nod, Black Suit topped up the glass. He then held the bottle questioningly toward Hope.

She stared at him, unsure what was expected of her.

"Well? Would you like some wine with your dinner?" her father demanded.

"I'm only seventeen," she squeaked.

"I know precisely how old you are. I was there when you were born, but that doesn't answer the question. Billings can't be standing there all night with the bottle in his hand."

"Um…no, thank you."

"Well, then." Her father took a long, appreciative drink of his own wine, while Billings removed her wine goblet and poured water from a silver pitcher into another glass. Next Billings placed bowls containing a rich, fragrant, ginger-colored soup in front of her and her father. A delicious aroma wafted up. Not having had anything to eat since she'd left Canyon Creek that morning, other than a couple of the cookies Priscilla had brought her, she could hear her stomach grumble in response. Mortified, she glanced at her father and clasped her hands across her belly.

Her father's eyes met hers. Without comment, he picked up the bread basket and offered it to her. She hesitantly selected a roll.

He kept his gaze on her, long and intense. Hope had the urge to squirm again.

"You look just like Rebecca," he finally proclaimed. "Your mother was an extraordinarily beautiful woman. You resemble her." He nodded, as if in approval, and reached a hand toward Hope. She nearly jumped when he took a lock of her hair and slid it through his fingers. "You've got her hair, too. It was, as they say, her crowning glory."

Hope thought his expression was wistful, but that was probably wishful thinking on her part. Her sense of grief and loss intensified, and she averted her eyes and spooned some soup into her mouth.

"Tell me about yourself," he commanded before she had a chance to swallow. "And let's see if you're like her in other ways, too." The last comment was flung at her like an insult. "Then we'll talk about how our living arrangement is going to work."

CHAPTER FOUR

SOMEHOW, HOPE MADE it through dinner. She couldn't remember what she'd eaten or much of the conversation. Stamped on her mind was a pair of hard, assessing eyes.

When she returned to her room, she found that Priscilla had unpacked her belongings.

Wandering around the beautifully furnished, spacious suite—lifting a ceramic bowl, trailing her fingers across the gleaming surface of a credenza—she felt completely adrift.

In the bedroom she noted that the bed had been turned down, the pillows fluffed, and her childhood teddy, Sebastian, well-worn from being well loved, sat in the center of the bed. That small gesture, from a woman who must've understood how lonely she was, made her want to cry.

She saw the photographs—of her and her mother, Aunt Clarissa, her and Luke together, and her other friends from Canyon Creek—

arranged on the dresser. Uncannily, her favorite picture of her mom had been placed on the nightstand. Next to it was a glass of milk and a small plate of cookies. Her mother used to do that when Hope hadn't been feeling well or just needed her spirits lifted.

She reached for the silver-framed photo on the nightstand and sat on the edge of the bed. She ran a fingertip across the image of her mother. Her father had it right; she did look like her, especially now that she was older. Pride crowded out some of the pain. But she was even prouder of *being* like her mother, something her father apparently derided. Her mother had been beautiful, but more important, she'd been lovely *inside*, a kind and gentle person. Hope missed her more than ever.

She wished her mother had told her about Jock. She knew very little about her father, and she couldn't understand his reaction. He had *wanted* her to live with him. Then why did he seem so cold and uncaring, so…hostile? It made no sense.

Her father thought she was like her mother, and that seemed to elicit his scorn. He had her future mapped out, too. The schools she'd attend, the courses she'd take, even the people she should be friends with. All of that he'd discussed—no, *discussed* was the wrong word. He'd *informed* her over dinner.

Hope sighed heavily. Replacing the picture frame, she reached for Sebastian and hugged him. Nestling back against the soft pillows, she closed her eyes.

HOPE BOLTED UP in bed and looked around, disoriented. Recognition came with a sense of alarm. She was in the room she'd been assigned in her father's house. She heard a soft knock on the door and realized that must have been what had awakened her. Her eyes felt gritty and her throat raw. She was still clutching Sebastian and placed him gently against the pillows, then swung her legs over the edge of the bed. The room was dark, except for the bedside lamp and the alarm clock's glowing red numbers, indicating it was ten minutes after seven.

She must have dozed off and slept right through the night, even neglecting to take off the dress she'd worn the evening before. All the sleepless nights must have been catching up with her.

The knock sounded again.

"Just a minute," she called out in a scratchy voice. Scooting off the bed, she rushed into the bathroom, brushed her hair and tried to smooth the wrinkles from her dress. When that didn't work, she grabbed her housecoat hanging on the back of the door and pulled it on, tying the belt snugly around her waist.

Hurrying through the dim living area of the suite, she bumped her shin against the corner of the coffee table and yelped. With a slight limp, she made her way to the door, opened it a crack.

"Good morning, Hope," Priscilla said cheerfully, balancing a large tray in her hands. "I brought you breakfast."

"Um…thanks."

Priscilla smiled. "You're going to have to open the door for me to bring it in."

"Oh, sorry." Hope stepped back.

Priscilla took the tray to the small table by a window in the sitting area. She pushed back the heavy drapes and bright sunshine flooded in.

Hope followed her. "So, I'm not having breakfast with my father?"

Priscilla glanced over her shoulder. "If you want to have breakfast with your father, you'll have to get up a lot earlier. He usually eats at five thirty and is generally out of the house by six."

"Oh." There was a tremor in Hope's voice. It was clear she hadn't made a great impression on her father the night before, and now she'd missed breakfast. "If I was expected downstairs at that time, no one told me." She knew she sounded petulant.

"Don't worry about it, miss. He wasn't expecting you. Sit down and eat."

Hope slid onto the chair and tugged the lapel of her housecoat up to cover the collar of her dress. "You didn't need to go to all this trouble. I can come down and get my own breakfast, once I know where everything is."

"It's no trouble. It's my job. But when you're ready, I'll show you around the house, so you can find your own way." Priscilla lifted the cover off the plate in front of Hope. "Is there anything else I can get you?"

Hope stared at the omelet, sausages, toast, orange juice and the cup of hot chocolate Priscilla was pouring from a thermos. It all looked and smelled wonderful, but she didn't have much of an appetite. "No, thank you."

"Fine, then." Priscilla did her little head-bob and moved to the door. "When you change, leave that pretty dress on your bed. I'll have it cleaned and pressed for you."

Hope's hand flew to her neck. Touching the collar of her dress peeking out above the housecoat, she felt the heat rise to her face.

"You don't have to worry about things with me, miss," Priscilla said softly.

"Thank you—and please call me Hope."

"Okay, Hope." Priscilla opened the door. "I'll be back in an hour, if that suits you."

Hope nodded, and Priscilla shut the door behind her.

AN HOUR LATER, Hope was dressed in jeans and a T-shirt. She'd pulled her hair back into a high ponytail and slipped on her sneakers. She smiled when Priscilla arrived and followed her out of the room. Soon, her head was spinning, and she still hadn't seen the entire house.

"Why don't we take a break?" Priscilla suggested. "You can sit outside, and I'll get you some iced tea."

It sounded heavenly to Hope. Priscilla led her to a flagstone patio and a small sheltered garden, edged by blooming shrubs. "Make yourself comfortable, and I'll be right back."

Compared to the grandness of everything she'd seen in the house, Hope liked the closed-in feel of the space. She stroked a velvety petal and inhaled the sweet and spicy scents of white gardenia and jasmine. She had her nose buried in the center of a bright red blossom, eyes closed, when the bush vibrated and she heard a scraping noise at its base. She stumbled back, causing both motion and sound to be repeated.

Crouching down, she cautiously pushed aside a large branch to have a look…and started to laugh. Unmindful of the damp grass, she fell to her knees. Still laughing, she reached under the base of the bush and hauled out a squirming, wiggling, mud-covered puppy. "What are you doing here?" she inquired of the little dog.

The puppy mewed and continued to wriggle. Hope leaned in to nuzzle him and pulled back quickly. "Wow! What they say about sweet puppy breath doesn't apply to you, does it? You stink! I bet that's more than just mud covering you."

In response, he slathered Hope's face with his tongue, landing one grimy paw on her white shirt and another on her cheek. "Thanks, pal," Hope exclaimed. She swiped her upper arm across her face, smearing the mud.

"I have our refreshments," Priscilla announced as she emerged from the house carrying a tray laden with a pitcher, glasses and a plate of sliced lemons. She almost dropped the tray when she noticed Hope kneeling on the grass. Depositing it on the patio table with a clatter, she rushed over. "Oh, I'm so sorry. Let me take him." She made a grab for the puppy, but Hope drew him back, streaking more dirt on her shirt and along her arms.

"Look at you! You're covered in muck," Priscilla said. "Morris was supposed to have taken that little dog to the pound a week ago."

Hope's eyes rounded, and she tightened her hold on the puppy. "To the *pound*?"

"Well, we didn't want to. Morris and I thought it would be nice to have a dog around, but your father..."

"He didn't want a dog," Hope concluded.

Priscilla nodded.

"Where did he come from?"

The puppy in question enthusiastically licked the side of Hope's neck.

"We have no idea. He just appeared a couple of weeks ago."

Sinking back on her heels, Hope placed the puppy on the ground, where he executed a somersault in pursuit of his tail, before clambering onto her lap again. Hope nudged him, and he rolled over on his back, where he remained with an expectant look on his face. When Hope obliged with a tummy rub, his gleeful squeals stole her heart. "So, he doesn't belong to anyone?" she asked.

"Not that we could determine." Priscilla squatted down, too, and patted the puppy on the top of his upside-down head.

Hope looked at her thoughtfully. "My father asked me last night if there was anything he could do to make me feel more comfortable here." She continued to rub the little dog's belly, while he nipped at her fingers with his needle-sharp teeth. "I've always wanted a dog, but I couldn't have one in Canyon Creek because Mom was allergic. What if I told my father I wanted to keep the pup?"

Priscilla smiled. "There's always a chance. Why don't we take the little guy into the mudroom and get him cleaned up first? Make him more presentable."

It took several cycles of lathering and rinsing until the bathwater finally ran clear. The pup was still mostly black, but the brown had washed away with the sudsy water to reveal a bright white belly and white boots on three of his paws.

"How big do you think he'll get when he's full grown?" Hope asked as she toweled him off.

Priscilla pursed her lips. "I'm no expert on dogs, but the shape of his face makes me think he's got some Irish wolfhound in him, but the rest of him looks like Labrador. If he's mostly Lab, he won't grow *too* large. Probably about sixty pounds when he's full grown."

"That's not so big. My father wouldn't object

to me keeping him, if I promise to take care of him and keep him out of his way, would he?"

Before Priscilla could answer, the outside door swung open and Morris strode in, the screen door slamming behind him. He took one look at the two women, the little dog between them, and started to back out.

"Not so fast, Morris!" Priscilla called.

He stopped in his tracks, but kept his hand on the door handle.

The puppy—having aptly demonstrated his displeasure with the entire bathing process—must have seen his opportunity to escape. He squirmed out of Hope's grasp and charged straight for the doorway, crashing headfirst into the screen. Fortunately, he bounced off it, landing ingloriously on his backside.

Hope rushed forward to make sure he was unharmed, but Morris was quicker. He held the puppy up and stared directly into his eyes. "Way to go, Einstein. I thought we'd learned about screen doors."

Hope grinned as Morris passed him to her. She studied the pup. "Why don't we call him Einstein?"

"I know him a little better than you do," Morris said, "and I can assure you, he's no genius."

"That's the point! He's exactly the opposite, which is why the name is perfect for him.

Hey, Einstein," Hope said, testing it. When the puppy's ears perked up in apparent recognition, she dropped a kiss on his now-sweet-smelling, fuzzy snout.

"Einstein it is," Priscilla concurred. She shifted her gaze to Morris. "Where were we?"

Morris started to back out of the room again.

Priscilla laid a hand on his arm. "Whoa, my friend. Weren't you supposed to have taken this little guy to the pound?"

"Well...yes," he replied, looking everywhere except into her eyes.

"And yet here he is," she said, stating the obvious. Annoyance flashed in her normally calm blue eyes. "He could've starved. Or worse, he could've wandered out into the road and been hit by a car."

"No, not really."

"And why would that be?"

Morris rubbed the back of his neck. "Well, because I was feeding him, and I set up a space in the garage for him. I'm not sure how he managed to get out, since it's fenced."

"You always did have a soft heart under that tough exterior, Morris, to go with your soft head!"

Hope grinned widely, watching the interplay between her father's two employees as she squatted down to finish towel-drying Einstein.

The pup had other ideas. With a series of rapid-fire yips, he barreled as fast as his over-size paws could carry him toward the screen door again. This time he landed spread-eagled on his belly.

Laughing, Hope gathered him back in her arms.

When she approached her father that evening about Einstein, he relented. She could have him, with the understanding that she'd keep "the pesky dog" out of his way.

That wasn't a problem, as Hope tried to avoid her father as much as possible. From that day onward, she and Einstein were inseparable.

THREE WEEKS AFTER Hope's arrival at Glencastle, the first call came. Hope was in her room, going through the frustrating exercise of teaching Einstein basic commands, when Priscilla appeared in her doorway. "You have a call, Hope."

"I do?"

"He says he knows you from Canyon Creek. His name is Luke."

"Luke?" Hope glanced at the telephone on her desk. "How did he get this number?"

"I have no idea, but he's on hold."

Hope scrambled up and backed away. Einstein, obviously thinking it was a game, gamboled after her and latched on to the bottom of her yoga pants, starting a determined game of tug-of-war. Hope pulled her pant leg loose, picked up the puppy and cuddled him. "I...I can't."

Priscilla raised an eyebrow. "He says he needs to talk to you. What would you like me to tell him?"

"I don't know. I don't care. *Please* just have him hang up."

Priscilla moved to the phone and lifted the receiver. "No," she said into the phone. "I'm sorry but she's—" She sent Hope a final questioning look, but Hope just shook her head emphatically and took a couple more steps back. "She's not available...No...Is there a message?...I see. Yes. Goodbye."

Hope placed Einstein on the floor. "What did he say? No. No, don't tell me. I don't want to know." She turned on her heel and rushed into her bedroom, Einstein scampering after her.

Luke's email arrived later that day. The subject line read: "Urgent." Hope's finger hovered over the mouse as she vacillated. Should she open it or not? Fleetingly she wondered if it could be about something more than her having left Canyon Creek, but she dismissed the thought. Eventually, she deleted the email unread and set up her mailbox to send any future emails from Luke directly to spam. It would be better—*easier*—for both of them if it was a clean break. That way Luke could get on with his life.

The first letter arrived a week later. Priscilla brought her the plain white envelope. Hope didn't need to see the return address to know it was from Luke. The handwriting was all too familiar. She threw it unopened in her wastebasket.

All future calls went unanswered and all future letters were relegated to the garbage.

CHAPTER FIVE

WITH NOT MUCH to do until school started, Hope was outdoors as much as possible. She couldn't deny the beauty of San Jose, especially in the area where her father's house was located. Being outside had the added benefit of making it less likely that she'd bump into her father. Glencastle had stunning grounds, yet he never seemed to venture out. The times they spent together tended to be what she considered command performances. If it wasn't mealtime—usually dinner—it was either because she'd displeased him in some way and was summoned or because there was some aspect of her future he hadn't fully resolved and he wished to "discuss" with her.

As summer passed, Hope gravitated more and more to Priscilla and Morris for companionship. The three of them kept their friendship to themselves, and Hope avoided her father's other employees as much as she could.

She sensed that they were different from Priscilla and Morris, and she didn't want to risk having them report on her.

She assisted Priscilla with her household chores and helped Morris wash and tinker with the cars. Soon after she had arrived, her father had bought her a sporty little Audi, which joined the collection of cars in the enormous garage.

She'd learned that Priscilla was a single mom to an adorable six-year-old named Molly, who was developmentally challenged. Priscilla's husband had died serving in the armed forces overseas. Priscilla said she was fortunate to have both her mother and her mother-in-law, who shared the responsibility of looking after Molly when she was at work and Molly wasn't in school.

Hope had met Molly on a couple of occasions when Priscilla had brought her to Glencastle; she was a happy child and sweet natured. It wasn't a hardship to look after Molly whenever Priscilla needed her to.

With every passing week, Einstein grew. And grew. But he didn't seem to be losing his clumsiness.

Finally, as summer neared its end, the phone calls from Luke dwindled, as did his letters.

Hope threw her energy into preparing for

the start of the school year, with a combination of nerves and excitement. Not just because it would get her out of the house, but she *enjoyed* learning. After only a brief conversation during that first dinner, it had been decided that she'd attend Los Gatos High School for twelfth grade and then San Jose State University the year after.

Early on in her relationship with her father, Hope had understood the importance of picking her battles. Since she had no objection to attending San Jose State, and since one high school in San Jose was the same as any other to her, it was easy to comply with her father's wishes in this regard.

For her last year of high school, her father allowed her some latitude in the courses she chose—and *what* she studied was more important to her than the actual school she attended—but they had a full-blown argument over what her major would be in university the following year.

He had retained his cold detachment, and Hope suspected that his desire for an heir had been the driving force behind his insistence on having her live with him. She'd discovered from Priscilla that he'd never had any serious relationships after her mother. With no other children, he intended to groom her to join his technology company. But Hope's interests lay elsewhere. She wanted to work with animals, in health sciences or research.

Hope put her father's long-term goals for her out of her mind and concentrated on the here and now. It was no longer possible to go back to Canyon Creek after she turned eighteen, considering how she'd departed and how people felt about her—but he'd still have less control over her at that age. If they couldn't come to some reasonable compromise regarding her education, she'd have to consider her options. When she talked it over with Aunt Clarissa during one of their periodic phone conversations, Clarissa agreed that Hope shouldn't concern herself about her first year of university yet. A lot could change in the intervening months. Why worry about something that might not happen?

Hope applied herself at school, but it didn't seem to matter how high her marks were or how much she tried to learn about her father's business; she just couldn't seem to please him.

Her phone calls with Aunt Clarissa were a source of comfort and support. But things had changed for Clarissa, too. She'd gotten a new job—a leadership position with a competing company—and had a boyfriend. Hope was happy for her. She knew Clarissa would always be there for her, but with the added management responsibilities and the new demands on her personal time, Hope accepted that their contact would be less frequent in the future.

At school, Hope kept to herself. She had no interest in making friends. She didn't want to expose herself to heartache again with her future so uncertain.

With summer approaching once more, she wanted to do something productive with her time. She was offered a job at the pet store where she shopped for Einstein. Nothing fancy. She'd be stocking shelves, helping customers, doing some grooming and, best of all, they'd let her bring Einstein to work. She'd never had a job before and she was over-the-moon happy! But when she mentioned it to her father, he *forbade* her to accept the position. He declared it *beneath* her. If she wanted a job, she could work for him. Start learning about the business.

Hope turned down the job at the pet store. Her father's resistance was just too great. She also declined the administrative position he offered her.

Priscilla came up with an idea that appealed to Hope and met with acceptance from her father. She volunteered at the local medical center to assist with the care of critically ill patients.

The passage of time might have dulled the pain, but Hope still missed her mother terribly. She knew that the upcoming one-year anniversary of her mother's death would be a particularly bad day for her.

Other than when Hope was in school, the hours she spent at the medical center were the rare occasions she and Einstein were separated. She tried to schedule her hospital visits for when her father was away from home. She preferred to leave Einstein with Priscilla in the house, rather than with Morris in the garage, especially since his duties required him to be in and out all the time.

It didn't always work out.

Hope received a call early one morning from the hospital, informing her that a regularly scheduled volunteer was unable to make his shift because of a family emergency. They needed her to fill in. She couldn't say no, despite being aware that her father was working from home most of the day. He'd said something about having legal contracts to review and had an evening appointment after that.

Eager to get Einstein out of the house, she went looking for Morris. Unfortunately, he was running errands for her father, and he wasn't due back until midafternoon.

She'd already made the commitment to the hospital, so she had to do it. Priscilla promised she'd watch Einstein and, above all, keep him out of her father's way. She told Hope not to worry. After all, Einstein might be big and ungainly, but he was a sweet, affectionate dog and no trouble at all.

WHAT THEY HADN'T counted on was a dustup in the front yard shortly after lunch between one of the housekeeping staff and a gardener, and they were heading, shoving and shouting, right toward the side of the house overlooked by Mr. Wilson's office window.

Noticing the altercation through the kitchen window, Priscilla gave Einstein a firm command to stay in the kitchen and rushed out the side door with the obvious intent of averting a disaster, and possibly two firings.

EINSTEIN WASN'T ACCUSTOMED to being on his own. His ears and tail drooped, and he pressed his big black nose against the glass insert of the door. He plopped down by the screen door, his huge sigh near-human, and his eyes tracked Priscilla as she hurried around the corner of the house. He waited…and waited…and waited.

Finally deciding he was on his own and not liking it at all, he rose with another big sigh. Pulling his leash from the hook by the door, he grasped it in his mouth and sauntered off in search of someone who could take him outside, where all the action was.

Jock was in his office reviewing legal papers when Einstein stuck his head through the door. A quiet dog when he wanted to be, Einstein padded into the office and plunked down next to the chair, without Jock's noticing. After sitting patiently for a few minutes, Einstein bumped Jock's knee with his nose.

Jock shoved Einstein away. "What are you doing in here?" he asked gruffly, as he brushed at the damp spot Einstein's nose had left on his trousers.

In response, Einstein raised one paw. His leash still clasped in his mouth, he thumped his tail expectantly.

"I don't have time to take you for a walk, nor do I want you in here. Go get one of the help."

Einstein whined, but taking Jock's position as a "not now" rather than a "no," he rolled onto his back, legs splayed.

Jock sent him a last dismissive look and turned his attention back to his document.

Not achieving the desired outcome, Einstein sat up again and crept a little closer to Jock.

Getting no reaction, he dropped the leash and once more butted Jock's knee.

"What the… If you insist on staying in here, be quiet and leave me alone to do my work. Just be thankful I haven't thrown you out on your ear!" Jock flipped a page and reached for the glass of red wine he had on his desk. As he raised the glass to take a sip, Einstein nudged his elbow, more insistently this time. The glass tipped and burgundy liquid splashed on the desk, the papers and down the front of Jock's shirt and tie.

Slamming the empty glass back on its coaster, Jock sprang up and dabbed at the spreading stain. "You!" He turned on the dog menacingly.

Not sure what he'd done wrong, but clearly appreciating that he was in trouble, Einstein cowered and backed away. "I've a mind to toss you out right now," Jock raged at the trembling dog, as he yanked off his ruined tie.

Retreating as he was, Einstein smacked against the door, shutting it as he did. Jock was narrowing the gap between them, and Einstein no longer had the option of fleeing. He drew himself in as much as he could, trying to become invisible—an impossible feat for a dog his size. Jock shot out a hand toward the doorknob just above Einstein's head. Fearing he was going to be struck, Einstein gave a sharp, terrified bark.

Jock pulled his hand back quickly, but his face was livid. "Threatening *me*, are you? We'll see who comes out on top." Moving swiftly, he looped his tie around Einstein's neck, twisted to tighten it and tugged the dog forward so he could open the door. He dragged the petrified dog along the hall, down the stairs and through the front vestibule past a wide-eyed Priscilla.

She hurried after him. "Mr. Wilson, what are you doing?"

"Taking this mongrel to the pound, where he should've been taken in the first place."

"You can't do that," she pleaded.

He threw her a contemptuous look. "Watch me."

"What about Hope? She'll be devastated! It's my fault. I was supposed to be watching him. Please let me have him, and I'll make sure he doesn't bother you again."

"Too late for that. This dog..." He yanked the tie, making Einstein whimper. "He spilled my wine, growled at me, and I'm sure if I wasn't quicker than he was, he would've taken a bite out of my hand, too."

Priscilla cast her eyes to the cringing, pitiful Einstein. "Please leave him with me," she implored. "I'll take him to the pound if that's what you really want."

"We're not going through that again. I can't trust you to do it. I'm personally taking him and having him put down like the dangerous animal he is."

"He's not dangerous—"

"Quiet!" Jock roared. "You *dare* to question me?" He wagged the index finger of his free hand at her. "Another word from you, and you'll be out on your ear, too."

"But Hope…"

"My daughter is *my* business. You two have gotten too close for my liking. But that's for later. Right now, this creature is going to the pound." He hauled Einstein across the floor and out the door, banging it shut behind him.

CHAPTER SIX

PRISCILLA PACED ANXIOUSLY in front of the window of the upstairs sitting room. It had an unobstructed view of the driveway, so she'd know right away when Hope returned. Why didn't that girl ever carry her mobile phone? But Priscilla knew the answer. She didn't have many people she wanted to talk to. Priscilla had tried reaching Hope at the hospital, but they'd sent her on an errand and couldn't reach her either.

Priscilla fretted that time was very much of the essence. She had no doubt that Mr. Wilson had taken Einstein to a pound and—true to his word—claimed him to be a threat and ordered him put down. By checking the last number dialed on his office phone, she'd identified the animal shelter Mr. Wilson had selected. She'd tried to call repeatedly, without success. If Hope wasn't home soon, Priscilla would go there, even though she knew she'd lose her job if Mr. Wilson found out. She worried about how she'd support Molly if that happened, but she had to do what was right. What kind of role model would she be to her beloved little girl if she didn't?

Just as Priscilla reached for the phone to call a taxi, Hope's Audi rounded the curve. Priscilla dashed down the stairs and outside, grabbing Hope's arms before she had a chance to get out of the car. "Something terrible has happened. Your father took Einstein—"

"Took him? Took him where?"

"He took Einstein to have him…put down."

"What are you talking about?" Hope screamed, shrugging free of Priscilla's hold. She was frantic. "Do you know where he took him?"

Priscilla reached in her pocket and pulled out a crumpled piece of paper. "Here. I wrote down their number, too. I've been calling and calling, but it goes to voice mail every time. I've left a few urgent messages."

"Okay, keep trying. Call me on my cell if you reach someone."

"You don't have it with you."

"Right." Hope was about to run inside.

"No. Don't waste time. Here." Priscilla took her own phone out of her pocket and handed it to Hope.

HOPE GRABBED THE phone and jumped back in her car. Speeding down the driveway, she was thankful for the first time that her father had bought her the little Audi. She hardly slowed at the foot of the drive and screeched out onto the road, cutting off another vehicle. A long, loud horn blast followed.

Glancing at the slip of paper on which Priscilla had written the address of the shelter, Hope set her navigation system through voice command. It wasn't that far, but rush-hour traffic was bound to slow her down.

Please don't let me be too late. Please don't let me be too late, she chanted. She would've shot through the changing lights if not for the person ahead of her, who stopped his vehicle when the light turned amber. She tapped the steering wheel impatiently. "Come on. *Come on.*" When the lights changed, she waited for oncoming traffic to clear and roared past the vehicle in front of her. An approaching van had to swerve to avoid colliding with her. Another horn blared just as she was pulling back into her own lane. Cutting it that close had scared her. She'd be no good to Einstein if she got in an accident while trying to get to him. She slowed her speed and prayed she'd get there in time.

When Hope finally reached the animal facility she was shaking uncontrollably. She leaped out of her vehicle and ran in through the front door. Not seeing anyone at the counter, she rushed around it and into the back, where she could hear animal noises. A tall, slender man was bent over a bag of kibble, measuring food into metal dishes. She called out to him and he straightened, surprise evident on his face. “You’re not allowed back here.”

Hope skidded to a stop, her eyes desperately searching the small, rusty cages around them, looking for Einstein. Not seeing him, she feared the worst. She grasped the man’s arms. “I’m sorry, but you have to help me,” she pleaded with dry, heaving sobs. “My dog was brought in here earlier today, to be put down. It’s a *huge* mistake. He’s not dangerous. He’s as gentle as they come. It was my father. He never liked him and I need to get him. My dog, I mean—not my father.”

“Whoa. Slow down, will you. I didn’t catch all of that, but we don’t have anyone here today who can euthanize animals.”

The relief that coursed through Hope was instantaneous. “Okay. Okay. So please show me where Einstein is, so I can take him home.”

“Einstein? The large black-and-white dog, looks mostly like a Lab?”

"Yes!" Hope almost cried with relief. "Please take me to him."

"I'm afraid I can't."

"What do you mean you can't?" She cried. "You *have* to."

"No. No. I would if I could. I *can't*. He's not here."

"Where is he?"

"I was just coming on shift when that dude dropped him off. He claimed the dog was vicious and unpredictable. Said the dog had tried to attack him."

"That is *such* a lie! Einstein wouldn't hurt a mouse. Where is he?"

"Nancy, the other staffer who was here, took him. I have to admit, he didn't seem mean to either of us. He was more terrified than anything, if you ask me. Well, since we don't have anyone here to euthanize animals, as I told you, and we're at capacity right now, Nancy arranged for the city's animal control department to pick him up."

"No!" Hope shouted. "He's *not* dangerous. Where did they take him?"

The man provided the address and directions.

"Phone them." She pointed a finger at him as she sprinted to the front door. "Please call them and tell them *not* to do anything to Einstein. I'm on my way to get him." She swung around just before she exited. Her voice turned hard and cold. "Tell them if they so much as harm a hair on him, I'm…I'm going to *sue* them for every penny they have." That would be no consolation if she lost Einstein, and she realized she sounded very much like her father, but she didn't know what else to say.

Her stomach was churning with nausea as she raced to get to the animal control facility. She didn't bother to park in the lot, just left her car in front of the building. She dashed up the steps to the door and pushed. It didn't budge. She tried again; it was definitely locked. That was when she noticed the sign. Fridays they closed at four. It was now approaching five. She rattled the door again and screamed in frustration.

Looking around, she saw a couple of cars parked behind the building. That meant there had to be people inside. She ran toward the back; peering through a window, she could see two people moving around. Hope banged on the glass with her fist, but they didn't seem to hear her. She continued around the side of the building, until she got to a large fenced yard. Inside the enclosure, there was a back door. Without hesitation, she climbed the chain-link fence, dropped down on the other side and ran to the door.

This time her pounding got the occupants' attention. The two women looked at the door, then at each other. The taller woman approached Hope. "We're closed," she yelled through the glass.

"I know, but it's urgent!" Hope shouted back. "*Please* open up."

"Come back tomorrow," the woman advised.

"No!" Hope pummeled the door again with both fists. "Please don't walk away. *Please*. You have my dog and there's been a terrible mistake." Tears were brimming in her eyes, blurring her vision.

The woman paused. "Which dog?"

Hope described Einstein. "You have to let me take him home," she finished, sobbing. "He's all I have. He's everything to me."

The woman glanced back at her companion, exchanged some words with her, and then Hope heard the lock disengage and the door opened. "Thank you," she breathed. "Please tell me he's all right."

The other woman joined them where they were standing. "He's fine," she assured Hope. "He was next on our list, but we couldn't believe he'd hurt anyone. He's such a sweet boy.

We were just discussing what we should do. He's scared, but he's fine."

Hope threw her arms around the woman, tears coursing down her face. "Oh, thank you." She hugged the other woman, too. "Please take me to him."

Einstein might have been big, but when he was released from his cage, he crawled into Hope's lap, licking every inch of her face and neck. She hugged him tight and buried her face in his fur. "You're okay, pal. You're okay," she murmured, attempting to soothe him as much as herself.

When she finally stood up, Einstein plastered himself to the side of her leg like Velcro.

"We're glad you got here in time." One of the women trailed a hand along Einstein's back. "We fell for the big guy."

"Believe me, we don't want to euthanize any animal," the other woman added. "But look at this place. We're out of room, as you can see, and we have more and more animals coming in. When they're hurt or sick, we can't tend them properly. The city just doesn't provide enough funding for veterinary services for all the strays and injureds we get."

"We wish there was more we could do," the taller woman interjected as they walked through the kennel area to the front office.

"But we just don't have the resources or the facilities."

Hope's heart broke as she looked around at the sad-eyed cats and dogs, resigned because they'd been there too long, and the eager new arrivals, trying to catch her attention, begging her to free them from their small, dank cages.

"I can't thank you enough," Hope said as she signed the paperwork to claim Einstein.

"We're happy to have you two reunited!" one of the women told her.

"Take care of each other." The other woman waved goodbye.

Outside, Hope took Einstein for a walk, letting him stretch his legs and work off some of his nervous energy. She also needed the fresh air.

The relief she felt that the unimaginable hadn't happened left her weak and a little dizzy. Now that Einstein was safely with her again, her anxiety was crowded out by an intense anger. How callous of her father to do what he did! Didn't he appreciate what Einstein meant to her? He knew full well that Einstein wasn't dangerous. Why hadn't he waited until she got home so they could have worked things out?

Hope couldn't take Einstein back to her father's house, now that she'd seen what he was capable of. But where could they go?

Did it really matter? Anywhere was better than living with such a dreadful man. He obviously didn't love her and never would. They simply coexisted beneath one roof…one very *big* roof!

She stopped suddenly. How could she have forgotten? Her birthday was next week! She would be eighteen years old. Legally an adult. That meant she could leave her father.

She let Einstein jump in the car and took her time driving home. She was no longer in a hurry, and she needed a chance to think. To figure things out. She didn't have to worry about facing her father that evening, because he was staying overnight at the hotel after his business function. Small blessings, she thought. If she just packed up and left that night, she wondered if he'd do anything about it.

Yes, he would, she decided. She was no more than a possession to him, and he was greedy with his possessions. He would find her if for no other reason than to prove that he was in control. That he *could.*

By the time Hope reached the house, she had a plan. She pulled up to the garage rather than the front of the house. Even though she knew her father wasn't home because he would've left for his evening engagement by now, she didn't want to risk Einstein being seen. She didn't trust all her father's employees the way she did Priscilla and Morris. Not that the others were bad people; they were just fearful of her father.

She left Einstein in the car. He whined and pawed at the window, obviously not wanting to be separated from her again so soon. She spoke to him reassuringly, then climbed the stairs at the side of the garage. She knocked and was about to knock again when Morris opened the door. Sitting inside on his sofa was Priscilla. From the look of her flushed, puffy face, Hope surmised that she'd been crying.

Seeing her, Priscilla shoved the soggy tissue she held into her pocket and rushed over. "Did you find Einstein? Is he okay?"

Hope nodded. "He's fine. He's in my car. I'm sorry—I should've called," she said regretfully.

"Oh, thank goodness you found him," Priscilla exclaimed, wrapping her arms around Hope. "I've been worried sick. It's all my fault. If anything had happened to him, I...I don't know how you'd ever forgive me. I don't know if I could've forgiven myself." She withdrew the tissue from her pocket and blew her nose loudly.

Morris touched Priscilla's shoulder. "Why don't the two of you sit down. I'll get Einstein. He shouldn't stay cramped up in that little car, especially after what he's been through."

Hope smiled at him gratefully. A moment later, the door opened again, and Einstein scurried into the room. Hope noted that Morris still looked glum, and it didn't seem to have anything to do with Einstein. "What's wrong?" she asked.

"You should tell her," Morris said to Priscilla. "She needs to know."

Priscilla stared intently at her hands. "It's not something she should worry about."

"It certainly is," Morris replied with more heat than Hope had ever seen the stoic chauffeur exhibit.

"I'm sitting right here! Please don't talk as if I am not. Tell me *what*?" Having already gone through the gamut of emotions, Hope felt her stomach tense once more. She slid her gaze from Morris to Priscilla.

Morris sat down and took Priscilla's hand in his. "She needs to know, since you'll both have to be careful."

"Careful about *what*?"

Priscilla drew in a huge breath. "Your father confronted me, when he got back from the pound. He said I was growing too close to you."

"I don't understand. We've been careful. He doesn't know we're friends."

Morris passed Priscilla a fresh tissue so she could dab at her eyes. "We have been, yes, but maybe not enough. You see, I defied him when he was taking Einstein to the pound. So when he got back, he reprimanded me for being… insubordinate."

Morris snorted.

"He said how dare I question his decision-making, and that I was forgetting my place because of our relationship. Yours and mine."

Morris cut in. "How could she forget? She works insanely long hours, even though she's supposed to be done by five."

Hope watched as Priscilla patted Morris's knee, and she wondered if she'd missed something between her two friends.

"Anyway, your father said I had to stop being friendly with you," Priscilla told her apologetically.

"Yeah. He said she was just the *help*, and if she didn't know her place, she'd be easy to replace."

Priscilla choked back a sob. "Your father pays very well, and even with all the help I get from Molly's grandmothers, I need the income for her."

Hope knew how dedicated Priscilla was to her daughter, and she was fully aware of Molly's special needs. "You won't lose your job," she assured her, and the plan she'd formulated on the drive home gelled in her mind. She had to leave her father's house, not only because of Einstein, but because of her friends. She couldn't let Priscilla or any of them suffer on her account. She was about to tell them about her decision, but if her father found out that they knew, he would just as likely fire them both.

No, she couldn't take them into her confidence. "I'll think of something," she said vaguely. She turned her attention to Morris. "I can't take Einstein into the house with me until I get things sorted out. Could we set up a space for him in the garage again, like you did when he was a puppy?" She forced a rueful smile. "But this time so he can't escape?"

Morris ran a hand along Einstein's back, as he lay at their feet. "That won't be necessary. He can stay here in my apartment for as long as you want. If he's here or out in the back, your father won't know."

"I appreciate it. Please keep him out of everyone's sight," Hope added as she stood, Einstein clambering up beside her. She hugged them both. “I promise it won’t be long.”

She already knew the issue would be resolved in a week. She and Einstein would be gone the day after she turned eighteen.

CHAPTER SEVEN

HOPE WAS UP early the morning of her birthday. Her father was throwing her a party, mostly for his business associates and their children. She hadn't really made any friends at school, but she'd given her father the names of some of her classmates for the invitation list. He'd offered to fly Aunt Clarissa to San Jose for the event, but Hope had declined, knowing it would've been too awkward for everyone involved when she left the next morning. She'd wake up early, tell her father over breakfast and be gone by nine.

She'd spent the past week preparing as much as possible. After seeing the conditions at the two animal shelters she'd visited to rescue Einstein, she realized more than ever that she wanted to work with animals. She found a posting online for a veterinary assistant in Monterey that appealed to her. She was excited when she was actually put through to the person who'd be hiring for the position. They had a short telephone chat, and Hope was asked to come for a formal interview. More from opportunity than design, she was going to Monterey, California.

She liked the idea of living in Monterey and being close to the ocean. Although she was optimistic about this job, if she didn't get it, she'd just keep looking. She could manage without a job for a while. She'd saved most of the allowance her father had given her. Combined with the money she'd received from the sale of her mother's house in Canyon Creek, which her father had invested on her behalf, she had a financial cushion.

Also through an online search, she'd found a reasonably priced bed-and-breakfast that accepted dogs. She and Einstein would stay there until she could find a more permanent place to live.

She wasn't taking the Audi with her, so she rented a van to drive to Monterey. Once she was halfway there, she'd call Morris and ask him to pick up her car from the rental place.

The day stretched ahead of her, but all she had to do was get through these next few hours, she reminded herself—her rite of passage to becoming an adult.

And to being free.

She took Einstein for a long walk and spent

the rest of the day packing. She wasn't taking much with her. She'd use the same four suitcases she'd brought with her. Once she'd packed, it was hardly noticeable that anything was missing from her closet. As with the Audi, all the things her father had bought her she'd leave behind.

Finally, it was time to get ready for her party. A glittery red Chanel gown was spread across her bed. She didn't want to think about how much the dress must have cost.

"Hope, are you in here?" Priscilla called from the sitting room.

Hope dragged her suitcases back to the closet and took a quick look around to make sure there was nothing out of place that might alert Priscilla to her plan. "Yes. In the bedroom."

"These came for you," Priscilla announced as she stepped through the doorway, holding two couriered packages.

The first one made Hope smile. Of course Aunt Clarissa wouldn't forget her birthday. When she looked at the second, her breath caught in her throat. It was from Luke. Her smile faded and she placed both packages on her bed.

"Aren't you going to open them?"

"Later," Hope said, although she probably wouldn't open the one from Luke.

"It's the same boy, isn't it?" Priscilla asked, as if reading her thoughts.

Hope nodded.

"He's persistent. You've never responded to him once, in all the time you've been here?"

Hope shook her head.

"And he hasn't given up trying to reach you. I remember the first time he called here. He said he really needed to talk to you. He…" She seemed to be searching her memory. "He sounded…distraught. There must've been something very special between the two of you."

Hope remained silent.

"It's up to you. I just thought a friend like that might be worth holding on to." She paused. "Is there anything I can do to help you get ready for the party?"

"No. I can manage." Hope hadn't intended to sound abrupt. Suddenly realizing that she might not have a chance to be alone with Priscilla again before she left, she hugged her fiercely. "I hope you know how much you mean to me. You and Morris."

Priscilla stroked the length of Hope's hair. "Now don't start crying, otherwise it'll show tonight. You don't want your eyes swollen at your celebration."

Hope sniffled. "You're right. I just wanted you to know."

"We feel the same about you. I'd better go now, before your father guesses where I am."

On her own once more, Hope glanced at the package from Luke. Over the past year, she'd tried hard to accept the loss of her mother and forget everything about Canyon Creek, put it all out of her mind. Although she'd be starting a new life in Monterey, she knew her greatest challenge would continue to be forgetting Luke. Or trying to… She was absolutely certain that it was in his best interest for her to be out of his life, although she still yearned for him in her heart.

But now wasn't the time for reflections and remembrances. She dreaded the party, and yet she embraced the undercurrent of anticipation at the thought of leaving in the morning. If the past year had taught her anything, it was independence and self-reliance. Those characteristics would serve her well. She took a quick shower, washed her hair and blow-dried it to a glossy mass. She pulled on her underthings and slipped into the red dress. When she turned to the full-length mirror, her own reflection shocked her.

Did her father realize she was only eighteen? For a man who hardly acknowledged her, he had the uncanny ability of knowing what suited her. The dress fit her perfectly. The clingy material hugged her slender frame, skimmed over her curves, flowed around her long legs. Its hemline ended just above the floor. She was a shimmering column of fire.

Because of the sophistication of the dress, she left her hair down. After all, she was just eighteen and in no rush to appear older. She glanced in the mirror again. When had she grown up? Excitement surged through her as she wondered what Luke would think of her in this dress. She was immediately appalled. Where had *that* come from? Luke had no place in her life any longer.

The momentary joy she'd felt at her new appearance vanished. It was a stranger staring back at her now. An adult. She straightened her skirt, squared her shoulders and walked out of the room to her party.

A RAY OF sunshine speared through the narrow gap between the curtains and danced across Hope's eyelids. She squeezed them more tightly shut and threw an arm over her face. A moment later, she shot up in bed. Pushing her hair back from her face, she twisted sideways to look at her alarm clock: 8:50! She'd missed breakfast with her father, and she'd planned to be on the road by nine. Clearly that wasn't going to happen.

The room spun and she clasped her head with both hands.

Had she really had champagne last night? Other than once sharing a bottle of beer with Luke at a Fourth of July barbecue, she'd never had anything alcoholic to drink in her life. What a time for her to start—the night before she wanted to break free of her father. She lay back against the pillows and moaned. Closing her eyes, she took several deep breaths.

She sat up again, slowly this time, and slid out of bed.

At least it was Sunday, and her father wouldn't have gone to work. She hoped he didn't have a golf game, otherwise she'd have to wait until he got home.

After a long shower, she pulled on her jeans and a blouse. She knew her father would be annoyed at seeing her dressed so casually on a Sunday, but he'd have much bigger things to be displeased about today.

Hope found him in the morning room, reading a newspaper. She'd often wondered why a man who'd made his fortune on the internet still read an actual paper, but she'd never had the audacity to ask.

"May I speak with you?" she asked.

He looked up, frown lines forming between his brows. "You know I don't like you wearing jeans."

"Yes. I know." Nerves skittered up her spine. "I'd like to talk to you."

He made a huge production of folding up his paper and placing it on the coffee table in front of him. He crossed one leg over the other and rested an elbow on the back of the sofa. "Well, come in, then."

Hope felt like a lamb walking into a lion's den. She perched on the edge of a chair, her back rigid, her hands linked and resting on her lap.

"Well, then?"

Hearing the cold indifference, she tried to remember if she'd ever heard warmth in his voice. Or approval? Not that she could recall.

Jock crossed and uncrossed his legs and checked his watch. Both gestures indicated his impatience.

"Is this going to take all morning?" he asked.

"No." She finally found her voice—and her courage. "It shouldn't take long." If he'd shown any kindness, even now, she wondered if she could've gone ahead with her plans. "Thank you for the party last night," she began formally. Manners were too deeply ingrained and she couldn't not express her appreciation, whether she wanted what he'd given her or not.

"You're welcome." He started to reach for his paper. "Are we done?"

"No. We're not." She realized her voice was a little sharp.

He leaned back, obviously surprised.

"I'm leaving," she announced.

"Fine. Have a nice time."

It was clear that he'd misunderstood. "I don't mean for the day. I mean for good. I'm moving out."

A short, sharp laugh burst forth and he waved a hand dismissively. "What kind of nonsense is this?"

"I'm eighteen. An adult. I no longer have to live with you."

"Where will you go? How are you going to live?" There was amusement in his voice. "You don't expect me to keep paying your expenses if you follow through with this ludicrous idea of yours, do you?"

Hope's resolve didn't diminish. "I don't want your money. I'll pay my own way."

"You can't be serious! How long do you think that'll last? Go clear your head of this ridiculous notion, and I'll see you at dinner.

We'll talk about whatever's bothering you." This time he did pick up his paper, unmistakably dismissing her.

Hope rose, holding her head high as she moved toward the door. "No." She bit back the word *father.* "You won't see me at dinner. I'll be leaving shortly."

"You're a foolish girl," Jock called after her. "Foolish and irresponsible, just like your mother."

Hope paused. He could belittle her all he wanted, but his careless, critical words about her mother cut deep. She turned back slowly. "My mother was a wonderful, caring person. Comparing me to her is one of the biggest compliments you can pay me. Thank you for that."

"Oh, if you only knew! Ungrateful girl," she heard him rant as she walked out. "You do this, don't you ever…*ever*…ask me for anything. Not money. Not anything."

His words taunted her but she refused to look back. It occurred to her how ironic it was that *she* was leaving *him* this time, much as she imagined he'd left her and her mother all those years ago. She expected him to fully shut her out of his life.

As he had once before.

CHAPTER EIGHT

July 2002

MONTEREY WASN'T WHAT Hope had imagined. It was more vibrant, somehow brighter, as if the sun shone more vividly on this stretch of California's central coast. The city, rising from the southern edge of Monterey Bay to pine-forested hillsides, was teeming with life, color and sound.

Then again, she didn't really know what she'd expected. She hadn't thought about it much. From decision to discussion to departure—everything had happened very fast. She just knew she needed to be out of her father's house. Out of his life.

Mission accomplished.

Tomorrow she had her interview at the veterinary clinic. Today her goal was to get settled at the bed-and-breakfast where she'd be staying. It was within walking distance to the ocean—admittedly a *long* walk. She had a ground-floor room, with its own bath and a door to the outside so she and Einstein could come and go without disturbing other guests. The owners were an elderly couple who loved animals but had lost their dog a few years back. When Hope explained Einstein's newly developed phobia of being left alone in confined spaces, they offered to watch him whenever she was out.

Hope didn't unpack more than her essentials, since a lot depended on her interview the next day. She'd done some research on the clinic and liked everything she'd learned. She was meeting with the two veterinarians who owned the practice and their office manager, the person she'd be reporting to, if the interview went well.

She hit it off with all three of them, felt good about the interview and was excited about the prospect of working at the practice. She was still on her way back to her room when the call came on her mobile phone. They were offering her the position of veterinary assistant.

Hope enjoyed her job, and she was a conscientious and hardworking employee. She quickly proved her value to her employers. They told her they were impressed with her intelligence and work ethic. When she expressed interest in taking on more responsibility after her first few months on the job, they suggested she consider becoming an accredited veterinary technologist. It was a two-year program at Central California College, and it allowed a degree of flexibility so she could complete it while still working. Her bosses believed in Hope so much that they offered to adjust her hours and to pay half her tuition. Hope was elated by the opportunity.

Since her interest wasn't in veterinary medicine itself but in the management and administrative end, she focused on the practice-management aspects of the program.

Even paying half the cost of tuition, she found that her income was sufficient to allow her and Einstein to move out of the bed-and-breakfast and into a small rental house on the outskirts of the city. She and Einstein enjoyed having their own space, and the property abutted the Los Padres National Forest, providing lots of space to roam.

With the passage of time and the more spacious living quarters, Einstein was gradually getting over his neurosis about being left alone. Hope was grateful to the owners of the bed-and-breakfast for helping out with Einstein while she'd stayed there, and they offered to watch him anytime she needed it.

How wrong she and Priscilla had been when they'd predicted that Einstein would be a mid-size dog. By the time he'd finally stopped growing at a lanky ninety-five pounds, his shoulder reached Hope's waist. He might have looked like a Labrador, but his size was that of an Irish wolfhound.

Hope thought of her mother often and continued to miss her. She hadn't had any contact with her father since the day she'd walked out of his house over six months ago. She'd stayed in touch with Priscilla and Morris. She got together with them occasionally, notably to celebrate their engagement. By tacit agreement, her father was seldom mentioned.

She'd wanted a clean break, and Luke had finally stopped trying to contact her. Priscilla confirmed that no further correspondence had been received at her father's place. She'd left behind the gift he'd sent her for her birthday. Unopened.

Hope spoke with Aunt Clarissa regularly. Clarissa's relationship had ended, but Hope was thrilled for her when she accepted a vice president's position with Premier Market Survey Solutions in New York City, even though it meant they'd be on opposite coasts.

Hope was happy with her job, the little house she and Einstein shared and her classes at the college. But she didn't feel truly settled. She was restless, as if she was still a visitor here, biding her time. Unlike her year at Los Gatos High School in San Jose, she let her guard down and made friends, but she drew the line at dating. Oh, the opportunities presented themselves. Now that she was more open and approachable, a number of young men showed interest in her, but Hope didn't reciprocate. She was too busy, she rationalized. Between school and work and Einstein, her days were full. It was almost three years since she'd left Canyon Creek, but if she was honest with herself, she had to admit that a large part of the reason she wasn't interested in a relationship was that she wasn't over Luke. She graciously deflected romantic advances, but managed to preserve the friendships.

Noah Drake was different.

Noah was a classmate in the veterinary technologist program at the college. He had a degree in biology and was two years older than Hope. Although he was focusing on the medical side of the program, they shared a number of classes.

Noah was smart, quick-witted, charming and undeniably attractive. He was popular with all the girls and for good reason. With his tall, athletic build and all-around California beach-boy looks, he attracted a lot of attention. His hair was on the longish side and sun-bleached by hours spent surfing. His eyes were a clear, sparkling blue in a tanned face, and his smile was just a bit lopsided but as endearing as any Hope had ever seen. There wasn't a girl in their class—on campus, for that matter—who wouldn't have been overjoyed to go out with him.

Except Hope.

She liked him. She respected his intelligence. Enjoyed being with him. But she didn't want anything more.

Noah wasn't as easily deterred as the others. Hope liked their banter and, surprisingly, his harmless flirtation. But it was just that to her. Harmless. Perhaps because she made it clear that she wanted to be no more than friends, she seemed to become a challenge for him. He wasn't accustomed to women saying no to him, and he continued to pursue Hope. She was flattered but definitely *not* receptive.

Hope couldn't take offense at Noah's good-natured interest, but she finally had to insist that it was friendship or nothing.

As cheerful as Noah had been in his pursuit, once Hope laid down her ultimatum, he accepted defeat. They developed a close friendship both were comfortable with.

During their final semester before graduation, over lattes at the campus coffee shop, Noah slid a piece of paper in front of Hope.

"What's this?" She picked it up as she sipped her coffee, smearing froth on her upper lip.

Noah chuckled and used a napkin to wipe the froth away. "You're almost twenty-one. You'd think you could drink a coffee by now without getting this stuff all over your face."

She swatted his hand but continued to read. When she finished, she looked up at him questioningly.

"Come on, Hope. Use your imagination! Think what the two of us could do with the place, what we could do for all its inhabitants."

"You want to buy the Monterey Animal Shelter?"

His grin was compelling. "Yeah. But I can't do it on my own."

"Don't look at me. First of all, I'm committed to the veterinary practice that's putting me through this program. I couldn't have done it without them. And you should think long and hard about this. There's a reason they're selling it and at the price they are. They can't afford to run it."

"See!" He playfully stabbed a finger toward her. "That's our business manager speaking. That's why I need you to do it with me. They're privately owned, so they don't receive government subsidies. They aren't businesspeople and they haven't capitalized on the fund-raising potential. And you—" he flicked a finger down her nose "—my little Einstein… Oh, wait, that's your dog. Okay, my little virtuoso, you're going to make sure we at least break even."

They talked it through as they finished their coffee. Over the next few weeks, they continued to discuss the possibility.

Hope was still reticent, but Noah was wearing her down. She thought about her savings and the fact that she could use most of it toward a down payment. Noah said he could match the amount. They'd have to see if they could finance the rest.

"Look, the timing is perfect," Noah said. "This is meant to be. We're a month away from graduating and the shelter is up for sale."

Eventually Hope acquiesced. "Okay. I'll run some numbers," she said. "See what I come up with. Can you arrange for us to look at their books and the facility?"

They went as far as kicking around some names. They wanted to send the message that it was under new management and have a name that was more appealing than the current one.

When they settled on Barkley Green, that

made it more real. "To our new business venture!" Noah announced as he raised his coffee cup in a toast.

"Don't count your chickens before they're hatched, so to speak," Hope responded, but laughed as she said it and touched her cup to his.

If this crazy idea of theirs came to be, she'd figure out how to handle it with her employers. They'd been so wonderful to her and she owed them. At a minimum, she'd pay back the half of her tuition that they'd covered. If she did leave, she'd find a way to do it respectfully and without compromising their friendship, but she'd cross that bridge if and when she came to it.

The idea of owning an animal shelter with Noah *was* crazy. And at the price they were prepared to offer, a long shot at best.

CHAPTER NINE

Monterey, California
March 2013

NOAH STROLLED INTO the back office of Barkley Green Animal Shelter. He tossed his keys on his desk and went to the sink, where Hope was scrubbing her hands. He leaned over her, took one whiff and drew back quickly. "Whew! Did you forget to shower for the last month or two?"

Hope flicked a hand at him, splashing sudsy water everywhere.

"Whoa!" Noah jumped back, avoiding most of the spray. "Careful!" He glanced down at himself. "This is a new shirt, and I'd like to wear it for at least a day before it gets stained."

Hope gave her partner an appraising look. He'd retained his classic beach-boy good looks although he'd turned thirty-one last month. She often thought, as she did now, that he didn't seem to have aged in the nine years they'd known each other.

Noah's hair was still a streaky blond and long enough to tie into a stubby ponytail. Right now, he had it tucked behind his ears. His skin was, as usual, tanned from devoting as much time to surfing as their schedules allowed. As for his new shirt and khaki pants, he had an uncanny way of spending very little on clothes—since neither of them had much disposable income—yet he was always well dressed.

"So, what have you been up to?" Noah inquired as he leaned back against his desk and crossed his legs at the ankles.

"Lucy had an upset stomach," she said, referring to the potbellied pig they'd recently acquired. "She finally started to feel better once she'd emptied her belly. Unfortunately, I wasn't quick enough to get entirely out of the way. Not only did I spend two hours nursing her through it, Tom didn't show for work again today, so after Lucy relieved herself, I had to clean out her pen, too."

Noah flashed his lopsided grin and nodded. "That would explain the stench." He gestured toward her shirt and jeans. "And the splotches of…well, you know…on your clothes."

Hope twisted to see where he was pointing.

"Oh, terrific. I thought I'd escaped the worst of it." She glanced up at him again. "So, why are you dressed as if you're going on a date rather than showing up for work at an animal shelter?" She reached forward as if to wipe her hand on his shirt.

Noah made a tsking noise and sidestepped her easily. "Because we have a meeting."

She grabbed a towel and dried her arms. "What meeting?"

He gave an exaggerated sigh. "You're the business brains of our little enterprise here. If you checked your calendar every once in a while, you wouldn't have to ask. We're meeting with the bank manager today."

Hope's face fell. "How could I have forgotten? And look at me!"

"My point, exactly."

"I need to get cleaned up. When's the meeting?"

Noah checked his watch. "Forty-five minutes from now."

"At the branch, right?"

"Correct."

"I can make it. I don't have a change of clothes here. I need to go home. I'll meet you there."

"Okay, but don't—"

"Be late. I know." Hope rushed over to her desk, pulled her handbag out of the bottom drawer and called Einstein, who'd been sleeping beside her chair.

Forty minutes later, Hope was leaning against her Jeep in the bank's parking lot. She wore slim black pants and a pale pink tuxedo shirt. She'd left her hair down for a change, and it cascaded past her shoulders in loose waves. Her arms were crossed and the index finger of her right hand was tapping a little tattoo on her left biceps when she saw Noah's car approach. As he parked in the spot next to hers, Hope unfolded her arms and glared at her watch.

Noah hopped out, flung an arm around Hope's shoulder and steered her toward the entrance of the bank. "I'm not late. I've got two minutes to spare. Besides, we don't want to be early, or Reeves might think we're too eager." Noah swept his gaze up and down the length of her. "How on earth do you do that?"

"Do what?"

"Transform yourself from Pig Pen to a pinup girl in the blink of an eye and starting from a deficit position. Factoring in your travel time, you couldn't have taken more than twenty minutes to shower and change." He leaned his head toward her. "No. It can't be true! You're wearing makeup." He took an exaggerated sniff of her neck. "And perfume."

Hope poked Noah's side playfully with her

elbow. “Looking a bit more put together than I usually do won’t hurt our cause today.”

“No argument.” Noah dropped his arm and opened the door for her. “Game time,” he whispered as she passed him.

“We’re here to see Mr. Scott Reeves,” he announced to the teller behind the counter.

“Is he expecting you?”

Noah nodded. “Hope Wilson and Noah Drake.”

“Just a minute, please.” The young woman hurried away and stepped into a small office, with Noah’s eyes following her movements appreciatively. When she popped back out, she motioned for them to go in.

Scott Reeves rose from behind his desk as they entered, and they shook hands. “You’re here about the Barkley Green Animal Shelter, correct?”

Hope refrained from rolling her eyes. What other reason would they have for seeing him?

“Yes,” Noah responded. “We’ve been operating the shelter for over seven years now. We’ve completed the restructuring, reducing expenses and overall debt, but we’ve also changed our business model. We don’t turn away any animal, and that means we’ve had to expand, requiring more space and staff.”

“Many of our personnel are volunteers,” Hope added, “and, as you know from our financial statements, Noah and I, as the principals, draw a modest salary, only enough for us to get by."

"We've been generating a steady stream of revenue through adoption fees, and we have aggressive plans to increase contributions from fund-raising, which of course remains our primary source of income," Noah explained.

"You would like to increase your borrowing capacity? Am I correct?" Reeves cut in.

"Yes, that's correct," Hope confirmed.

Reeves consulted his notes. "When we last raised the limit for your line of credit two years ago, you assured me that it was more of a safety net. You said then, too, that you'd have less reliance on borrowing, since you had plans to augment the revenue you generated through donations. Yet you've been hovering very close to your limit for some time."

"We've increased revenues from both adoption fees and donations but we've also expanded, as we just explained," Noah said. "We're working on the new fund-raising campaign. In the meantime, we need access to more capital. We've never defaulted on a payment."

"True. That's true." Reeves nodded while thumbing through the pages in the folder in front of him. He glanced up. "And if you misjudge again? How will you service your increased level of debt? You're barely making it now. Instead of asking for more money, why not stop accepting animals when you reach your capacity?"

"We couldn't do that," Hope protested. "These animals *need* us. Without Barkley Green, where would they go? Some would have to be euthanized."

Reeves raised his eyebrows in a "so what" expression.

"That would defeat the whole purpose of our shelter," she rushed on. "We can't turn animals away! We heal or rehabilitate as quickly as we can for adoption or—with wild animals—for release, but we won't turn away a single creature."

"Doesn't sound very businesslike." Reeves flipped the file folder closed. "I'm sorry I can't help you. You're already heavily leveraged, the shelter's primary source of income is donations and the two of you draw your salaries, modest though they might be, from the shelter." He linked his hands and rested them on the folder. "I appreciate what you're trying to do, but I just can't increase your borrowing capacity any more than I already have. I'm sorry."

"WHAT ARE WE going to do now?" Hope asked Noah plaintively. Her shoulders sagged as she leaned against her Jeep, hands tucked in her pockets. She kicked a pebble across the asphalt.

"First, I'm going to buy you a drink. Then we can discuss where we go from here." When she didn't smile or budge, he opened her door. "C'mon. Follow me to the Blue Fin. You don't want to pass up a free drink, do you?" When she still didn't move, he braced his hands on either side of her, forcing her to look into his eyes. "*It's going to be okay.* We haven't let anything deter us so far, and we won't let this beat us either."

"If we can't get more funding, it might be the last drink we'll have for a long time," she grumbled, meaning it to be humorous, but neither of them laughed.

Sitting on the outside patio of the Blue Fin Café on Cannery Row, Hope twirled her wineglass on the table, leaving little curlicues of moisture. "This isn't how we imagined it would be when we were in college," she lamented.

"Yeah, well, I also thought you wouldn't have been able to resist my extraordinary charm, you'd fall madly in love with me, and we'd be married with six kids by now." He shrugged, his grin assuring her there were no hurt feelings. "But that didn't happen either. So we make the most of our circumstances."

Noah had always been able to coax her out of her dark moods. Finally she managed a shaky smile. "If I hadn't resisted you back then, I would've been another Drake casualty—along with those dozens of other girls. Which means you and I wouldn't be friends or business partners now."

He placed his hand on top of hers. "I have to say, hard as it is for me to get these words out, I'm glad you turned me down. Our friendship means the world to me."

"It does to me, too." She took a sip of her wine before continuing. "As for the partnership, what do we do about money?"

"This isn't our first challenge, nor will it be our last. We'll get through it."

"I appreciate the confidence, but do you have any ideas how?"

"Like we told Reeves, we'll intensify our fund-raising efforts." He gestured with his bottle of beer. "Hey, do you remember when we did that charity dance-a-thon two years ago? Everyone thought we were a couple and it worked to our advantage, because of all the media we got, which led to more donations."

Hope laughed. "Yeah. That picture of you dipping me made all the local papers. Remember the one with the caption 'Fred and Ginger'? Everyone—even our friends and volunteers—thought we'd been holding back on them because we looked like we were in… You know. Together."

Noah chuckled, too. "You just can't say the 'L' word, can you? So, we proceed as planned with the fund-raising, and we approach other financial institutions."

Hope shook her head. "Even our most consistent benefactors aren't giving as much anymore. The economic downturn hit people hard. As for other banks, if the one we do business with won't extend additional credit, it's unlikely another one will."

"Well, aren't you full of good cheer and optimism?" He tugged on her hair. "How about we focus on the positive, okay?" Opening the folio he'd brought into the bar with them, he unclipped his pen. "Let's make a list of what we *can* do."

A WEEK LATER, sitting in the small office they shared at the shelter, Noah crossed the final item off the list they'd compiled over drinks at the Blue Fin Café. "That's the last of our ideas."

"Much as I hate to say this, not only can we not expand, we have to seriously consider downsizing. We've cut our salaries to the minimum. Any more and we won't be able to pay our own rents. It's a good thing that we get most of our veterinary services pro bono through the local clinics." Hope sighed, grateful as always that her former employers continued to support their efforts. "We suspended all discretionary spending," she went on. "Not that anything we had really fit that category." She rubbed her tired eyes. "I'm sorry. I'm out of ideas, and we have to face reality."

At a light knock on the door, they both glanced up.

"Come in," Noah said.

Gillian, their part-time administrative assistant and office manager, cracked the door open. She looked from one long face to the other and didn't bother entering. "I'm sorry to disturb you, but I just signed for a registered letter from a law firm. I thought it might be important and you'd want it right away."

Hope turned to Noah, and she knew they both expected it to be more bad news. With a flirtatious smile, Noah reached out a hand for the courier pouch. Gillian, her cheeks pink, passed it to him, but added, "It's actually for Hope."

"Not both of us?" Noah asked in surprise. "Huh. Well, look at that."

He passed the pouch to Hope, and she felt the blood drain from her face. Why would *she* be getting a registered letter from a lawyer as opposed to both of them? They were equal partners in the shelter. "Thanks, Gillian," she said softly. Gillian nodded and closed the door behind her.

Hope stared at the pouch in her hands. The return address in San Jose caught her attention and she immediately worried that something had happened to Priscilla or Morris. Why else would she be getting a letter from a law firm in San Jose? She opened the flap and took out a letter-size envelope.

She read the two-page letter once, then reread it, before looking up at Noah. He glanced from Hope's face to her trembling hands, got quickly out of his chair and crouched down beside her. "What is it?"

"It's…it's from my father's lawyer." She swallowed audibly. "Here." She handed the letter to Noah. "Read it."

Noah took the sheets of paper and propped one hip against the desk. He scanned the letter quickly. His brows shot up as he handed it back to Hope. "Is this for real?"

Hope, suddenly and inexplicably, wanted to cry. Her vision was blurred by the tears in her eyes.

Noah's face sobered instantly. "I'm sorry. I wasn't thinking…"

"No, please don't feel bad. You're aware of my relationship—or lack thereof—with my father. Believe me, it surprises me that I feel like crying. Realistically, I never had any expectation that we'd reconcile, but to have the possibility arise at a time like this, when he's *dying...*"

"I'm sorry," Noah repeated.

"I knew from Priscilla that my father had some health problems over the years..." She felt the corners of her mouth curve upward. "Did I tell you she and Morris are expecting a baby? Sorry. I digress. Anyway, Priscilla told me my father had some issues but I supposed he'd gotten better. I never thought he'd have a stroke with no hope of recovery. Whatever our differences were," she said, "and they were considerable, knowing he's in the state he is still hurts. He was always so vital. I guess I thought he'd live forever."

Noah reached for Hope's hand and squeezed it as silence hung in the air between them. Finally, he pointed to the letter. "The reference to you being his sole beneficiary? And the part about his net worth? Is that possible?"

She shrugged. "If the lawyer says so, it must be. My father was always an astute businessman. According to the letter—well, you read it—my father was shrewd enough that when many of the dot-com billionaires went bankrupt in the late 1990s, he protected enough of his net worth and invested it outside the technology sector. I never realized how rich he was the year I spent with him. It might be just a fraction of what he was worth at his wealthiest, but nearly two hundred million dollars is more than I can imagine. It's a lot of money. Money that could help us here and solve all our problems."

Noah laughed. "That much money could solve the entire city's problems!" His expression grew thoughtful. "But what about the conditions?"

Hope sighed. "Yeah. There is that. Who would've thought that in his final days, my father would want to see me—and make amends to the town of Canyon Creek?"

Noah's smile was a little awkward. "Seeing your father might help you, too. Bring some closure…and give you the opportunity to say goodbye to him. As for the second condition, two years isn't such a long time, is it?"

JOCK'S STROKE WAS SEVERE. His lawyer had stressed that Jock didn't have much time left. Days at most. Although his brain was still sharp, his body was significantly compromised. Hope drove to the hospital in San Jose the next morning.

She was stunned by her father's physical condition. More than half his body was paralyzed. His face was a frozen mask, a trickle of drool running down his chin.

Her strong-willed, coldhearted father had tears spilling from his eyes when he saw Hope, making her wonder about his mental state. But—as the lawyer had assured her—Jock's mind was as sharp as ever. He rested his petrified hand in Hope's warm ones and told her a story that made her weep.

He apologized for not having been there for her and for not being truthful with her when she'd lived with him during that brief period in her teens. He explained that his departure from Canyon Creek wasn't mercenary and self-serving in the way he let people believe. He had, in fact, loved Hope's mother deeply and passionately, but had suspected that when they'd gone through a rough patch as a couple, she'd had a short and discreet relationship with another man. When they reconciled, Jock had insisted they marry and without delay. Jock was overjoyed to learn of Rebecca's pregnancy early in their marriage.

Hope arrived several weeks premature, by

Jock's calculation, but was a healthy weight and size, arousing his suspicions. A DNA test confirmed that Hope was not his child and he confronted Rebecca.

She confessed to having an affair during the period they'd been apart, as he'd speculated. Jock was shattered, but his love for Rebecca was so great, he thought he could forgive her anything and was willing to raise Hope as his own. To appease his jealousy—and to circumvent possible legal challenges to Hope's paternity in the future—he hired a private investigator to locate the father. The investigator reported that the man had died in a skiing accident not long after Rebecca had ended the relationship.

As time passed, Jock had tried to overcome his jealousy.

He told Hope that she was a sweet and beautiful baby, but he simply couldn't open his heart to her, since she was a constant reminder of his wife's transgression. Although no one else knew, the thought of Rebecca with another man ate away at him. For his own sanity, Jock saw no alternative than to leave his hometown and the woman he loved. His pain and resentment had built to the point that he wanted to lash out. Uncaring of the consequences to the town, he closed his business with the sole purpose of minimizing the financial settlement Rebecca—and therefore Hope—would receive.

Yet in all the years after he walked out on Rebecca, Jock had never gotten over his feelings for her nor had he been capable of loving another woman. Instead, he'd buried himself in work.

Learning of Rebecca's death, Jock had grieved, despite the passage of time. He'd brought Hope to him with the intention of being a father to her and at least having part of Rebecca to treasure.

But just as when Hope was an infant, the sight of her—bearing such an uncanny resemblance to Rebecca—inflamed his bitterness and heartbreak. In Hope, he saw Rebecca. He could not forget or forgive.

His cheeks wet with tears, Jock begged Hope's forgiveness for the way he'd treated her.

Confronted with the certainty of death, he'd come to realize how wrong he'd been. He should never have left Rebecca—he said it again and again—and he should've been there for Hope. By seeking to punish them, he'd deprived himself of a lifetime of love, hurting so many people in the process.

His dying wish, he insisted, was for Hope to find it in her heart to forgive him. Everything he had was hers; all he asked was that she make restitution to the town of Canyon Creek on his behalf. He wanted to give the town a much-needed new school and community center. He wanted her to return, to compensate for what he'd done. Talking it through with her, he saw the error of making it a condition in his will. He'd forced her to leave when she was a teen and now he was forcing her to go back. He planned to change that. He wanted her to do it of her own free will rather than out of obligation. He said he'd have his lawyers draft a codicil.

Hope saw a tortured, troubled, sad man, so unlike the one she'd lived with for nearly a year. The feelings she'd harbored for her father were tempered by seeing him as fallible and capable of a lifelong love. In this new and kinder light, she understood that his abandonment of her and her mother was not as straightforward as it had seemed.

She would have to reconcile herself to her mother's role in the circumstances. Regardless, going back to Canyon Creek for two years, to try to make restitution on behalf of her father and in the manner he asked, was a daunting task. Before she could argue with him, Jock took a shaky breath, closed his eyes and drifted into a peaceful sleep.

CHAPTER TEN

Canyon Creek, Texas

HOPE PULLED HER Jeep over to the side of the road next to a meadow, just where the road crested as it wound toward Canyon Creek. The Jeep was packed to the roof, and she'd even strapped some duffel bags on top. The only available space inside was for her and Einstein. The drive from Monterey had been almost exactly twenty-four hours, spread over three days with short, intermittent stops to rest or sleep.

She still found it hard to believe that she was on her way back to Canyon Creek.

Her father had fallen into a coma, never to wake again. He didn't have the chance to change his will before his death. It stood as written. To receive her inheritance, she had to satisfy his original condition; she had to move back to Canyon Creek for a minimum of two years and use a portion of his assets, bequeathed to her in trust, to establish a new school and community center within the stipulated time frame.

Although she could have chosen to walk away from the money, the inheritance would not only solve her and Noah's financial issues with Barkley Green, it offered an unprecedented opportunity to modernize and expand the shelter in ways they could only have dreamed of. They could add a much-needed veterinary hospital, enlarge and upgrade the kennel area, and fund it all in perpetuity through a trust. It meant they'd never have to turn an animal away, and they could have full-time medical care right on the premises.

On a personal level, the condition presented a huge challenge for Hope. In all the years she'd been gone, she'd never imagined that she'd have to return to her hometown and face all the people who believed she disdained them. Not to mention seeing Luke Carter again.

She had no choice.

Although she wouldn't see a penny of the inheritance for her own use until she'd fulfilled the condition in her father's will, his estate paid all costs related to "the project," which thankfully included her gas for the trip. They would've paid for airfare, but she was *not* putting Einstein in the cargo hold of a plane.

She would also be reimbursed for her periodic visits to Monterey to be able to maintain her business interests there. She and Noah had agreed that she'd continue to oversee the bookkeeping and would fly home every four to six weeks to handle other business matters.

Hope stretched her legs, then her back. The final portion of the trip had been five hours of nonstop driving. They'd started out before sunrise. What a glorious vision it had been when the bright orange globe rose on the eastern horizon, shrouding them in the warmth of its glow. Stifling a yawn, she opened the passenger door for Einstein. He wasn't as agile as he used to be, but he was still healthy and jumped out of the truck without hesitation. Once she'd led him to the grassy area, where he sauntered off, nose to the ground, Hope turned back toward the town.

Had it really been more than a decade since she'd last seen Canyon Creek?

From where she stood, it looked so familiar. The slow-flowing Gulch River that snaked its way along the town's eastern periphery. She could just make out the red roof on the stone church. The board-and-batten Elenore Hotel. Center Street with its quaint shops, restaurants and bars. And outside the town, the patchwork of ranches.

The buoyancy she'd felt as she'd driven toward the rising sun faded, and she felt a ripple of apprehension. In tune with her mood as always, Einstein ambled over and nuzzled her hand. She automatically stroked the top of his head. "Well, we might as well get this over with," she murmured.

Hope let Einstein back in the Jeep, then climbed into the driver's seat.

As they approached Center Street, she slowed. Part of her yearned to drive down Center Street. To see close-up how much had changed and how much had stayed the same. But that would have to wait. They'd been on the road for three days; they needed some rest.

At the first set of lights—one of only three in town—she took a sharp right.

She'd booked a room at a motel on County Road 93, twenty minutes from downtown Canyon Creek. Hope had chosen to stay there rather than at the Elenore Hotel to avoid being noticed. At the motel, she was close enough to do what she needed to, but far enough to keep a low profile.

A half mile down, the road changed to gravel and she reduced her speed further to avoid kicking up too much dust. She had a vague recollection of where the motel was. She and Luke used to ride a couple of his neighbor's horses along this road when they were kids. Unexpectedly, her eyes stung and her throat constricted.

It shocked her that after all these years, she'd still feel the pain and regret of losing Luke. Being back unearthed all the memories and feelings she'd tried to bury.

She blinked rapidly to keep the tears from forming and sighed in relief when the motel came into view.

It was an unadorned, one-story brick structure, with maybe a dozen rooms. It backed onto a field and allowed dogs, both of which were important considerations for her. The room she'd reserved had a kitchenette, so she could make her own meals.

Hope pulled into a parking spot in front of the motel office. She smoothed down her hair and glanced at Einstein. "Wait here. I'll be right back." He emitted a soft, resigned moan. "You'll be fine. I won't be long," she assured him.

True to her word, she was back in the Jeep less than ten minutes later, with a room key in her hand. She backed out of the spot and drove slowly to the end unit. Parking in front of it, she glanced over again. "Ready, pal?"

Some heavy panting and a short bark were her answer. "Let's go, then."

She released Einstein, got a couple of bags out of the Jeep and unlocked the door to their room.

It was small, the decor dated. The carpet had seen better days, and the bed had a distinct sag in the middle, but it would do.

Hope unloaded her vehicle. She wouldn't unpack everything, but she couldn't very well drive around with her Jeep full of her belongings. She'd go into town to pick up some groceries and other essentials, enough to keep her and Einstein going for a few days, but her first priority was to take Einstein for a walk. In deference to the heat, she tucked her hair under a baseball cap to keep it off her neck and shoulders.

They wandered along the dirt road and across the overgrown field without running into a single person. All the while, Hope tried without success to sort through her muddled emotions about being back in Canyon Creek. Since she'd learned that she'd have to return, not a single day had passed that thoughts of Luke hadn't intruded on her consciousness.

Leaving Einstein in the room to rest, she drove into town with those unsettling thoughts still circling in her mind.

The grocery-shopping excursion went without incident—and without seeing anyone she knew. Not having anticipated how all the dust and pollen they'd encountered on their walk would affect her, she decided to buy some allergy medication while she was in town. Entering The Apothecary, the local pharmacy, she recognized Miranda Stewart, one of her former schoolmates, standing behind the counter. Miranda stared at Hope, as if trying to decide whether her eyes were deceiving her. Finally Miranda placed her hands on her hips. "Well, well, well. If it isn't Hope Wilson." She almost purred the words.

"It's nice to see you, Miranda. How are you?" Hope asked, trying her best to be friendly.

"Fine. Just fine."

Hope began to feel awkward under Miranda's obvious appraisal. She had a strong urge to get what she came for and leave. "Could I have a package of Claritin, please?"

Miranda didn't blink an eye. "I'm *so* sorry, but we're all out."

Hope shifted her gaze to the shelf behind Miranda. An ample supply of the distinct blue packages were neatly lined up. "It's right there, behind you." Hope pointed.

Miranda turned slowly, took some time to study all the products, then faced Hope again. "As I said, we're all out."

"But—" Hope didn't have a chance to finish what she'd been about to say as Miranda stalked off.

Hope watched with disbelief as the other woman exited through a swinging door behind the counter. "You've got to be kidding me," she murmured. She and Miranda had never been close friends, but they'd gotten along well enough. Her encounter with Miranda did not bode well for how she'd be received. If this was any indication of what was to come, it would be a very long two years. Her thoughts drifted back to Luke and what his reaction might be. She just wanted to return to the motel but, like it or not, she had to make one more stop to buy the premium dog food Einstein required for his aging joints.

In the pet store, she pushed the shopping cart up and down the aisles and tried to set her negative thoughts aside. But she found it more challenging to put Luke out of her mind.

"That's a lot of dog food," the young clerk behind the counter commented as she rang up the two thirty-pound bags, a box of dog treats and a couple of chew toys.

"Yeah, and you'll be seeing me back sooner than you'd think," Hope said as she slipped her credit card and the receipt in her wallet. The clerk was too young to know her. After the encounter with Miranda, it was nice to have a pleasant interaction, free of tension. Hope slid the shopping bag over her arm, then hefted the first of the two large bags of kibble.

"Let me give you a hand with that." The clerk came around to help just as the phone started ringing.

"Go ahead and answer that. I can manage," Hope told her.

"You sure?"

Hope nodded.

"Thanks," the clerk said as she rushed to answer the phone.

Hope pushed the plastic bag farther up her arm and hoisted the other bag of dog food. Weighed down and barely able to see over her load, she was glad her Jeep was only a few steps outside the shop. She maneuvered one of the bags farther up as it began to slide and raised her leg to balance the other one so she could reach for the door. Just as she was about to open it, the door was pulled out of her grasp. She lurched forward and tumbled out the doorway. She hit the sidewalk hard, landing inelegantly on her hands and knees, her purchases scattered about. One of the bags of dog food had split and kibble was strewn around her.

Hope pushed to her knees and winced as raw skin scraped across the rough cement.

"I'm so sorry. Here, let me help..." A pair

of large hands reached toward her. They froze and withdrew abruptly as Hope looked up and, from under the brim of her baseball cap, made eye contact with a pair of gold-flecked amber eyes—Luke Carter's lion eyes.

The man before her was tall and fit. His face had matured in a rugged, handsome way. He looked the same and yet he didn't.

Hope's immediate reaction was excitement, that little thrill she'd always experienced when she'd been with him as a teen.

She lowered her head. "Great. Just great," she muttered. Those mischievous fates just had to have another go at her today, didn't they? Of all the people they could've thrown in her path, it had to be Luke. Probably served her right for not being able to keep her mind off him.

"Hope? Ah...hi. It's really you? What are you doing here?"

A range of emotions—not all of which Hope could decipher—passed across Luke's face, finally settling on concern.

"Let me help you up." He reached out. With the utmost care, he clasped Hope's elbow to assist her.

"Thank you," she mumbled and became absorbed with brushing off her legs and her clothes. Drops of blood welled on her knees. Luke pulled a blue-checked bandanna out of his back pocket and held it out to her. Hope's eyes shifted from the bandanna to Luke's hand…free of a wedding ring. Dismayed by her own thoughts, she frowned.

"It's clean," he assured her. "Go ahead. Use it."

Hope's look had nothing to do with the condition of the bandanna and everything to do with bumping—literally—into the one person she was least prepared to see.

When she didn't move to accept the bandanna, Luke bent down and, placing one hand behind her knee, gently dabbed at the abrasions. That simple, impersonal touch made her feel as if a two-hundred-and-twenty-volt electric current surged through her body. She tried to spring back, but Luke's hand on her leg prevented her, and she nearly lost her balance again.

Her sharply indrawn breath caused him to release her. "Did I hurt you?"

Hope stepped back to put some distance between them. "It's fine. I'm fine. I just need to…to get my things." Her words tumbled over each other.

Luke rose and, unmindful of the blood on his bandanna, stuck it back in his pocket.

Hope hurriedly gathered everything that had fallen out of the shopping bag, as Luke folded over the top of the torn bag to keep more kibble from spilling before lifting it into his arms.

"You don't have to do that," Hope protested. "I can manage. Really."

Disregarding her objection, he grabbed the undamaged bag, as well. "Where's your car?"

Hope wanted to protest again, but her legs felt like lead weights and she was worried her voice would crack. She decided it was easiest just to get her purchases loaded and be gone as quickly as possible. She pointed to the red Jeep. "Right there."

Luke carried over the two bags as Hope rummaged through her shoulder bag for her keys and opened the back door. He placed the bags inside. Then he went to clean up the spilled kibble, tossing it into a nearby trash receptacle. Tucking his thumbs into the front pockets of his jeans, he strode back to Hope. His eyes were steady on hers, and she was distinctly uncomfortable under his scrutiny. She wanted to run, to hide, but her legs now seemed to have grown roots, too, and she was—ha—rooted to the spot.

"It's good to see you, Hope." The initial shock of seeing her seemed to have worn off.

"Uh…thanks." Her tongue felt swollen and too big for her mouth. Her inability to control her limbs and her speech was frustrating and absurd.

Luke shifted his gaze down to her boots and up to her face again. A sheepish smile raised the corners of his mouth. "You're even more beautiful than you were at seventeen. What brought you home?"

The years certainly hadn't hurt his looks. He was still broad-shouldered, with that thick crop of chestnut-brown hair, intense lion's eyes and beguiling smile.

"Oh, stuff," she mumbled. She didn't understand what was happening to her, but she felt hot and clammy at the same time. She closed her fist over her keys, hoping the sharp points stabbing into her palm would restore her self-control. She had to get away from Luke, or she'd make a bigger fool of herself than she already had. It was too disconcerting to see him. And he'd said "home." That unsettled her in an entirely different way.

She fumbled with her keys. "Thanks again, Luke." His name on her lips felt odd but also… familiar. "Take care." She succeeded in getting her legs to cooperate, climbed into her Jeep and started the engine.

With an uncharacteristic and mortifying grinding of the gears, she hastened away from the curb.

A glance in her rearview mirror showed Luke still standing as he had been, thumbs in his pockets, hip cocked. He was watching her rapidly departing vehicle.

But his smile had turned into a frown.

CHAPTER ELEVEN

LUKE CARTER SAT behind his desk in his office at Whispering Springs Ranch. Ignoring the financial statements in front of him, he stared out the window at his pastures and barns, watched a couple of his ranch hands work with one of his horses. He smiled fleetingly as he noticed one of his dogs chasing a butterfly.

It was common knowledge that Hope was back in Canyon Creek. How could it not have been? Everyone in town had been buzzing about it since she'd shown up at The Apothecary a few days ago. If he'd heard she was back in town rather than actually seeing her—bumping into her—outside the pet store, his immediate thought would've been to seek her out. How ridiculous would that have been?

Thankfully, he hadn't had the opportunity to rush all over town like a lovesick puppy, hoping to catch a glimpse of her.

What were the odds of running into her accidentally the way he had? He shouldn't have been surprised that the beautiful girl he remembered from high school had grown up to be a stunner. He'd been so happy, unreasonably happy, to see her, despite everything she and her father had done…and she'd acted as if he had a communicable disease. She rushed off in a hurry, making it abundantly clear where he stood with her. It was obvious that she didn't have any residual feelings for him or any remorse for the way she'd abandoned him.

Luke leaned back in his chair and gazed up at the ceiling.

It was for the best, he mused, because he hadn't realized until after his recent encounter with Hope how much pent-up resentment he still felt about her not being there for him when he'd needed her so badly. He could still remember reaching out to her, despite her having left him, when his world had caved in shortly after her departure from Canyon Creek. He'd called her, pleaded with her in his letters and emails, because she was the one person who could've helped him make sense of what had happened. He was ashamed of how desperate he must have sounded in his notes.

She'd completely ignored him.

Luke thought back to the day he'd lost his

father in that fiery crash on I-35 S outside Fort Worth. Only days earlier, Philip Carter had sent him a letter, again placing the blame for his troubles on Hope's father. Yeah, maybe it wasn't all her father's fault, but his own dad's downward spiral had started with the loss of his job when Jock closed his manufacturing plant. Luke had poured it all out to Hope in his correspondence. There hadn't been a single call, email or letter from her in response.

That had shown him how much she cared—or rather, didn't. Maybe she *was* just like her father, as everyone said. He'd finally stopped his futile attempts to reach her and dealt with his grief and pain in his own way. But based on his reaction now, he'd never fully resolved his feelings for her.

Luke would rather have been branded with a cattle iron than admit to anyone that he'd kept track of her, even after he'd stopped trying to get in touch with her.

He knew she lived in Monterey, owned an animal shelter and was seeing the guy she ran the shelter with. He'd tried to block out the bitterness he'd felt toward that Drake character whenever he'd seen pictures of him with Hope, arm in arm at some event. The last person he would've expected her to be with was some California pretty boy.

Still, he couldn't help feeling proud of what Hope had accomplished with the animal shelter, but the sting of her desertion lingered. Just like her father, she'd left without a second thought for the people she had left behind.

Despite everything, Luke had treated every picture of her that he'd come across—usually taken at a charitable event or industry function—as a precious drop of life-sustaining water for a thirsty man lost in a desert. Somewhere along the way, he'd been able to develop a degree of detachment, from both the longing and the hurt, but he never stopped checking periodically for updates about her life.

Did that make him some sort of weird cyber stalker? he wondered uneasily. Another good reason not to let anyone—including the lady in question—find out what he'd been doing.

He dragged a hand through his hair. What kind of fool was he, anyway? The woman couldn't have been more obvious about her feelings, and here he was, *twelve years* later, still not over her.

In all the years she'd been gone, he'd never forgotten that one brilliant summer of young love they'd shared. Even her callous treatment of him afterward hadn't dimmed its shine. For his own sanity, or what was left of it where she was concerned, he decided it would be best to keep things polite and friendly, but avoid her as much as he could.

Luke rubbed a hand over his chest. The roast beef sandwich he'd had for lunch must not have agreed with him. He felt a definite burning, right above his heart.

He needed some air. And maybe some hard manual labor would help. He pushed out of his chair and headed off.

AS IT TURNED OUT, Hope's run-in with Miranda Stewart was just the tip of the iceberg. Hope might've been hesitant about seeing her former friends and acquaintances after so many years, but she'd never expected the cold reception that met her wherever she went. Every trip she made into town caused her some unease.

It was obvious that the rumor mill hadn't changed in the years she'd been gone. After the first few encounters, it was obvious that people were aware of her presence. When asked a couple of times why she'd returned, she'd answered truthfully, saying she wanted to build a school and community center. Although she remained vague about the details, there was no point in hiding her purpose, since people would find out sooner or later anyway.

It didn't surprise her that this news, too, spread through Canyon Creek like wildfire.

If her business—her *project*—was to be public knowledge, she wished it would warm the townspeople's view of her. She didn't dream of friendship or acceptance, but she didn't think tolerance would've been too much to ask. After all, she was here to do something good for the town.

If she'd thought—hoped—that most people would have forgotten her, that wasn't the case. If she'd hoped—prayed—that they'd forgiven her, that was even more unrealistic. Not only did the residents of Canyon Creek shun her, they didn't want to have anything to do with her project, simply because it was being funded by her father's money. She regretted letting that particular detail slip. While opening a bank account, she'd mentioned how her return to Canyon Creek had come about while explaining why money would be transferred regularly by a law firm to cover her expenses.

Regardless of the source of funding, she would've expected the townspeople would welcome a new school and community center complex. But apparently their anger was profound and enduring.

As a teen, she hadn't fully grasped how deeply everyone in town had reviled her father. And they'd turned their anger on her, too, when she'd left Canyon Creek. That was her own fault; she'd flaunted her father's wealth and her desire to emulate him. Like her father, she hadn't looked back and—just as in his case—the townspeople had no way of knowing her true reasons for leaving.

The next two years stretched endlessly ahead of Hope. If not for the animals that depended on Barkley Green in Monterey, she would've been tempted to pack up and go back there. But the money mattered a great deal to her and Noah and the animals they cared for. And she'd made a commitment. If Noah was willing to keep things going mostly single-handedly during her absence—a considerable additional burden for him—how could she renege on her side of the bargain?

Over the past couple of weeks, Hope had focused her time and energies on the preliminaries associated with getting her project started. It helped occupy her mind. If she needed to go into town, as she had that morning, she tended to do it early, while most of the residents were still at home or occupied with chores at their ranches. Although it was a small town, she hadn't seen Luke since the pet shop incident. She hadn't realized that she'd expected him to seek her out—until she'd felt the pang of disappointment that he hadn't. Based on her instant reaction to him, she'd fleetingly wondered if there could be something between them again, but there was no point in thinking about that. Her place was in Monterey, and the last thing she needed was more heartache. Maybe they could be friends, but she had her doubts, since it seemed that Luke was avoiding her.

Almost as if she'd willed Luke to appear, she saw him cross the street and walk in the direction of the Canyon Creek Mocha Shoppe. Watching his fluid gait, she felt a hum of excitement.

Two years was a long time to avoid each other. She deliberated for a moment, then picked up her pace and called out. "Luke!" He paused and looked over at her. She waved as she hurried toward him. "Can I buy you a coffee?" she asked.

His eyes were hard, his mouth unsmiling. "A coffee?"

"Yes, a coffee. Or a bagel." Hope gave a nervous giggle and gestured toward the Canyon Mocha Shoppe. "That's where you're going, right?"

"Well, yeah."

Hope smiled and reached for the door. She felt his touch on her arm and turned, but he abruptly withdrew his hand. "You don't have to buy me a coffee," he said, his voice low and serious.

Hope's smile faltered. She really wanted them to get along. She'd hoped that her effort to be friendly would sway him, but it didn't appear to be the case. "All right. Then why don't you join me and pay for your own coffee?" she suggested uncertainly.

"Hope..." His face reflected some inner battle. "Don't do this," he said finally. "Not after everything." He opened the door and walked into the coffee shop.

AFTER EVERYTHING? HOPE was troubled by Luke's choice of words as she drove home. She knew she'd hurt him when she'd left, but hadn't realized how much. They were teenagers back then, and twelve years had passed. She'd hoped that time would have done its healing, and they could put their history behind them. That didn't seem to be the case with Luke.

She mulled that over for most of the trip. Forcing thoughts of Luke aside, Hope couldn't resist a smile as she turned her Jeep into the driveway. One positive development since she'd been back in Canyon Creek was that she'd managed to get an exceptional deal on a small rental house outside town. As a bonus, the house had come furnished. It was only a little more expensive than the motel room, but it had far more privacy. It was on a good-size lot that provided plenty of room for Einstein to explore. And it was bordered by undeveloped land and a ranch, so she had no close neighbors to concern herself with.

Hope adored the house, with its rickety wraparound porch, overgrown garden teeming with drought-resistant perennials, faded cream-colored siding and emerald-green shutters.

The inside was cozy and comfortable. There was a combined living/dining area, kitchen and two-piece bath on the main floor and two bedrooms and a full bath on the second. Both upstairs rooms had a view of the backyard and the enormous white ash and bald cypress trees edging it.

Hope used one bedroom to sleep in and set the other one up as an office. That was where she went now, cup of tea in hand, and sat down at her desk situated beneath the window.

Gazing out, she found her thoughts wandering back to Luke. When they'd met outside the pet store that first day, he'd been friendly and helpful, and she'd been...well, curt at best, bordering on rude at worst. Seeing him so unexpectedly had thrown her off. Her response to him was purely physical, or so she tried to rationalize. Luke was a more mature version of the boy she'd loved when they were in high school. The crinkle lines around his eyes when he smiled were new and oh, so sexy. No ring on his finger meant he wasn't married; she was sure he was the type of guy who'd wear a wedding ring. She wondered if the way she'd reacted was enough to prompt his cold rejection of her at the coffee shop. Whatever the cause, it had left her embarrassed and regretful.

Hope took a sip of tea, leaned on her crossed arms and smiled at a couple of blue jays squabbling over the bird feeder she'd hung.

She turned her thoughts to her project. She'd discovered that the small school she'd attended as a kid had been outgrown long ago. It hadn't been updated since she went there, nor had it been expanded to accommodate the increased population. It was dated and overcrowded. Kids spent several classes a day in trailers on the school property. And the nearest community center was forty-five miles away in Tudhope. If she was giving up two years of her life for this, she wanted it to be worthwhile. She believed the school and community center would do that—make a big difference to the town and its residents. Her father must have known that, since he'd incorporated it in his will.

And that led her to think about her father. She felt grateful that they'd reconciled, at least to some degree. He'd slipped away peacefully while she held his hand.

Once the astonishment of what he'd revealed about her paternity had worn off, Hope was surprised by a couple of things. First, her feelings for Jock had changed. Now she felt sorry for him more than anything and tried not to resent her mother for her role. Second, she wondered why she wasn't motivated to discover the identity of her biological father or search out his family. Jock hadn't mentioned his name, nor had she thought to ask him at the time. All he'd told her was that the man had died shortly after her mother had ended the relationship and that he likely never knew he'd fathered a child. Hope doubted her mother had confided in Clarissa or anyone else, so the identity of her biological father was lost to her with Jock's death.

She supposed she could have hired a private investigator, too, but after so many years what would he have to go on? Also, having lived her life essentially without a father, she had no strong desire to learn the identity of one who was inaccessible to her regardless.

She watched a blue jay fly off on an erratic trajectory, another in hot pursuit.

Even in the short time she'd been here, she was starting to think of the project as *hers* as much as her father's. It had come to matter to her, and she wanted to do the very best she could. She still seemed to think of the town as hers, too. With sentiments like that, how was she going to make it through the two years? Or even more disturbing, what about all the years after that? It had taken her a long time to adjust to leaving Canyon Creek as a teen. What would it be like to start all over again at the end of the two-year period?

Einstein, who'd been lying beside her, rolled over in his sleep, bumping into the folding doors of the closet. The rattling noise startled him awake. He righted himself as quickly as his aging joints would allow and released what Hope thought of as a trying-to-be-tough-but-missing-by-a-mile series of staccato barks. The barking did manage to snap her out of her ruminations. She turned on her computer and studied the short list of local real-estate agents she'd compiled. With a good idea of what she was looking for, she was ready to start the search for a development site.

After narrowing it down to three real-estate agents, Hope chose Joanna Westwood. Joanna's credentials were solid. She'd moved to Canyon Creek from San Antonio less than five years ago. She had no firsthand knowledge of Hope's history. That meant there'd be no animosity.

Hope stressed the importance of timing, and Joanna didn't waste any time. She did her research quickly and soon they were out viewing properties.

A couple of days after they'd begun, Hope and Joanna were standing adjacent to a split-rail fence fronting a large parcel of vacant land. Hope leaned on the railing, rested a booted foot on the bottom rung and considered the property. It was a flat, ten-acre parcel, unused at present for grain or grazing. The long grass swayed gracefully in the wind, and the combination of bright sun and intense heat caused lovely little shimmers to dance across the tips. The backdrop of a working ranch, with horses and steer feeding in the distance, only enhanced its appeal.

"This is it," Hope announced. The brisk north-easterly wind blew her hair wildly around and she shook it back. A grin spread across her face. "I really think this is it!"

Joanna nodded. "Yeah. I thought this might work for you. I don't think you'll have to worry about zoning. It shouldn't be a problem, not with this location and your proposed use."

Hope turned to face Joanna. "Okay. What's next?"

Joanna slipped an arm in the crook of Hope's

elbow and led her back to her car. "We go to my office and write up the offer."

Hope felt a giddy sense of anticipation as she watched Joanna enter the details in her computer and then send the document to print. She pulled the sheets of paper out of her printer and scanned them. Satisfied, she handed them to Hope. "There you go. Look it over carefully before you sign. Make sure I got everything you wanted in there."

Hope took the pages and started reading. Almost immediately, her smile waned. She looked up at Joanna. "Carter Enterprises?"

"Yes. Carter Enterprises is the current owner."

"As in *Luke* Carter?"

"Why, yes. I believe so."

Hope almost groaned. "I thought he was a rancher." At least that was what she'd heard around town.

"He is, and quite successful, from what I understand. But he's also a businessman. Some of our most prosperous ranchers are, to cushion them against fluctuating market prices."

Hope abruptly dropped the papers on the desktop.

Joanna angled her head. "Is there a problem?"

Hope's laugh was brittle. What were the odds? She wouldn't have imagined that she'd find the perfect piece of property, and it would be owned by Luke. After the coffee shop incident, she knew she wasn't in his good graces. Even if she went ahead with the offer, would he accept it?

If not, she couldn't blame him. She wanted to believe that he wouldn't be holding a grudge after twelve years, but if everyone else did—people who hadn't cared about her nearly as much—wouldn't it make sense that he would, too? And yet, he'd started out being nice to her during their very first encounter...and she'd spoiled his attempt.

Ideal as the property was, she couldn't proceed with it. Hope knew she wasn't being rational, but she nudged the pages toward Joanna. "I've changed my mind. I'm sorry, but we're going to have to keep looking."

Joanna tapped her bright red fingernails on her desk. "Okay. Are you looking for something different?"

A property not owned by Luke Carter? Hope shrugged. How could she explain if it didn't even make sense to her? Telling Joanna that her connection to Luke was the reason she couldn't go ahead with the transaction would only make her sound foolish. She knew it was her heart and not her head that was driving her decision. She just couldn't see herself conducting a civilized business transaction with

Luke. "No. I'd like to buy something similar. Just not *that* property."

Joanna raised an eyebrow. "Okay. Let me see what I can find."

She continued to show Hope properties, but two things were clear. With her illogical behavior, Hope had managed to drive a wedge between her and Joanna. She could sense the agent's withdrawal from her on a personal level. The lighthearted mood that had existed between the two of them was gone. Just great! The one person in Canyon Creek she thought she was developing a friendship with, and she'd blown that, too. Second, she'd already seen most of the available land that satisfied her search criteria.

As Hope continued to view properties without much success, she started the process of hiring an architect. Since there were no firms in Canyon Creek that could undertake the work for her, she researched architectural practices in a broader area. As none of the firms were known to her, based on qualifications and expertise, she narrowed it down to four, with a strong preference for one. To do her due diligence, she requested expressions of interest from all four. One declined, but reviewing the information submitted by the other three, Hope selected the firm she'd favored from the beginning: Harry Gifford Architects, or HGA, as they referred to themselves.

HGA was a boutique shop with only a handful of employees, owned and operated by the principal architect, Harry Gifford. The practice was headquartered in nearby Northcliffe, but they'd done work in Canyon Creek before and were interested in doing more. The firm was small enough to provide personal service, but large enough to take on a project the magnitude of hers.

She liked the work Harry did. With him as the lead architect, she had confidence in what she'd be getting. Hers would be the largest project HGA had handled, but not by much. It meant that they had demonstrated capability but would consider her job an important one. As an added advantage, Harry proposed to set up a small local office for her project. It was as convenient as she could have expected.

She and Harry agreed to meet for a coffee at the Long Horn Grillhouse. Hope entered the restaurant close to the appointed time. Head down, mumbling a quiet greeting to the waitress, she made her way to a corner booth. She sat so that her back was to the room but she could keep an eye on the front door.

"There's a sight for sore eyes! I heard you'd returned."

Startled, Hope glanced up. Travis Carter stood by her table, a dish towel slung over his shoulder. He'd tucked his hands in the front pockets of his jeans, much like his brother tended to do. Travis was Luke's brother, younger by four years. Although he'd been only thirteen when she left, there was no mistaking the impish grin and the sparking blue eyes.

"Travis…you…you're all grown up!" He seemed friendly, even happy to see her, but Hope steeled herself for disappointment. His laughter alleviated some of her uneasiness.

"That's a good thing, considering I'm twenty-six now." He held a hand out to her. "Let me have a look at you."

Hope placed her hand in his. He drew her to her feet, turned her to one side, then the other and gave a low whistle. "You've grown up, too, and you're still as pretty as I remember."

Feeling self-conscious, Hope pulled free and sat down again. She scanned the room, hoping they hadn't attracted too much attention, then glanced toward the door, wondering what was keeping Harry. Travis's eyes followed hers and returned to her face. "Mind if I join you until whoever you're waiting for shows up?"

Hope motioned to the other side of the table. "Sure."

Travis slid in and signaled the waitress to

bring him a coffee. Hope noted the towel still draped over his shoulder. “You work here?”

His laugh burst forth again. “You bet I do! Nearly as many hours as there are in a day.”

Could things have been so tight for him that he had to work in a kitchen? Was Luke struggling, too?

Only now did Travis seem to realize he had the towel over his shoulder. He yanked it off and tossed it on the seat next to him. “I think you misunderstood. I own the Long Horn Grillhouse.”

“Really? Good for you!” Hope took a more careful look around. “Nice place.”

“Who would’ve thought I’d end up owning a restaurant and bar? When we were kids, I’d do anything to get out of helping Mom in the kitchen.”

Hope smiled. She remembered it well, including the number of times she’d offered to help Mrs. Carter just to spare him. “How is your mother?” she asked.

Travis’s expression sobered. “I guess you haven’t heard. Mom passed away, oh, nearly three years ago.”

“I’m so sorry.”

“Yeah. Thanks. We still miss her every single day.”

“And your father? How is he?” Hope knew

that Luke and Travis had stayed in contact with him after he'd left Canyon Creek, and wondered if he'd ever returned.

"He's gone, too," Travis muttered.

Before Hope could say anything, he changed the subject.

"I understand you're back to build a school and a community center."

"That's right."

"Terrific!"

Hope laughed without humor. "You're probably the only person this side of Stillhouse Hollow Lake who thinks so."

"People haven't been very welcoming, huh?"

"That's an understatement."

"They'll come around."

"We'll see. So far I haven't had much cause for optimism."

The waitress placed Travis's coffee in front of him. "Thanks, Carly," he said and turned to Hope again. "I'm sorry they're giving you a hard time."

When Hope remained silent, he continued. "What I don't get is what's going on between you and Luke."

Hope's eyes shot up. "There's nothing between Luke and me." Her voice had taken on a sharp tone.

Travis sipped his coffee. "See? That's what

I mean. Hear how your tone changed? I ask Luke about you, and he's surly as a bear and just about bites my head off. And it can't all be because of, well..." He paused. "Obviously, there are still feelings involved. Don't you think the two of you should talk things through?"

Hope didn't have a chance to answer as the front door opened and Harry walked in. Travis glanced over his shoulder, grabbed the towel and rose. He leaned forward, one arm braced on the table, and placed a light kiss on Hope's forehead. "For what it's worth, *I'm* happy to see you." Straightening, he introduced himself to Harry, then headed to the kitchen.

HOPE AND HARRY made an immediate connection. She offered him the contract at the conclusion of that first face-to-face meeting.

She wished the property search was going as smoothly. Four futile days later, Hope was again sitting in Joanna's office.

"That's about all that's on the market right now in the area you specified," Joanna said. "I wouldn't recommend going outside those boundaries. People aren't going to want to drive that far to get their kid to school or to play a game of basketball."

"Can you think of any properties that might

be suitable but aren't currently on the market?" Hope caught Joanna rolling her eyes, but to her credit she took some time to consider.

Finally, she shook her head. "Sorry, I can't. If you want to wait, I can keep an eye out and call you if anything comes on the market over the next few months."

Hope thought about the weeks of her allotted time she'd already used with nothing to show for it other than having hired HGA. She knew there wasn't a lot of slack in the stipulated two-year time frame. Sure, she could start with the design, but doing that without knowing the site was far from ideal. Just sitting back and hoping another suitable parcel of land would come on the market was definitely not a wise move.

Hope took a deep breath. "Let's go ahead with the offer on the parcel owned by Carter Enterprises."

Joanna nodded in acknowledgment and turned to her computer. "Same terms we discussed previously?"

"Yes," she said resignedly.

CHAPTER TWELVE

"EVERYTHING OKAY, LUKE?"

Luke spun around to face his friend and sometime real-estate agent. He hadn't heard Joe enter the office.

"Is…everything…okay?" Joe repeated, spacing the words out.

Luke had no idea how long Joe had been standing there while he was lost in his own thoughts, but if the grin on Joe's face was any indication, it had been a while. "Yeah. Fine," he grumbled.

Joe made himself comfortable in the chair opposite Luke's desk. They'd worked together on Luke's property transactions for the better part of seven years, had been friends longer than that. "When I couldn't reach you on the phone, I thought I'd stop by. I don't want the offer on that property at the corner of your ranch to expire before you decide."

"Okay."

"So…?"

"So what?"

Joe threw back his head and laughed. "Where did you go when you were staring out the window? You're always on top of things. Heck, you usually have the answer before I ask the question. So what do you think of the offer?"

"Hold on a second." Luke picked up the printout of the document Joe had emailed him earlier that day, scanned the pages, noted the dollar amount. He hadn't gotten past Hope's name when he'd first looked at it. The amount was fair. More than fair, actually.

He glanced at Joe. "Any other interest in the property you're aware of?"

Joe stuck one of his ever-present toothpicks between his teeth and maneuvered it to the left side of his mouth. "Nope. Not for months, and you know it. It's too small to ranch. Too remote and rural for most businesses. The last nibble we had was that guy from Houston wanting to build a house on it, remember? But it fell through when he looked into the cost of construction."

"Yeah, I recall." Luke stared at Hope's signature.

"You should accept it. You're not gonna get a better offer, that's for sure."

Luke raised his eyes to meet Joe's. Joe might have been older than him, having finished school a couple of years before, but he knew about Luke's connection to Hope. Who in Canyon Creek didn't? Luke appreciated Joe's not bringing it up. "Leave this with me for a day, will you?"

"That's all you've got—a day—before the offer is null and void." Joe rose. "I've got to get going. I have a showing in a little while. Call me when you've thought about it. But keep in mind that after midnight tomorrow, the offer will have expired, and she might not come back in."

"Yeah. I realize that. Thanks."

After Joe left, Luke stared at the document. Just thinking about Hope made him want her, but then the hurt of her rejection pushed through the desire. Why did she have to return? At this rate, he'd go crazy before she left again.

He ran a fingertip over Hope's signature. Hadn't changed much over the years. Maybe a bit more authoritative. He left the document on his desk and strode out.

Climbing into his pickup truck, he put on a Tim McGraw CD as he drove into town, cranking up the volume, hoping the music would jolt some sense into his brain. When the song "Felt Good on My Lips" started to play, it immediately brought Hope to mind.

And kissing her. He abruptly popped out the CD, but it was too late. He was thinking about Hope again…

He should tear up her offer and be done with it, wait for someone else to buy his property.

He wasn't mean-spirited. Wasn't he always the one stepping up to *help* a neighbor or a friend? But with his emotions all twisted up the way they were, he couldn't see himself selling his land to Hope, shaking her hand politely and saying "Have a nice day."

As he turned onto Center Street, he'd changed his mind again. He'd sell her the property. He'd be an idiot not to. And why should he let her rattle him like this? He knew why she wanted his land. And he also knew there was little else on the market that would suit her needs.

If she wanted the property, she'd have to pay for it. Besides, it wasn't her own money, but her rich daddy's. That was all over town after she'd told the bank teller that transfers would be made into her account by her father's lawyer.

It wouldn't be a matter of her not being able to afford his property, but he wanted to send a message that all was not forgotten…or forgiven. If he set the price high enough, maybe she'd leave again. That would be better for him, for his peace of mind.

But that wasn't realistic, nor was it in the best interests of the town. Hope was determined. She had been when he'd known her and still was, judging by what he'd learned about her work with the animal shelter in Monterey.

He pulled into a spot near the Long Horn. It was a safe bet that his brother would be around. Since Travis had bought the old bar and grill and fixed it up, he'd more or less lived there. Actually, he *did* live there. In the apartment right above the restaurant. Luke thought that seeing his kid brother might improve his mood. As he walked up the sidewalk toward the restaurant, he yanked his iPhone out of its holster and called Joe.

HOPE THREW UP her hands. "Is he *joking*?"

"If only he was," Joanna replied. "His agent says 'that's the price. Take it or leave it.'"

"But that's nearly *25 percent* higher than what we offered. It's way more than what you said was fair market value." Hope glared at the agent.

Joanna held her palms up. "Whoa! I'm just quoting."

She pointed at the agreement on Joanna's desk. "That's just ridiculous! It's more than his asking price."

"I know it."

"I would've been willing to go to his asking price. But this? It's unreasonable!"

Joanna leaned back in her chair. "Do you want the property?"

"Yes."

"Can you afford his price?"

"Well, yes."

"Then I suggest you accept it."

"How do I justify spending that much more?" She thought about her father's lawyer and how she'd address the increase in the monthly progress reports she was required to submit to him.

"First of all, if you want it, grab it now. Luke's agent told me Luke wanted to put a 50 percent premium on it when he learned you were the buyer, but Joe talked him down. I know Joe pretty well, and he wouldn't tell me that if it wasn't true. As for justifying the price, when Luke first listed the property, it was higher. The market value really isn't that far off from what he's asking. He'd just lowered the price a couple of times because he wasn't getting any offers."

Hope strode to the window, stared at the sun-dappled park across the street from Joanna's office, the hazy outline of the mountains in the distance. She thought of a dazzling day much like today, a lifetime ago, when she and Luke had ridden out to the base of those mountains.

While their horses drank from the crystal clear stream, they'd pulled off their boots and sat on a rock, feet dangling in the cool water. Along with the memory, there was an echo of sheer contentment, even happiness she hadn't felt in a long time. The feeling faded before the memory did. "I'll pay him what he's asking," she declared.

HOPE LET HERSELF into the house and dropped her keys on the small table in the entryway. She gave Einstein—still exuberant despite his thirteen years—his obligatory greeting. The ritual was complete only when the big dog flopped down, gingerly rolled onto his back and she rubbed his belly.

Hope hadn't expected life to be comfortable, coming *home* after all this time, but she'd never bargained on it being quite like this either. The feelings she'd had for Luke in high school had never been extinguished during the intervening years. She'd felt it when she'd run into him outside the pet store and even after he'd rejected her outside the coffee shop. Now he seemed to be punishing her with his unreasonable attitude to the sale of his land.

She wasn't sure how to define her feelings for Luke at this point, but there was nothing she could do about them anyway. And it hurt to see his reaction to her.

Well, she'd set a quick closing date for the property. It would be done, and she wouldn't have to deal with him again. She'd keep her visits to town to a minimum. If she was lucky, she wouldn't run into him often.

The best way to keep her mind off things was to get busy. The next task on her project schedule was to start the design, and she dived right in.

LUKE DIDN'T KNOW what had compelled him to go for his Saturday-morning run along Yardley Drive and up to Promontory Park. As he turned onto the gravel path from the sidewalk, he came to an abrupt halt. Sitting on the bench with her back to him was Hope. There was no mistaking that long, mahogany hair, even in a ponytail and under a ball cap. Next to her feet was a large mostly black dog, lying on his side.

Just seeing her now, her back so straight and proud, and yet looking so forlorn and alone in the quiet park, made him want to…talk to her. Touch her.

He yanked his T-shirt out of the waistband of his shorts and used the bottom to wipe the sweat from his forehead. Tucking it back in, he approached Hope at a jog. “Nice morning,” he greeted her.

She and her dog both raised their heads and gazed up at him. “Hi, Luke,” she said hesitantly.

He stooped down in front of the dog, held a hand out to him, then rubbed behind his ears. “What’s his name?”

“Einstein.”

“Hey, big fella.” He spoke quietly to the dog as he continued to rub his ears, eliciting soft moans of pleasure. Finally, he rose. “Am I interrupting?”

“Ah, no. We were just taking a rest before we start back.” She laid a hand on Einstein’s head. “He doesn’t have as much stamina as he used to.”

Luke nodded. It was obvious the dog was elderly. “Mind if I join you?”

“Um…no. Not at all.”

He dropped down next to her and rested his elbows on his knees. They sat side by side, staring off toward Stillhouse Hollow Lake.

“How does it feel to be back?” he asked, still looking ahead.

He heard her sigh. “Strange.” She paused. “I never thought I’d come back. Now that I have, part of me wishes I’d never left.”

Luke noticed the remnants of her Texas

twang but he also heard regret in her voice. He turned his head toward her. Even in profile, and sad as she appeared to be, she was gorgeous. She was twelve years older now—and sexy as all get-out. He felt his heart kick. He wanted to ask her why she'd rejected him, but as strong as his need to know was, he wanted to preserve the current atmosphere between them. He moved to a safer subject.

"How's your project going?"

Surprise was evident on her face. He couldn't blame her if she hadn't expected him to be friendly. She had good reason.

"It's coming along." Her lips curved upward in a faint smile. "I like the design my architect's developing. It should work nicely on the site."

Luke nodded, asked some questions about it and listened intently. Her face was animated and excited as she spoke about her plans. Watching her like that, it was easy to forget that she'd become as hard and calloused as her father had been.

"It's going to be wonderful!" she concluded, a bright smile lighting up her face, her deep brown eyes glowing.

Those eyes transported him back in time.

Before he could reconsider he blurted out, "Have dinner with me."

She looked startled, then seemed to settle down again. “That would be nice,” she responded softly.

“How about next Saturday? If you’re free.”

“I’m sorry, but next weekend I have to go home to Monterey. I run an animal shelter there. I have some…commitments.”

Luke thought of Drake and was on the verge of asking about him, but once again he didn’t want to spoil the mood. His next inclination was to let the matter drop and put it down as a bad idea.

“How about the following Saturday?” she suggested.

He’d boxed himself in, but couldn’t say he was sorry about it. “Great.” He rose, feeling unsure all of a sudden. “What if I pick you up at seven?”

She nodded and gave him her address. He said goodbye to her and her dog and took off at a brisk run in the direction he’d come from.

His mind was on her relationship with Drake, and he wondered how big a mistake he’d made.

CHAPTER THIRTEEN

TWO WEEKS FLEW BY. Hope hadn't heard from or seen Luke, either before or after her trip to Monterey. She wasn't entirely sure that she hadn't imagined Luke's asking her out or, if he had, that he'd follow through and pick her up that night. Even with these doubts, she couldn't deny her schoolgirl excitement at the prospect of seeing him. She'd brought one of the few dresses she owned back with her from Monterey the weekend before.

Hope was ready and waiting when she heard the knock. Einstein scrambled to the door ahead of her. She counted to ten before she followed him.

"You look great," Luke said as he handed her a brightly colored gift bag and bent down to greet Einstein.

"Thanks." She smiled as she pulled tissue paper out of the bag.

"I took a gamble that you'd still like those

chocolate-covered almonds, and I figured I couldn't go wrong with dog treats."

"You sure know the way to a girl's heart!"

While Hope put the chocolates aside, Einstein accepted a large chew bone from Luke. He was so delighted with his prize, he didn't even bother to lift his head as they walked out the door.

Luke had made reservations at a French restaurant. They were seated at a quiet corner table. To Hope it felt like a dream, to be sitting with Luke in the flickering candlelight. She was fascinated by the man he'd become. She sensed a reserve in him, but encouraged him to talk about his business interests as they ate their appetizers. "And you're a rancher," she observed with a grin.

"I bought Whispering Springs Ranch about eight years ago. I purchased the eastern half of the property first, then had a chance to consolidate when the Wilkinsons decided to retire and move out of state. I bought their property, which is also when I got the piece of land you're building on. In total, I have just over five hundred acres now."

"You've accomplished a lot. I bet your parents would be proud."

A shadow crossed his face. "My father wasn't around long enough." Luke sounded resentful, but then shrugged. "Yeah, Mom was proud. She lived at the ranch with me. Travis did, too, until he got the crazy notion of running a restaurant and moved into the apartment above the Long Horn."

He may have used the word *crazy*, but she could see he was proud of his brother. "He's done well for himself," Hope interjected.

"You're right. The Long Horn is successful and Travis loves what he does."

They paused while the waiter cleared their plates, served their main course and topped up their glasses.

"What do you think of Canyon Creek after all these years?" Luke asked when they were alone again.

Hope toyed with her pasta while she considered her answer. She weighed her feelings about the place against the hurt caused by the townspeople's reaction. "I'll always love Texas, but I've built a life in Monterey. I have friends and my work there." She smiled gently. "It's nice to make a difference," she said, referring to all the animals she and Noah had helped over the years.

"You'll be making a difference here, too, with the school and community center."

Hope took a bite of her chicken parmigiana, smiled again. "That's the plan." She felt relaxed and comfortable. The tension she'd sensed on the previous occasions she'd seen Luke wasn't evident now. "It really mattered to my father that I do this." She looked down for a moment, then continued. "He wanted to make a difference, too."

Luke made a scoffing sound and her eyes flew back to his.

"He made a difference, all right."

Hope was sure the sarcasm in his voice had to do with her father's closing the plant. She had a newfound understanding of Jock and what had driven him, and she had to defend him. "My father's motivations were complex."

"You're being kind. You couldn't tolerate your father for more than a year when you lived with him."

Hope was mildly surprised he'd known that; she surmised that Priscilla must have told him, even though she didn't think he'd tried to reach her after she'd left. "It wasn't working for either of us," she said vaguely. She thought of the wretched, tortured man she'd seen on his deathbed and his disclosure to her. Her heart cried for him. "But now?" she continued quietly. "I wish I'd made an effort to understand him while I was there."

Luke's face hardened. "I can't believe you wanted to live with him in the first place."

Hope was taken aback by his vehemence. She thought about the false pretenses under which she, too, had left Canyon Creek. "I guess we all do what we think is right at the time."

"Perhaps. But I can't see anything right about living with that tyrant."

"Luke, please." The admonishment came out more sharply than she'd intended.

His expression remained cynical. "I'm just stating a fact."

Hope was sorry the mood was shattered, but she wouldn't let him speak ill of her father. Although no one else knew what he'd been through and why, she did. It was unfair of people to judge him so severely, despite the damage he'd done. "My father had his reasons."

"Maybe," Luke responded.

With his apparent hostility, there was no point getting into the particulars and ruining their evening. They avoided personal topics, and the pleasant atmosphere was restored by the time dessert was served.

After dinner, Luke drove Hope home. They took Einstein out together, and he held her hand companionably as they walked along the country road. The gesture felt friendly, nothing more, but Hope loved the feel of her hand in his. Memories flooded her, as they strolled leisurely back to her house.

Luke walked up the steps to the front porch with her and rested his hands lightly on her shoulders. "Thank you for having dinner with me."

"Thank you for taking me," she said. "I enjoyed it."

He raised a hand and grazed a fingertip along her cheek. "I did, too." As he leaned forward, Hope closed her eyes and a little sigh escaped her lips. Disappointment seared through her when she felt his lips brush her temple.

"We'll have to do it again sometime," he suggested.

"I…I'd like that."

"Good night, Hope," he said, then turned to leave.

With Einstein trailing behind her, Hope went inside. Wrapping her arms tightly around herself, she leaned heavily against the door and closed her eyes.

HOPE WAS BUSY and so was Luke, yet they still made time to see each other. There was no question in her mind that she still had feelings for Luke, but she was getting mixed signals from him.

She sensed that he was attracted to her, and yet he was treating her more like a sister or a friend. Certainly not as a romantic interest. Whenever he touched her, it was very proper and innocent. If he gave her an occasional kiss it was on her brow or cheek.

Maybe that was all there could ever be between them—friendship, which would make it easier for both of them when she returned to Monterey, as she ultimately would. That was where her life was—Barkley Green, Noah, her other friends.

Hope watched Luke across the table at the Mocha Shoppe and tried not to wince as he stirred a heaping teaspoonful of sugar into his coffee. "Would you like a little coffee with your sugar?" she teased.

He smiled. "I've cut back the amount of sugar I used to put in it."

That was true enough, she mused, remembering coffee dates in high school.

"How's your project coming along?" Luke asked.

"Really well. I'm on schedule, which is good news, and within budget, too."

"Not that money would be a problem, thanks to your father." His tone was brusque.

"I want to do it right, but I don't want to be wasteful. My father wanted this project to happen in a certain time frame, and he wanted it to be well executed."

"It's hard to believe he would've given us a second thought, let alone want you to build a school and community center for us."

Hope frowned. Instinct told her she should change the subject, but she thought of her father during his last days, opening up to her for the first time in his life. *Appealing* to her. She couldn't ignore Luke's reaction, his bitterness. It kept coming up between them and seemed to be getting worse. "My father realized he hurt a lot of people. It was very important to him that I do this, help him make things right." Hope thought about sharing with Luke what she'd learned about her paternity. The secret was a heavy burden she carried, but based on his reactions whenever her father was mentioned, she didn't trust him to accept it and not judge.

"There are some things you can never make right," Luke retorted.

Hope's gaze met his. There was animosity in his voice again. She didn't remember him being that antagonistic back in high school, back when the loss of his father's job would have been much fresher in his mind. She thought again about the broken, lonely, remorseful man she'd seen that final day, and her protective instincts kicked in. "My father didn't intend to hurt those people! He felt bad about it. This project isn't so much about wanting to be forgiven, more about simply making a small restitution."

Luke's brows drew together. "This isn't something we should talk about."

Hope felt that his anger was out of proportion, based on what had happened nearly three decades before. She considered it unfair to her father's memory, when he'd had such regret over it all. She thought of her father's lonely, loveless life—more than enough punishment, in her opinion—and placed a hand on Luke's. "My father was an old man who realized he'd made some serious mistakes. In his own way, he suffered as much as anyone. Is it so wrong to forgive him?"

Luke drew his hand back. "I said we shouldn't talk about this. Let me be clear—no, I can't forgive him. You, of all people, should understand."

Hope put her suddenly cold hand in her lap. This wasn't how she'd expected or wanted the evening to end. She didn't understand his vehemence, and with her relatively new loyalty to her father, she couldn't let it go. "Luke, you're not being reasonable."

"*I'm* not being reasonable? You sound as if you love him. You never did when you lived here."

"*Love* is a strong word. I may not love him, but I care about him and his memory. Can't you just—"

"No. Let's leave it at that, okay?"

Confused and disappointed, Hope asked if he wanted more coffee when she saw the barista approaching. He declined politely and couldn't seem to get back to his truck—and away from her—fast enough.

HOPE TOSSED TWO shirts and a pair of jeans into her duffel. In the four months she'd been in Canyon Creek, she'd returned to Monterey for a few days every four or five weeks, as she'd promised Noah. It helped him out and afforded her some much-needed respite. She added toiletries and a pair of sandals and zipped up the bag. Einstein sat next to the bed, his eyes sad and intent, shoulders hunched, if that was possible for a dog.

"Look, pal. Can we not go through the guilt trip this time?"

Einstein's head drooped a little farther and he heaved a huge sigh. So did Hope. She moved over to him and sat on the edge of the bed. Einstein immediately laid his head on her lap. "So clearly we *are* going to go through it again, huh?" She slid one hand under his snout and lifted it slightly to make eye contact. "I honestly can't help it, and we've had this discussion before. Not that it's done any good." She placed a kiss on his nose. "I have to go back. Noah needs me, and it's the least I can do. How do you think he feels about having to run the whole place by himself, when we could barely manage between the two of us? And we've got all the planning to do for our expansion. On top of that, I have to be at the fund-raiser Saturday night. They expect both of us there. I'm sorry, but I really have to go."

The response was a drawn-out moan.

"You know Harry will take good care of you." Hope was grateful that the very first time she'd made the trip back to Monterey, Harry had offered to watch Einstein. Harry liked dogs. If he didn't need to be in Northcliffe for business reasons, he stayed at her house, so Einstein could remain in his own space.

"I'll be back in a couple of days," she assured the dog. "Besides, you can't tell the passage of time. As soon as I close the door behind me, as far as you know, I'll be walking right back in."

Einstein tilted his head and looked at her mournfully.

"Well, that's what they say, and who am I to argue?"

The sound Einstein made was almost a gasp.

"Right. Sorry. How could I forget you're not an ordinary dog?" She rose. "Gotta go or I'll miss my flight." At the gleam in his eyes, she chuckled. "Yeah, wouldn't that make you happy?"

NOAH MET HOPE at the airport and gave her a bear hug. She loved the comfort and friendship he offered. He always seemed to smell of salt water, fresh air and, well, sunshine—or what she imagined sunshine would smell like—and it made her smile. He grabbed her carry-on and draped an arm around her shoulders as they walked out of the terminal building. "How're things?"

Hope sighed.

Noah stopped, concern in his eyes. "Problem with the project?"

She tugged on his arm to get him moving again. "No. Not in the way you think. Everything's going reasonably well and on schedule. We've got the design completed, and the tender documents and specifications are almost done, too."

He fell in step with her again. "So what was the big sigh for?"

She thought about Luke, about how all those old feelings had returned with a vengeance. How painfully polite he'd been after their last date had ended on such an odd and angry note. She hadn't heard from him since. "Oh, I don't know."

"Sorry, but I don't buy it."

As they reached his car, he stowed her bag in the trunk. Once they were inside, he started the engine to get the air-conditioning working and turned to her. "You knew going back wouldn't be easy," he reminded her gently.

"Yeah, but in some ways it's worse than I expected. In others, better."

"Huh. Do you want to elaborate now or over dinner?"

Hope felt unbearably weary all of a sudden. She rested her head against the seat back. "Why don't we wait until dinner?"

Noah put the car in gear and gave her a sheepish grin. "Speaking of dinner, do you mind if we make it a threesome?"

There was something unusual in his tone. Hope glanced over at him. "Who's joining us?"

"Gillian."

"Our office manager?"

"Yeah."

"Okay. But why? Is there a problem with the shelter I need to know about?"

He checked to make sure the road was clear before pulling out. Hope got the impression he was stalling. "Noah?"

Safely in the lane with the flow of traffic, he finally replied. "We're…ah…dating."

Noah was always going out, but never with one of their employees before. Nor had he ever wanted to bring one of his dates to dinner with them. "Is it serious?"

He grinned again. "Maybe."

The simple statement delighted Hope. There was a different tone here. "Sure. That'd be nice." She almost breathed a sigh of relief, thinking she wouldn't have to discuss her muddled feelings about Canyon Creek and how confused she was about Luke. She hadn't meant to let her guard down with Noah. It just felt so darn good to see a friendly face.

"I'll ask her to join us later, so we have some time to talk first."

She wouldn't get out of sharing what was bothering her, after all, Hope thought.

MARSDEN'S WAS HOPE and Noah's favorite restaurant. The ambience was comfortable, they knew most of the staff and many of the regulars, and the food was terrific.

Noah took a long draw of his beer. “So, tell me.”

He didn’t need to say more. They knew each other well and often communicated in what they considered their own personal shorthand.

Hope swirled the wine in her glass. Watched the little eddies form and dissipate. “I’m not sure where to start.”

“Start with the ‘better’ part.”

Yeah. That would be easier…maybe. “In the time I’ve been there,” she began, “I’ve discovered a few things. Top of the list, and on the plus side, somewhere along the way, the school and community center complex has become more than an obligation.”

Noah raised his eyebrows. “Meaning?”

“Meaning I’ve found that establishing the school and community center is not only about carrying out my father’s wishes. It’s also about doing something good for the town and the people. It matters to me.”

Noah made a noncommittal sound.

“That’s the positive.” She sipped her wine.

“What’s the negative, then?”

“It’s that I still care. A lot.”

“Care about what? The town?”

"Yeah, the town. The people." With downcast eyes, she added, "Luke Carter."

"Luke Carter?" Noah echoed. "Isn't that the guy who was your boyfriend when you lived there as a kid?"

"I wasn't a kid. I was a *teenager*," she said primly. "But yeah. That's him."

"I've known you for over ten years, and in all that time you've never shown any real interest in a guy. Not the 'L' word type of interest, anyway. Now you're telling me you're still hung up on the guy you dated a lifetime ago?"

Hope nodded.

"You loved this guy, Carter, didn't you?" Noah's gaze was steady.

She nodded again.

"And what are your feelings now?"

"*Love* may be overstating it, but I definitely have strong feelings. I know it's absurd. It's been *twelve years*! What did I know back then?" She described their conversation at the coffee shop, telling Noah what Luke had said, grateful that he was aware of her reconciliation with her father.

Noah lowered his head to make eye contact again. "That doesn't sound rational, feeling that way over what your father did so long ago. Did you ask him about it?"

"I didn't get the chance."

"Then I think you should—"

"Good thing I'm not the jealous type." Whatever Noah was going to say was forestalled as Gillian joined them. Her voice was teasing and held no rancor. Noah released Hope's hand and took Gillian's. She brushed her lips across his. "Hi," she greeted him in a breathy little voice. Noah's look was nothing short of besotted.

This was new, Hope thought. There was a genuine affection between these two. Noah sent her a questioning look apparently to determine whether she wanted to continue the conversation. She shook her head.

Gillian settled in the chair next to Noah's, and the two of them leaned toward each other, as if drawn like magnets. Hope suddenly felt like a fifth wheel. She was happy for Noah and Gillian, but seeing them together just made her feel lonelier. She had Noah and Aunt Clarissa, and Morris and Priscilla, and she had Einstein. But that was it. That was her little world.

After dinner, although it was still shy of eight o'clock, she made her excuses and said goodnight.

She went back to her hotel and got to bed

early. She slept soundly, feeling more relaxed and less sullen in the morning.

Hope grinned when she saw Noah in the office, pouring himself a cup of coffee. She walked over to him and bumped his shoulder with her own. His mug wobbled but he was able to keep the coffee from spilling. "You and Gillian are really an item?"

"So it seems."

"I'm glad for you." She passed on the coffee and they walked out of the office, into the animal containment area. "You've done a fabulous job here." She noted the painting and refinishing he'd done with the help of their volunteers. The space was so much brighter and cleaner. Hope squatted down in front of a kennel to reach in and rub the ears of a little terrier pushing its snout through the bars. She glanced up at the name on the door. "Hey, Hogan. How're you doing?"

"Since the little guy hasn't mastered the art of speech yet, I'll translate… He's doing great," Noah supplied. "We've got a family interested in him. We're just checking their vet history and references. If all goes well, Hogan should be in his forever home by next weekend."

"That's terrific. Way to go, pal!" She scratched

the terrier's head a final time before she straightened and they moved on. "Our adoption rates seem— Oh, no!" she exclaimed and dashed to a kennel on her right, fumbling to unlatch the door.

Noah laughed and placed a hand over hers. "Stop! It's okay."

Hope was horrified. "What are you talking about? That dog is mauling that rabbit."

Noah was still laughing. Hope sent him an indignant look and reached for the latch again. This time Noah took both her hands in his. "Wait... You know I wouldn't let an animal get hurt." She focused on the enclosure. Pulling her hands free, she crouched down. She'd thought the dog, a husky mix, had the rabbit by the neck, but upon closer inspection, she saw that the dog's large pink tongue was stroking over the rabbit's sable-brown fur. He was actually grooming it. Eyebrows raised, she turned to Noah.

"They're best buds," Noah explained. "Sasha—that's the dog—was out in the exercise yard when the rabbit hopped in." His expression turned serious. "In fact, he *dragged* himself in. The rabbit had been badly injured, probably ran into some barbwire. Anyway, it happened while I was called away for a minute. When I went back to the yard, all I saw was Sasha lying on the grass, his back to me. He was whimpering. I rushed over thinking something had happened to Sasha." He chuckled again. "Imagine my surprise when I got to him and found him curled around a rabbit. Clarence, that's the rabbit, was nestled against his chest. Sasha was tending to his wounds. From that moment on, Sasha became the rabbit's self-appointed nursemaid and guardian, and they've been inseparable. Whoever adopts Sasha will have to take Clarence, too, unless they want to listen to his incessant howling."

The dog and rabbit had gone from grooming to playing. She'd never seen anything like it, not with two such diverse creatures that had not been raised together from a young age. The miracles of the animal kingdom never ceased to move and amaze her. And sometimes wounded souls just had a way of finding each other…

Luke came to mind, along with a deep-rooted yearning.

Hope suppressed the feeling, and she and Noah finished their tour. It was apparent that they were at, if not over, capacity. Makeshift kennels had been erected in some of the office areas.

There was no question that they desperately

needed her inheritance; she just hoped they could keep things going until then.

She spent another day in Monterey, working on the books and reviewing the expansion plans with Noah. All would be well—if only they could get through the next eighteen months.

CHAPTER FOURTEEN

LUKE WAS IN a corner booth at the Long Horn. He stared into his coffee, trying to think of anything but Hope. He knew exactly when she left for Monterey—at least he had to assume that was where she went each month—and when she returned. He knew her daily routine probably as well as she did. Not that he actually kept tabs on her. But it was a small town. The development site was adjacent to his property, and her house was on his way to… well, on the way when he decided to go for a drive. Or a ride.

Whenever her Jeep wasn't at either location or at the architect's local office, and the architect was walking her dog, he knew she'd driven to the airport in Austin. He'd see her vehicle again in two or three days.

He considered everything he'd learned about her partner in Monterey. If she and Drake were so crazy about each other that they couldn't bear to be apart for more than four or five weeks, why didn't he move here with her or at least come and visit? Why was she always the one doing the traveling?

And why did that concern him? Was he so messed up that he couldn't stand the thought of her being away for a few days? Not that he saw her when she *was* here. She kept mostly to herself.

What he did know was that other than those regular few days she spent in Monterey, she never seemed to stop. From what he'd seen and heard, the woman had limitless energy. She was applying herself to this project of hers nonstop. He wasn't aware of her having taken a day off, weekends included, and she didn't participate in any of the community social activities. He knew, because he had been attending most of them. If that was completely out of character for him, so what? He had a right to socialize now and again, didn't he? He'd gone from trying to make sure he didn't bump into her, to dropping in at event after event just in case she was there. And that was senseless. She was in a relationship, and that meant she was off-limits. Still, he had to admire her determination. She worked diligently, prevailing over every hardship that presented itself to make her father's wishes come true.

But he couldn't believe she'd gone soft on her father. Hope had reason enough not to defend her father because of the way he'd treated her and her mother, but knowing about the circumstances of his own father's death, how could she not be sympathetic to his feelings? He'd certainly told her all about it in those long and painful letters, those anguished emails.

Luke slouched forward and held his cup in both hands. He nearly jumped when he felt a tap on his shoulder. He cast angry eyes up into his brother's dancing ones.

"I guess now I know what people mean when they say 'if looks could kill!'" Obviously not the least bit perturbed, Travis took a seat opposite his brother and signaled Carly to bring them a couple of beers. "So what's put you in such a foul mood?"

"What makes you think I'm in a foul mood?" Luke grumbled, and Travis burst into laughter. Luke narrowed his eyes.

"Sorry, but I haven't seen you like this very often—until recently, that is. I'm the moody one, remember?"

Luke thanked Carly when she brought his beer, replacing the empty coffee cup.

"You want to talk about it?" Travis prompted, after Carly left.

Luke frowned.

"Okay. Let's try this. Does it have anything to do with Hope Wilson?"

Luke's scowl became more pronounced.

"I'll take that as a yes."

They both took sips of their beers.

"So what are you going to do about it?" Travis asked.

"Why would I do anything?"

Travis stared at him, unblinking.

"She left me years ago. What's past is past."

"No," Travis corrected him. "She left Canyon Creek, not you specifically. And from what I can see, what the two of you had back then is unresolved."

"It's as resolved as it's going to get. Besides, she's with someone else." That was a big part of the reason—and a good excuse. Travis knew nothing about Luke's desperate attempts to reach Hope when their father died. As a result, he was also unaware that she'd ignored those attempts, essentially turned her back on him. Since Travis had been only a kid at the time, his recollection of their father's death was sketchy, and he wasn't as resentful about Hope's father's role.

"Is she?" Travis asked. "But what about the two of you?"

Luke gave Travis a look that used to put fear

into his brother when they were kids. But Travis only grinned.

Luke pushed his beer bottle away. “If I wasn’t in a bad mood before, you’re doing a great job of putting me in one now. Can we agree on something?”

“As I just pointed out, you were already in a bad mood. As far as agreeing…” Travis shrugged. “Depends.”

“It’s simple. Don’t talk to me about Hope.”

When the front door opened, Travis grinned and waved at the newcomer. “Hey, Rutledge. Come on over. Beer’s on the house if you can get your pal here to lighten up a bit.”

“Sounds like an offer I can’t refuse,” Malcolm said with a laugh as he joined the brothers.

Malcolm might have been Luke’s best friend since high school, but right now Luke didn’t feel like company. He couldn’t seem to escape it, though.

“There’s only one thing I can think of that would put that sour look on your face,” Malcolm observed after Travis left them to get back to work. “It has to do with Hope—and your father’s death. Am I correct?”

Malcolm was the only person who knew that Luke tried countless times to contact Hope when his father died.

"I *want* to forgive her. I really do," Luke told him. "I can even get over her not being there for me when we were kids and my father was killed in that crash. I know she was dealing with her own issues." He took a sip of his beer and thought back to the letter he'd received from his father, mailed just days before his death, and tried not to let his resentment get the better of him again.

"Then what's holding you back?"

Luke shook his head.

"You know you can talk to me."

"Yeah." He gave a heavy sigh. "What I can't understand is the way she feels about her father now. She was always indifferent to him when we were kids. He was like a stranger to her… She didn't last a year living with him when she was seventeen and, to the best of my knowledge, they were estranged again after that. But now she seems to *care* about him. She *defends* him. I don't get how she can do that. And especially to me. That's hard to accept when she knows he was responsible for my father's death."

"Whoa. Now you're overstating things."

Luke sighed again. "Maybe. But I'm completely turned inside out by this."

"Have you talked to her about it?"

Luke threw up his hands. "What's the point?

She knows it all. I told her everything in my letters and emails. She knows about my dad's depression after he lost his job, and the DUIs." He cast his eyes down and hunched in on himself. "I told her in no uncertain terms that my father blamed hers. I explained that losing his job caused his depression, which led him to drink and drive. How he slammed his car into that bridge's concrete abutment."

Malcolm waited.

"The worst of it is I'll never know if it was an accident or intentional. My father was a solid man. A great father. A good provider." Luke raised his eyes to meet Malcolm's. "He was all those things *before* he lost his job when Jock Wilson shut down the plant. Then he left us, started drinking, and in the letter he sent me he laid the blame squarely at Jock's feet. True or not, that was his reality." His voice was raw. "And for Hope not to understand how I'd feel about her father? To defend her father to me?" He dropped his gaze again. "Sorry, I'm not a big enough person to accept that."

HAVING JUST RETURNED from Monterey, Hope was unpacking when there was a knock on the door. She opened it to a broadly smiling Harry. He held out a set of rolled-up drawings and wiggled it.

"We're done?"

"Uh-huh. Want to have a look?" He handed them over and bent down to ruffle Einstein's fur, then glanced back up at Hope. "Is it possible this guy's still growing?" he joked. "He seemed bigger to me this weekend."

Hope chuckled. "Oh, no! He's big enough already." She ran a hand affectionately along Einstein's back. "Besides, he's a senior citizen now. He stopped growing years ago."

Hope walked over to the kitchen table, with Harry and Einstein following. She sat down and unrolled the drawings. Einstein plunked down beside her and rested his head on her lap.

She started to flip through the pages. "So explain it all to me, please," she said as Harry pulled out the other chair.

He took her through the various sheets—the site plan, the elevation, the floor plans, and finished off with a rough rendering. Hope made a number of suggestions, and Harry said he thought they were all great ideas.

The more Hope immersed herself in the planning, the more excited she got. "So now what?"

"With your sign-off, we can put together the package for rezoning."

"Rezoning?" she asked hesitantly. "I thought we were okay with the zoning."

"No, we aren't."

"But the real-estate agent said..."

"Yeah. I know. She wasn't wrong. As per the preliminary review, the *use* conforms with the zoning bylaw. It's the size and characteristics of the building that are outside the specified limits." He gestured to the architectural drawings. "To be able to build this, we need to get the property rezoned."

"Will that delay us?" Hope's face must have shown her disappointment, because he patted her hand.

"It shouldn't take too long."

FRIDAY-MORNING COFFEE with his brother was a regular event for Luke. As much as he wished it wouldn't, the conversation turned to Hope—as it invariably did ever since her return. Even without his personal history, she and her project were big news in their small town. And Travis seemed to be fond of her. For his part, Luke preferred not to have anything more to do with her and didn't mind saying so, but Travis was persistent.

"You know Hope's having a hard time. She could use a friend," Travis was saying.

"What do you mean?"

"She's trying to do some good here, and we're making it hard on her."

"In what way?" He thought about the extra amount he'd asked for the land and felt a wave of guilt.

Travis chuckled, and Luke wondered if his brother had read his mind. He was about to snap back, but Travis raised a hand. "Well, she's doing all this work and Town Council is planning to play hardball with her over the rezoning."

"How'd you find that out?"

"Tim mentioned it last time he was in here," he said, referring to the mayor. "You know how he's always felt about Hope's father and the closing of the plant."

Luke was aware that it had taken the mayor's father two years to find another comparable job, and that was in a town sixty miles away. "Tim's never been able to get past the impact it had on his family."

"That's right. He apparently has no desire to help Hope out with the project, to see her succeed."

The consequences for Tim's family hadn't been nearly as devastating as the ones their family had suffered, Luke thought. "That's carrying his resentment a little too far," he protested, but felt that stab of guilt again.

"I've been told that not only is Tim not willing to support the project, he wants retribution because of what her father did and how Hope… What did he say? How she *aligned* herself with Jock when she left Canyon Creek. And he might not be alone in that feeling."

"She was just a kid. He can't seriously blame her," he muttered, but the words sounded false to his own ears.

"Tim can't seem to let it go. Hope's presence brought it all to the forefront again."

Great. Now Luke felt sorry for Hope, on top of everything else.

TRUE TO HIS WORD, Harry delivered the package for rezoning in record time, nearly five months into her schedule. "I think you should attend the council meeting with me," he suggested.

"Me? Why would I need to be there?" The idea of going to such a public place, where so many people could see her, was daunting. "You said it was going to be straightforward."

"I thought so. I don't understand it, but now the town council seems to have some concerns."

She got up to pace. "Why? They don't want a school and a community center? Don't those guys have kids? Have they *seen* what their current school looks like? How jammed it is? And the nearest community center right now is forty-five miles away in Tudhope!"

"Take it easy, Hope. They have no concern with the planned use."

"Then what's their problem?"

"What I understand from the town clerk is that it's...you."

Hope felt her mouth drop open.

"It's mostly the mayor who has concerns, from what I hear."

She sat back down. The mayor was a few years older, but she remembered him from high school. "What possible issues could he have? This isn't about me. This is about new facilities for the town."

Harry got up and poured two cups of coffee, added some milk to one, the way she liked it, and took them over to the table. "This is only hearsay, but it's what I've been able to find out. It's not just you. I think it's more about your father."

"My father? But he's dead, and it's his money that's going to pay for this project!"

"I understand there's a lot of resentment toward him. The mayor's father was the manager at a computer parts plant that your father owned?" He looked at her questioningly.

She nodded. "Yes, my father did own a plant. That was, what, almost *thirty* years ago! I realize some people here have sore feelings, but are they willing to stop the project over them?"

"People seem to have long memories in this town. So your father… Jock, is it?"

Hope nodded again.

"I was told when Jock closed the plant, it affected a great many people. So I guess there are some who want to see you fail."

"But isn't that shortsighted? Shouldn't the council's priority be to do the right thing for the people?"

"You'd think." Harry fiddled with his coffee mug. "This is just what I've heard. You didn't tell me any of this, Hope. It's definitely going to complicate things for us. Have you considered building somewhere else? Where they'd welcome the project?"

Hope shook her head slowly. "No. It has to be here. I'm sorry I didn't tell you about the situation and why I'm doing what I'm doing, but I didn't foresee this level of resistance."

"It would've been helpful to know *why* you're doing it."

"I'm excited about the project but it didn't start out that way. I'm doing it to satisfy a condition in my father's will. If I don't complete the project in two years—well, eighteen months at this point—I lose my inheritance."

"So you're doing it for the money?" Harry asked, sounding disappointed.

"It's not that simple," Hope murmured. She considered telling Harry about the shelter in Monterey and why the inheritance was so important to her. She also considered explaining the situation with her father and how she felt she was doing something good for the town—but she didn't think there was any point. It would just sound defensive and not make any difference to Harry.

Harry watched her intently. "Okay. But I'm going to have to reassess the fees I quoted you. Working with this kind of opposition is going to take extra time and effort."

"How much more are you going to charge?" she asked cautiously.

"Let me think about it, and I'll work up a revised estimate for you. It won't be a lot more. I just have to make sure I cover my costs. We'll get through this. It's a great project. One the town needs without question." His grin flashed. "And besides, the design is masterful."

Hope managed a smile, too. "See, that's why I enjoy working with you."

"Because of my masterful design?"

"No. Because of your oversize ego!"

When Harry laughed, Hope found she was able to laugh with him.

LUKE COULDN'T STOP thinking about Hope. Or the conversation he'd had with Travis—which had brought him to the mayor's office. He tapped lightly on the door frame.

When Timothy Grieves looked up from the papers he was perusing, Luke asked, "Do you have a minute, Tim?"

"Sure, Luke. What can I do for you?" Tim asked, gesturing to the guest chair.

"Why are you trying to block the rezoning application for Hope Wilson's school and community center project?"

"You certainly know how to get to the point." Tim leaned back in his chair and linked his hands across his ample belly. He seemed genuinely surprised. "You should understand. After what her father did to this town? To our *families*? And then Hope left without a backward glance, wanting to be just like him?"

"So it's because of Hope?" Luke's words were measured. "Isn't your responsibility to the town?"

Tim leaned forward again. "Of course it is! Do you know of anyone in Canyon Creek who wants her back here including you?" A smirk appeared on his face. "I heard how much you made her pay for your land."

Luke shifted in his chair. "I know how hard it was on you and your family when your father lost his job. And, yeah, mine up and left." And died, but he didn't mention that. "We were all affected. But Hope was just a kid then. She and her mother suffered the aftereffects, too. This can't be about Hope's father, our fathers or even Hope. She wants to build us a school and a community center. Could we use them? Do we *need* them?"

Tim nodded slowly.

"Darn right. Do we really care who builds it or pays for it? In the end, Hope'll be gone and we'll have a school and a community center. Do we want to risk having her leave without finishing what she started? Who'd lose then?"

Tim's eyes narrowed, but he remained silent.

Luke rose. "Just some food for thought, Tim. Thanks for your time."

HOPE SANK INTO the armchair in Harry's Canyon Creek office. "We did it!"

In the end she hadn't gone to last night's council meeting; instead, she'd waited anxiously for Harry's call.

He offered her a bottle of water from his mini-fridge.

"Thanks. With everything you'd said, I worried they were going to vote against us. What do you think swayed them?"

Harry sat down in the chair opposite her. "My good looks and charm?"

She rolled her eyes. "Yeah. I'm sure that had a *lot* to do with it."

"It surprised me, too, but here's what I think. First, they had no legal basis for denying it. They knew that from the start, but wanted to play games. They had a change of heart. Not sure what prompted it, but we should be thankful." He took a long drink from his bottle. "I'd say they're aware that people are starting to appreciate the benefits a community center and school complex would bring to the town. The source of the funding is becoming less significant to people than the outcome. The council members, after all, are elected officials. They don't want to risk losing their seats on council because they insisted on holding a grudge. Finally, most of them have kids. They see the value, and that outweighed their obstinacy."

It all made sense, but Hope was disappointed. Yes, the townspeople were seeing the worth of her project, but she'd still wished they were starting to accept *her*, too. Being back made her long for the carefree days of her youth. Even made her want to come back for good—but that was impossible. Her life and her obligations were in Monterey.

"Now we can start the site work," Harry continued. "But we're going to need a right-of-way easement across a portion of the adjoining ranch."

"An easement? Why?" Hope knew the adjacent ranch was Luke's Whispering Springs. With the way things were between them now, she didn't relish the prospect of broaching the subject with him.

"For servicing the site. We can get hydro directly from the road, but to get natural gas to the site, we'll need the adjoining property owner's cooperation."

"Why do we have to get it from that end? Can't we get it from the road?" she asked. "The same as hydro?"

"The hydro's already there, but since we're on the outskirts of town, there's no natural gas line. You wouldn't want to use hydro or an alternate fuel for heating a building that size. It would be too expensive and impractical. The best solution is to bring it in from the other side."

"Acquiring the easement from the owner—is that something you'll do?" she asked hopefully, not wanting to deal with Luke again.

"Not normally. It generally isn't a big deal. We'll restore the site once we're done and the owner will never know it's there. Here." Harry passed her a sheet of paper. "I did a quick calculation of what the cost should be."

She scanned the sheet of paper. "All right. We'll need to talk about your fees again," she said. "You're going to have to do the negotiation for the easement."

LUKE'S TEMPER WAS UP. He'd sold her his land. Okay, she might not have known it, but he was responsible for getting her rezoning through. And now? When she needed something from him again? She didn't even have the courtesy to approach him personally.

True, he'd raised the price of his land, but he'd assuaged his guilt over that by smoothing the way for her rezoning. He'd thought that would be it. He'd tried, with a modicum of success, to put her out of his mind again. There was just too much history between them. His father and hers. How she felt about Jock now. The fact that she'd turned her back on Luke when he'd needed her. Her relationship with Drake. All good reasons to stay clear of her.

Now he'd have to deal with her once more. The easement wouldn't have been an issue for him in the long run. The construction noise and mess would be a temporary nuisance, but what really aggravated him was that she had her *architect approach him about it.*

They were adults now. Shouldn't they be able to get along well enough to deal with something as simple as this? He'd show her! He'd sent her architect—nice guy though he seemed to be—on his way. Luke made it clear that he wouldn't deal with anyone but Hope. She had his land. She'd gotten her rezoning. If she wanted the easement, she'd have to talk to him personally.

He couldn't rationalize why he'd insisted on it. He could even call his actions foolhardy. Because seeing her would only stir up his emotions, confuse them more than they already were.

"WHY ON EARTH would Luke want to negotiate the easement with me?" Hope shoved her hands in the pockets of her shorts. "Or why wouldn't he have one of his people deal with it?"

"At what point are you going to stop asking me questions that only you know the answers to?" Harry asked mildly.

Hope was about to retort but thought better of it. Harry was right. She and Luke had managed to stay out of each other's way. So why was he doing this? What was the point?

Was he trying to block her efforts to build the school and community center?

With all her unresolved emotions, the risk in seeing him was that she'd break down like a blubbering idiot. That would be mortifying for both of them and make the rest of her time in Canyon Creek even less tolerable.

"Can't you go back and try again?" she pleaded.

Harry sighed. "It would be a waste of my time—and your money. More important, if it didn't move things forward, it would impact your schedule negatively, as well. If you ask me, I think it would just annoy Carter. I don't know what the situation is between you two, but he's made his position clear. It's up to you."

"Okay," she said resignedly. "Will you arrange it?"

He looked exasperated. "Hope, don't put me in the middle of this. Just call him. I'm going to grab a bite to eat at the Long Horn before heading home. Do you want to join me?"

"No, thanks. I might as well see if I can set something up with Luke."

Harry packed up the papers he'd be taking home with him and rose along with Hope. "Don't look so gloomy. It's just a business transaction."

"If only," Hope murmured to herself.

"BRING ME A BEER, would you, Carly? A Corona."

"Sure, Harry." The waitress bent her head to get a look at his papers. "You never come in here just to relax. You always have papers with you. What are you working on?"

"Revising the budget numbers for the school and community center project for Hope Wilson."

"It's really something, isn't it? Hope coming back after all this time and doing this." She glanced up as the door opened, then said, "I'll be back with your Corona."

Carly waved to Suzie Walbridge, who'd just entered. "Be right with you, Suz. Have a seat anywhere you like."

Harry watched the attractive woman with the short cap of bright blond hair as she sat down at another booth. Carly swung by to take Suzie's drink order and was back at Harry's table with a frosty bottle and the requisite slice of lime.

"You know, I don't have any issues with Hope." Carly continued where she'd left off. "And what she's doing is a good thing for the town. But I don't get it."

Harry had gone back to calculating the construction costs and lost track of the conversation. "Get what?"

Carly sat down opposite him. He wasn't surprised. He'd gotten used to the informality of the people in this small town. She propped her elbows on the table and rested her chin on her fists. "I don't understand why Hope would be doing all this. She left, what…a dozen or more years ago? No contact with anyone in all that time. Now she's spending a couple of years here and is building us a school? I know it's her daddy's money and all, but…"

Harry ran another column of numbers and only half listened to Carly. "Oh, it's the condition," he said thoughtlessly.

"Condition?"

He looked up at her and lost his place. Darn, he'd have to start that column again. When Suzie called her, Carly glanced over her shoulder. "Just a minute, Suz," she said. "So, you were saying…?"

"Yeah. Her father put a condition in his will. She doesn't get a cent of her inheritance if she doesn't finish the project. I understand there's a lot at stake." He started running the numbers again.

Carly stood up. "Seriously?"

"Yes." The waitress's reaction surprised

him. He'd thought people would know, since Hope was originally from the town and everyone seemed to know everyone else's business.

"Huh. Well, how about that." She hurried over to Suzie's table.

CHAPTER FIFTEEN

LUKE SAT BEHIND the well-worn desk in his office at Whispering Springs Ranch. Hope, her back straight as a poker—with that yard of thick, dark hair loose and tumbling over her shoulders—perched on the wooden chair across from him. She was wearing a simple white shirt, jeans and cowboy boots. He could recall her dressing in a similar fashion when they were teenagers.

She was here about the easement. He'd gotten what he'd asked for.

The amount she'd offered for it was more than fair, yet he'd forced this meeting. He thought of himself as a logical, reasonable person, but his actions where she was concerned seemed to defy common sense.

Hope ran her tongue across her lip. The simple gesture made Luke feel as if someone had planted a large fist in his gut. He reproached himself once again for insisting on this meeting.

Hope cleared her throat. "You have my offer. Which of the terms did you want to talk about?"

He was struck again by the way her voice retained the faint remnants of a Texas twang, but was deeper, sultrier than he remembered. He tried to focus on her words, not her voice. Or her looks. He didn't have any issues with any of the terms, but he couldn't very well tell her that. "The price and the construction," he improvised.

"All right. The price we offered is fair market value. I can show you the independent appraisal if you want."

She had him there. He'd have to do some fast talking. "If I was interested in giving away an easement then, yeah, it would be reasonable. But it's my land and *I* don't need the easement. You do. That puts me in a position of strength. My bigger concern is the construction. The easement would traverse a working ranch—mine. That means noise, dust, inconvenience. I want a covenant saying that the impact will be minimized to the greatest extent possible. And I want an assurance that when you're done, the site will look *exactly* as it did before you started." Luke thought that sounded credible, but the longer she sat there, her back so straight, her full lips in that irresistible pout, her luminous deep brown eyes focused on him, the more he wanted to lunge out of his chair and…and *what*? Was he really thinking he wanted to take her into his arms and hold her? Crazy.

"Sorry. What?" He'd been so caught up in his reflections, he'd missed what she'd said.

Hope sent him an exasperated look. "I said I have no problem with a covenant to restore your property." With a snarky little smile she added, "Even though it's at the very edge of your land and shouldn't have much, if any, impact on your operation. After the excavation, we'll reseed, but it'll take time for the grass to grow back."

Luke nodded slowly. She knew what she was talking about. The peculiar ache in his chest warred with that sense of pride he couldn't shake. He masked both with a gruff voice. "I can accept that. Now the price. I want double."

"You've got to be—"

She'd let her impeccable control slip for a moment but recovered admirably. Still, it felt good to see her temper, to know that she wasn't as unaffected as she seemed. It reminded him of the impulsive seventeen-year-old Hope he had loved. A memory of Hope losing her cool when town gossip Suzie Walbridge first spread rumors about them being a couple came to mind. Hope had flown off the handle, face flushed, eyes flashing. Oddly, the memory made him want to grin. Instead he kept his features impassive.

"That's just not reasonable," she countered, her voice restrained again. "You got a 25 percent premium on the sale of the land and now you're asking for a 100 percent premium on the easement?"

"It's *my* land. *You* need the easement," he said again. He could see her struggle to maintain control.

"I don't mind paying a premium, but double is out of the question."

He crossed his arms. Waited.

"I'll increase my offer by 25 percent. The same premium you got on the land."

He was practiced at the art of negotiation. He hadn't even had to try to get her up to twenty-five, which was more than generous. If only he could stop wondering what it would be like to kiss her. The fact that he *remembered* with uncanny clarity what it had been like over a decade ago irritated him. It made him want to see if he could push her further.

"Fifty percent."

Because he was watching her so intently, he saw the regret and some other emotion he couldn't identify flit across her face.

"Luke, why are you doing this?" The cool, composed persona was gone. Her voice was soft, almost pleading. Suddenly she looked fragile. Unsure. That indefinable emotion shone in her eyes.

Her question was the same one he'd been asking himself, and he had no answer. He struggled to come up with a plausible response. Finding none, he felt defensive and snapped, "Because I can."

She recoiled. It was slight but it was definite. The other emotion, the one he'd noticed a moment earlier, was more dominant on her face now. Was it...hurt?

He had to wrap this up and now. Otherwise he *would* get out of his chair, take her in his arms and promise her whatever she wanted. He rose and walked to the window. "Thirty-five percent."

"Agreed. Are we done?"

There was a quaver in her voice.

If he hadn't known her so well at one time, he wouldn't have recognized it.

He shoved his hands in his pockets and clenched his fists. "Yes. Send the papers over when they're ready."

"Fine."

Luke heard the chair creak; she must have pushed it back. He realized he should shake hands on the deal, but he didn't think he could face the sadness he'd see in her eyes. He turned only when the door closed softly behind her, and he wondered yet again if he was losing his mind.

The edgy feeling persisted even after she'd left. He tried to answer some emails, review the financials for the month, but he couldn't concentrate. Whenever he wanted to clear his head, there was one sure way to do it. Ride the range.

Luke surged out of his chair and grabbed the Stetson hanging on the back of his door.

He strode into the barn. "Hey, Ronnie," he greeted one of his ranch hands and tossed a treat to one of the dogs. Ronnie was barely more than a kid, born and raised in Chicago, who got tired of city life and severe winters. He seemed to have found his calling working on the ranch. Ronnie'd been with Whispering Springs two years now. Luke liked to pat himself on the back for having taken a chance on a greenhorn. Ronnie was one of his best workers.

Ronnie stopped grooming the gelding and grinned. "How's it going, boss?"

"Good. Thanks." Luke gestured to the horse. "Is Barney still favoring that rear leg?"

Ronnie gently stroked the horse's flank. "No. I took him out to the corral. Walked him a bit.

He seems fine today. Do you want to have a look?"

"I trust your judgment." Ronnie's whole face lit up at the vote of confidence, making Luke smile. "I'm glad he's better."

"Can I do anything for you, boss?"

"Nah. I think I'll take Dante out for a ride." The spirited stallion should take his mind off Hope. "Check the fences."

"Did you want me to saddle him for you?"

"Thanks, but I can do it."

As Luke approached Dante's stall with a blanket and saddle, the stallion tossed his head with a bad-tempered snort.

"You're having one of those days, too, huh?"

They eyed each other stubbornly for a long moment before the horse finally tossed his head again, more for show, and averted his gaze.

Dante was a breathtakingly handsome horse, and Luke was convinced he knew it. He stood a good seventeen hands tall and had a glossy ebony coat.

Luke entered the stall cautiously. He always exercised a degree of care around Dante. Although the stallion wasn't mean-spirited, Luke didn't entirely trust him. Dante would take any opportunity to test his will against Luke's. He was acutely aware that if Dante chose to kick out, he could do considerable damage, especially in the confined space of a stall. It was one of the reasons he preferred to saddle Dante himself. The other was that he loved and admired the independent-minded stallion.

Once they were outside with Luke on Dante's back, he let the horse have his head. Dante lunged forward as if shot out of a gun. They proceeded northwest to the farthest corner of the ranch. Luke knew it was the least likely place to encounter any of his ranch hands and the most seldom-checked length of fence line. Going there would serve two purposes: he would avoid other people and ensure that there was no breach in that section of his fence.

The farther they traveled, the more the tightness in his chest eased, but Hope was still firmly entrenched in his mind.

The memory of the look on her face caused his guilt to resurface.

It astonished him that he still had feelings for Hope despite everything that lay between them. Feelings that had never really gone away. Was *that* what made him act so crazy and irrational?

They had been *seventeen*, for Pete's sake! He'd tried to forget her. He'd dated—lots. Ultimately, he resigned himself to the idea that only time would heal, and he'd gradually settled into a quieter existence. Now he dated occasionally, but seldom for long and never seriously. He pulled Dante up so suddenly that the horse reared. Luke held his seat, but the realization that had dawned on him—that he'd *never* gotten over Hope, not at all, not the slightest bit—was troubling.

Picking up on his emotions, Dante pranced skittishly beneath him.

To appease them both, Luke gave Dante free rein for a canter.

Hope had clearly moved on with Noah Drake. Even the name rubbed him wrong. He'd seen enough pictures of them at various charity functions. He could tell from the way they were always gazing at each other, the way Drake always had an arm around Hope's shoulders or waist, that their relationship was more than a business partnership. The captions that accompanied those pictures on newspaper websites underlined the fact that they were a couple. Luke had to admit—grudgingly—that they looked good together. Hope darkly exotic and Drake's pretty-boy blond looks. Clearly Hope had no "type" when it came to men, since Drake was about as different from Luke as day was from night. Well, good for her.

Luke pulled back on the reins a bit when Dante tested him for a full-out gallop. He'd thought the ride was helping, but now he had those images stuck in his head. The one that riled him the most was of Hope wearing some long, sleek dress in a steel-blue color that flowed over her body like molten metal. And Drake in a tux. Luke didn't even *own* a tuxedo. And they'd been dancing, with Drake dipping Hope so far back that her hair seemed to sweep the floor. Their eyes were locked on each other and they were both laughing.

Luke did a quick calculation from the time he'd first seen a picture of the two of them. They must've been together for at least eight or nine years. You'd think Drake would have married her by now.

So...he was a fool twice over. Still hung up on his high-school girlfriend, when she was obviously in love with someone else. Even if she wasn't, could he *trust* her again? A rhetorical question at best.

The smart thing to do was to put her out of his mind.

As Luke felt the tightness in his chest again, he finally let Dante gallop and they raced toward the farthest corner of his ranch.

HOPE SAT ON the back steps of her house and kept an eye on Einstein. She held the phone to her ear with one hand, a mug of tea with the other.

"Luke's turned into such an angry, mean person, Aunt Clarissa," she said.

"He always struck me as a balanced, decent, levelheaded young man," Clarissa said. "Your mother thought so, too. Are you sure you're not misreading him?"

Hope groaned and explained to Clarissa what had happened in Luke's office that afternoon. "And even though he got his 35 percent premium and the stronger covenant—basically everything he asked for—forget about thanking me. He didn't have the decency to say goodbye or look at me when we were done."

"I don't know what to say. Maybe he just had a bad day?"

"He was unreasonable over the sale of his property, too. Aside from the business issues, we seemed to be getting along. We went out a couple of times and it was…nice. But then he'd suddenly get grumpy, and everything would change. Now we barely talk, and he's just so…different." Hope felt her heart sink. "Unless he's still the same person and I'm the one who brings out this side of him. Do you think it's possible for someone to be that resentful for that long? Silly question." She answered her own query before Clarissa could respond. “I’m proof positive, based on how the people here feel about me, that it *is* possible. Yeah, it’s probably me,” she concluded glumly. And if she could still have feelings for Luke all these years later, why couldn’t *he* still be angry with her?

“Oh, honey.” Clarissa’s voice was solicitous. “I’m sure that’s not it, but I’m afraid I can’t help you. Why don’t you ask him? You’re going to be there a lot longer. Things could be very uncomfortable for both of you if you don’t reach an understanding.”

Hope had thought about that, too. If she tried to talk to him, appeal to him, it would likely have two negative consequences. First, she’d probably set him off again. Second, with her emotions in such turmoil, she might not be able to keep her own feelings from showing. That would embarrass them both. “No. I’ll leave things as they are and do a better job of avoiding him.”

“If you think that’s best.” Clarissa didn’t sound convinced. “Please don’t let it get you down.”

“I won’t,” Hope responded, but despite the bright sunshine, she felt as if a dark cloud had descended over her. Yes, that *was* the best thing—to put Luke out of her mind.

AS USUAL, NOAH met Hope at the Monterey Regional Airport. It didn’t matter that she’d already been gone for more than five months; they stayed in touch by phone and email, and their friendship never changed. She doubted that she could've been closer to a brother. They walked through the terminal and Noah pointed to a poster. "You up for that again?"

Hope looked at it. The poster, which showed an elegantly dressed couple executing some intricate dance move, had her laughing. "No way! Do you remember how many hours of practice we put in to be competent, let alone good enough to win that charity dance-off?"

Noah smiled. "Yeah. I do. But it was fun. Except when you kept stomping on my feet."

"*I* stomped on *your* feet? You must be losing your memory. *You* stepped on *mine*! Incessantly."

Noah laughed. "I guess that means no to entering this year."

"Correct."

"We could use the prize money, though."

"No!"

"Oh, well, it was worth a shot." They'd reached his car and he held the door open for her. "So how are things going in Canyon Creek?" he asked once they were both seated. "Any risk of not getting your inheritance?"

"There's always a risk, but I think I'll make it."

"That's good." His voice was subdued.

Yes, she knew him well. "What's wrong?"

He pulled out of the parking lot onto Fred Kane Drive and threw her a quick look. "We can talk later."

She rested a hand on his arm. "There *is* something wrong."

He kept his eyes on the road but she could see the tensing of his muscles, the pulse at his temple. "Talk to me," she encouraged him.

"Well, remember Reeves from the bank? He's threatening to cut our line of credit."

Hope twisted in her seat. "*What?* Why?"

"He's worried about our ability to pay."

"That's ridiculous!" she exploded. "We've always made our payments. We haven't defaulted or been late a single time!"

"He says we're overleveraged."

"Did you tell him about my inheritance?"

"Yeah. He wants to see a copy of the will. Have the bank's lawyers look at it. But I also told him about the condition." He shrugged. "Full disclosure. Better he hear it from us than have the bank's lawyers tell him after they've reviewed the will. He didn't like that, and he doesn't think their lawyers will either."

Hope's happy mood had vanished.

"Hope… He's talking about a significant reduction. If you don't get the inheritance…" He reached over and touched her hand. "We might lose Barkley Green. At a minimum we'd have to downsize."

Hope couldn't think of a single thing to say.

"You sure you don't want to enter the charity dance contest?" he inquired, an obvious attempt to lighten the mood.

It fell short of the mark.

CHAPTER SIXTEEN

"I CAN'T BELIEVE we're ready to hire a contractor!" Hope exclaimed. "Once the first shovel's in the ground, so to speak, it's going to seem real."

"No question about that," Harry said.

"And timing-wise, we're okay?"

"We should be..."

"That doesn't sound very reassuring."

Harry scratched his head. "It shouldn't take more than sixteen, seventeen months...for a good-size contractor. What I wasn't counting on until I started looking is that there's only one contractor in the area that's large enough to handle this. I should've thought of it before."

"But that's all right, then. We'll hire him."

Harry's lips curved in a smile. "Hold on a second. Your enthusiasm is admirable, but there are a couple of considerations. The company is large enough, but they'll have other jobs. Which means they can't take on your job until their workload allows. Or they take it, but they won't have their full resources available, so it'll go slower than we want."

"But you *know* I have a deadline!"

"The other consideration is that if *they* know they're the only one in town big enough for us, you might not get a competitive bid from them. Then again, you might want to pay a little extra to make your job a priority."

"I don't want to throw money away. But I have no flexibility with the timing." She thought of the millions of dollars at her disposal. "I do have some room in the budget. What's your recommendation?"

"Let's take it one step at a time. I'll set up a meeting with the owner, and we'll see what he says. I'd like to think he'd want to work on this project. It's big. It promises to be a beautiful structure." Harry smiled playfully. "Exquisite design that it is! But seriously, it's an important project for the town. I imagine he'd want in."

"How soon can we meet?"

"I'll call him after we're done here."

Hope was barely back at her house when her phone rang.

"We can see the owner of the construction company on Thursday at ten," Harry told her.

"That's great! Did he sound interested?"

"Interested enough to meet with us. I couldn't

tell any more from his voice. It was a short conversation."

Hope bit her lip. She just wanted the contract signed and construction under way. Then she could finally relax. "But it's not bad news, right?"

"No. I don't think so. Stop worrying about things that might not happen. Everything I heard about this guy is that he's solid. Very professional and his word is good."

Hope's breathing came a little easier.

"Rutledge said we should come to his office."

Hope felt the blood drain from her head. She sank back against the sofa cushions and stared up at the ceiling.

"His office is located on Green Briar Road. I'll pick you up, okay?"

There was silence.

"Hope? Are you still there?"

She sighed hugely. "Yeah, I'm here. It wouldn't be *Malcolm* Rutledge we're meeting with, would it?"

"Yes, it is." Harry sounded hesitant. "Is this another one of those things you should've told me about?"

"Yeah," she whispered. "It probably is." She sighed again. "Don't worry about it. I'll see you on Thursday."

Hope hung up the phone and leaned down to stroke Einstein's head. "What are the odds, huh, pal?" Einstein's look was unconcerned. "No sympathy from you, then?" The dog managed to twist around in the narrow gap between the sofa and coffee table to expose his stomach. Knowing her dog well, Hope scratched his belly.

What were the chances that there'd be only one contractor in town large enough to handle her project—and the company was owned by Malcolm Rutledge? Malcolm and Luke had been best friends in high school. Malcolm had also been her friend. Who would've thought the Malcolm she knew back then would be running a construction company?

Canyon Creek might be a small town, but it was a cruel twist of fate that had forced her to deal first with Luke and now with Malcolm.

Malcolm had been a shy, awkward, unpopular kid who idolized Luke. One of the things that had originally appealed to her about Luke was that he didn't care whether Malcolm was popular or not. Luke had, at least in those days, a real soft spot for the underdog. She'd found it endearing how devoted Malcolm was to him because of that simple offer of friendship. When people talked about having someone's back, that was Luke and Malcolm. They always had each other's backs.

If that was still the case—and she had no reason to suspect otherwise—it wasn't promising for the project. She was sure Malcolm knew it was *her* project when he'd made the appointment with Harry. Did that mean he'd want a huge premium, as Luke had with the land?

Hope thought back. Not the Malcolm she'd known then. He'd been such a decent kid. Luke used to say Malcolm had a secret infatuation with her. That had been absurd. Mal was just a sweet, good-hearted boy who wanted to fit in.

She pictured an older version of the scrawny kid she'd liked so much and had a hard time imagining him running a business.

Oh, well. People changed, and maybe Malcolm had, too.

HOPE'S THOUGHT ABOUT people changing echoed in her mind as she shook hands with Malcolm Rutledge a few days later.

She'd never imagined anyone could change *that* much. The skinny, geeky kid had transformed into a...well, a gorgeous, self-confident man.

Malcolm had to be six foot if not more. He certainly wasn't skinny. His shoulders and chest had filled out enough to rival those of any Dallas Cowboys defensive back. Without the attractive stubble on his face, he'd probably look almost too pretty for a man. What hadn't changed were his astute blue eyes.

Malcolm's handshake was firm. Businesslike. "I'd heard you were back" was his curt greeting. It wasn't rude. It wasn't friendly either, but there was something questioning, searching in his eyes.

"I like your work," he said to Harry. "Come. Sit down." He gestured to the small meeting table in the corner of the room. "Can I get you some coffee? Water?" When they both declined, Malcolm sat down across from them. "So, you're looking for a contractor to build your school and community center?" Malcolm directed the question to Harry, making Hope wonder why she'd bothered to come. When Harry looked at her and she nodded in reply, Malcolm spared her a brief glance, draped an arm over the back of the empty chair next to him and turned to Harry.

"Closer to forty," Harry corrected him.

Malcolm whistled appreciatively. "That's going to be some building. Do you have a construction budget yet?"

"I do."

Malcolm shrugged. "You're not going to tell

me what it is? I'm curious, but I don't need to know." Hope saw the mixed emotions on his face, in his eyes. Then he said, "My business is doing well. I don't need your money."

Hope felt a chill run down her spine. Was he going to turn them down without even considering the project? She was thankful when Harry broke the silence.

"I have the plans with me, if you want to see them?" Harry's voice had a slight edge. Clearly, he'd detected the undercurrent, too.

Malcolm straightened and looked at Harry again. "As I said, I like your work. You have style, but your designs are functional, too. I'm intrigued." Harry reached for his folio, but Malcolm stopped him. "But there's no point. They might tempt me."

Harry's bafflement showed on his face. "You're not interested?"

Malcolm glanced at Hope and this time held her gaze. "No" was his flat reply. Something shadowed his eyes once more—some inner conflict perhaps. His features softened and Hope detected in the man something of the boy she used to know. "I'm sorry," he added, his voice sounding genuine. "It won't work."

"But..." Harry sputtered. Hope understood what this was about. Apparently the kind-hearted boy still lived inside the man, but his loyalty to Luke outweighed everything else. The heat crept up to her face, and she knew her cheeks would be flushed red. She rose and slid the strap of her handbag back on her shoulder. "Thank you for your time," she mumbled as she strode toward the door and turned to wait for Harry.

Harry stood, too, and held his arms out, one toward Malcolm, the other toward Hope in a conciliatory gesture. "Wait... Why did you agree to meet with us, then?"

"I'm sorry," Malcolm repeated. "I thought I might be able to do it. But I can't." He shrugged again. "I can't deny I was curious."

"Then look at the drawings at least. Can't we talk about this?"

"No," Hope and Malcolm replied in unison, and Hope walked out, Harry rushing after her.

"I don't get it," Harry said as they got into his car. "He likes my work. This could be a job of a lifetime, and he isn't *interested*?"

"It's got nothing to do with the project."

"Then what?"

"It's me."

"That same issue again, huh?"

"Yeah." She stared straight ahead. Her voice was hollow, matter-of-fact. "Let's move to plan B?"

"Using a small local contractor could put

your schedule in real jeopardy. Finding a larger contractor nearby is our best chance, but we have to move fast."

Hope felt all her and Noah's plans for the animal shelter slipping out of her grasp. She remembered Noah's caution about Reeves, the bank manager, wanting to reduce their line of credit. The possibility that they would lose Barkley Green terrified her. It was her life, helping those animals. She *wouldn't* let that happen.

She hadn't realized how much she'd come to count on the inheritance money until the very real prospect of not being able to meet the condition of her father's will loomed before her.

CHAPTER SEVENTEEN

"YOU UP FOR A BEER?" Malcolm asked without preamble when Luke picked up the phone.

Luke detected something odd in his friend's voice and checked his watch. "Sure."

"Great. I'll meet you at the Long Horn in an hour."

Malcolm was already sitting in a booth at the back of the restaurant, sipping a beer, when Luke walked in. He was staring down at his bottle, brow furrowed and his mouth drawn into a hard, straight line. The fact that he wasn't flirting with the ladies was a sure sign that something was bothering him.

Luke slid onto the bench seat opposite Malcolm and motioned to Carly to bring him a beer, too. It was out of character for his friend to knock off work early. "To the best of my knowledge, it's a weekday and before five. What's up?"

Luke's smile only made Malcolm glower

more. "I own the damn business. I'm entitled to quit early once in a while."

When Carly brought Luke's beer, Luke took a drink. "Lighten up, will you? Nothing can be that bad."

Malcolm rolled his eyes before they both drank.

"So, what's wrong?" Luke asked.

"Ever kicked a puppy?"

"Can't say I have."

"Well, that's how I feel."

"What brought that on?"

"I don't think you want to know."

"Sure I do. And if you didn't want to talk about it, you wouldn't have asked me over here."

"Yeah. I guess." He paused, then blurted out, "I saw Hope today."

Luke's hand stilled as he was lifting his bottle.

"I told you, you wouldn't want to know."

Luke crossed his arms and leaned back. "Does it have something to do with her project?"

"Yeah. She and her architect came to see me today. They want me to build it for them."

Luke realized he should've seen that coming. "Makes sense, since you're the only game in town for a project of that size," he said carefully. "Why would that upset you?"

"Because I can't do it."

"You're not so busy you can't take on the largest project you'll probably see around here for years."

"Nah. It's got nothing to do with that. I could get the crews mobilized and some of it would be subcontracted work anyway."

"Then what?"

"It's because of Hope and everything that happened. She hurt a lot of people back in the day. And then there's what her father did. Now that she's come home, she's got you all tied up in knots again. I can't work with her," he concluded. "It just doesn't seem right. It seems…disloyal. To the town. To *you*. But when I said no, it felt a lot like kicking that proverbial puppy."

Luke understood what Malcolm was talking about. Hadn't he started out with that perspective himself when Hope first wanted to buy his land? But he'd relented on the land. Then he'd started to admire her for the way she met obstacle after obstacle head-on, admittedly a couple of them of his making. She just wasn't giving up. The spirit of the young girl he loved—*had* loved, he corrected himself—seemed to be very much part of the woman she was today.

How he handled this conversation with Malcolm would be pivotal. His response could impose further hardship on Hope, and it could have a negative impact on Malcolm and his business. What kind of friend would he be then? Or…he could do the right thing for both of them. "So you'd like to do the job?"

"Oh, yeah! It would be the biggest we've had. Knowing the work of the architect, it'll be an exceptional building. There is the conundrum."

"Okay. Look at the big picture. You want the contract. It would be good for you and your employees. Think of the benefits to the town. To have a state-of-the-art school for our kids. You and I don't have kids yet, but think about when we do. Do you want them to go to an overcrowded, dilapidated school? Or do you want them in a facility designed by that architect you admire?"

"Yeah. I know all that," Malcolm muttered. "And now you're making me feel like even more of a jerk than I already am."

"Happy to do my part." His attempt at levity didn't work.

"Hope was my friend when no one else was, other than you. Now *she* has no one and I kicked her when she was down." Malcolm took a drink. He grimaced as if the beer tasted bitter in his mouth. "I wanted to help her. I was really tempted.

But she hurt so many people." He gestured toward Luke with his bottle. "*You* suffered for months. Maybe years."

Luke tried to wave it away.

"You can't do that with me," Malcolm said. "I was the only person, other than Travis, who had any idea what you were going through. You weren't the same for a long, long time." Malcolm put down his bottle. "Come to think of it, as far as your relationships with women are concerned, I don't think you've been the same—ever.

"But you seem very forgiving about it." Malcolm raised his eyes to meet Luke's.

Luke considered his own struggle to figure out why, after all this time, he had such a strong emotional reaction to her. "Do you really think I'm carrying a grudge?"

Malcolm nodded slowly. "I do think there's still a lot of baggage there. But I also think you're not carrying a grudge as much as…a torch."

Luke choked on his beer. He leaned forward and coughed. "C'mon, Mal!" Was he so transparent that his friend could read him so easily? See the very same thing he'd been grappling with?

"Yeah." Malcolm kept his eyes steady on Luke's. "But that doesn't mean your feelings weren't genuine. Or lasting. Who're you dating now?"

"Who're *you* dating?" Luke tossed back at Malcolm. "Just because I'm not in a relationship doesn't mean anything. Forget it, will you?"

"It's something," Malcolm said, changing the topic. "Hope coming back all these years later to build a school and community center." Malcolm glanced at the waitress as she walked by, and a look passed over his face, as if he'd just remembered something. "Speaking of her doing this… It's all rather self-serving, don't you think?"

"What are you talking about?"

"You haven't heard? Carly had a chat with the architect. He said Hope's doing this to get her inheritance."

"What?" This was news to Luke. "What do you mean?"

"There's a condition in her father's will. If she doesn't complete this project by the deadline he established, she doesn't get a cent. So it isn't altruism that's driving her. And that look on your face? That's why I'm not going to help her," Malcolm concluded with an emphatic nod.

More evidence that she was like her father, Luke thought—as he had numerous times before—but it wasn't his concern why she was doing this. "Let's get back to the point. You're a contractor. You're the biggest and the best in the area. You're in business to make money. This job can make you a truckload of it. The town needs a school and could benefit from a community center. She'll get it built—one way or another—so it might as well be you. Do it for yourself. Do it for the town. Or look at it this way. You'd be helping Hope do something good. Is that so wrong?"

"No," Malcolm conceded.

"Besides," Luke added quietly, "she hasn't had any breaks since she got here. No one wants anything to do with her."

"Yeah, that's got to be tough."

"Don't pass up the chance on my account, Mal," Luke went on. He could see that Malcolm was relenting. "Don't *not* do it because of me. My feelings for Hope are well in the past." His last statement set off a little alarm in the back of his mind. But if he was lying to his friend, it was for a good reason.

"I don't know, Luke. You're different since she's been back."

Luke forced a laugh. "What kind of sap do you think I am? Do you *really* believe I'd be pining over some girl I was in love with when I was seventeen? I'm completely over Hope.

Like I said, don't make the decision based on me. It's not practical, nor is it necessary. And remember, if you decide not to do it and it doesn't get built, it isn't just Hope you'd be hurting."

"The job *is* a terrific business opportunity," Malcolm conceded, then fell silent, his eyes downcast. "All right. I'll have a chat with her and the architect." He tapped his bottle against Luke's. "Thanks."

"I'm glad you came to your senses."

"Yeah. And speaking of senses, she's quite the looker, isn't she?"

Luke shifted in his seat. "Yeah, I guess she is."

They both remained quiet for a few minutes.

"You know, if you really *are* over her, you wouldn't mind if I asked her out, would you?"

Luke stared at Malcolm. "You mean Hope?" With the decision about the project behind him, Mal's thoughts appeared to have taken a turn that wasn't altogether comfortable for Luke. His own assurance that he had no romantic feelings for Hope must have gotten Malcolm thinking. Luke suddenly remembered that he'd always suspected Mal had a crush on Hope back in high school.

"I certainly don't mean the architect," Malcolm retorted. "We've just discussed the fact that neither one of us is seeing anyone right now. Since you're not interested, what harm would there be if I tested the waters with Hope? See if she'd be willing to go out?"

Even if there was nothing between him and Hope now, she'd been his girlfriend. In the intervening years, both he and Malcolm had always thought of her that way. Malcolm's mood had improved considerably. Luke moistened his suddenly dry throat with a sip of beer. This was why he *never* lied. No good ever came of it. He couldn't very well object, now that he'd claimed he had no feelings for Hope. It certainly wasn't true. He just hadn't figured out exactly what those feelings were or what to do about them. "I'm not going to stop you, if that's what you're asking."

"Good to hear it."

"You should know she's seeing someone in Monterey."

Malcolm tilted his head. "And why would *you* know this?"

"As you said, everyone talks about her," Luke told him, to cover up his own prying. "She's big news in our little town. It's the guy she runs the animal shelter with. She's been going back to see him for a few days every month or so since she got here."

Malcolm flashed a grin. "That's one way to make sure she doesn't get too serious about me."

Luke narrowed his eyes.

"Hey, lighten up. If you don't want me seeing her, just say so. Our friendship is too important to me."

"It's none of my business," Luke said curtly, preventing any further discussion of the topic.

After they finished their drinks and settled their tab, they walked out of the Long Horn.

"You've had a few beers. You're not planning to drive, are you?" Luke asked.

"Naw," Malcolm assured him. "Just gonna get something from the truck and head to the office for a bit. Have a look at my schedule, see how I can fit in Hope's project." He grinned. "Besides, now that we've cleared the air, I might just give her a call and suggest another meeting."

CHAPTER EIGHTEEN

HOPE DIDN'T KNOW what to make of Malcolm's apparent change of heart and his desire to meet with her and Harry again. She picked the first available day Malcolm had offered, and she and Harry made another trip to his office.

They went over the drawings in detail, and Malcolm declared that he was prepared to put in a bid for the project. He understood the tight schedule they were working with and said he'd get his bid to Harry by the end of the week.

Hope was with Harry in his office when Malcolm's call came in.

"It looks like we've got a deal!" Harry announced as he hung up the phone. "Rutledge's bid is reasonable, and it's well within our budget. He also confirmed that he can meet our schedule."

Hope jumped out of her chair and threw her arms around Harry.

Harry returned the hug, but then looked at her with unease. "There's just one thing..."

"What?"

"Rutledge wants to address some final points before he signs the contract—and he wants to do it over dinner."

"He wants to have dinner with us?"

"Not us. *You.*"

Hope felt her face go pale. *"Me?"*

"Don't look so distressed. You can handle a dinner with Rutledge in the interest of the project, can't you? Remember, we thought we couldn't get him. A dinner isn't such a high price to pay."

"I suppose you're right," she said, but with everything else that had happened, she was worried it wouldn't be as straightforward as it seemed.

"Rutledge suggested Friday night. I took the liberty of agreeing. I know you're not going to Monterey this weekend, and we need to move quickly."

"*This* Friday?"

Harry chortled. "Yes, *this* Friday! As in tomorrow."

MENDOCINO'S WAS A new restaurant. New in Hope's context, at least, in that it had not existed when she'd lived in Canyon Creek. Hope hadn't known what to expect, but it certainly wasn't the elegant setting, muted lighting, soft music and discreetly spaced tables.

Malcolm ordered wine, despite Hope's objections. She tasted the sauvignon blanc when the waiter served it, mostly to be polite, but pushed the glass aside as soon as he was gone. She wasn't much of a drinker, and this dinner was strictly business. She didn't want a fuzzy head.

She reached down beside her chair to pull a folder out of her bag and passed it to Malcolm. Malcolm placed his hand on top of hers. "Can this wait until after dinner? Better yet…" He took the file folder from under her hand and leaned it against the leg of his chair. "Leave it with me and I'll review it with my lawyer on Monday. If everything's in order, I'll get the signed contract back to you by end of day."

Hope tried to tug her hand back but he curled his fingers around hers and held tight.

"Why don't we have a toast?" he suggested.

"Malcolm…"

"Let me finish, please? To our relationship… in business." He lifted his wineglass and motioned for her to do the same. "And for old times' sake."

With a sigh, she reluctantly did as he asked, and they touched glasses.

LUKE FOLLOWED THE maître d' to a table where his broker, Jim, was already seated. Hearing the faint clink of glass over the ebb and flow of hushed conversation, he glanced over toward the sound. The woman might have had her back to him, but he instantly recognized that long, luxurious cascade of rich mahogany hair. There was also no mistaking the fact that she was holding his pal Malcolm's hand. Malcolm had a self-satisfied smile on his face and a definite gleam in his eyes.

His friend sure moved fast. It wasn't a full week since they'd spoken about Hope, and now the two of them seemed very cozy.

Luke had a visceral urge to head over, yank Malcolm out of his chair and ask what he was doing. He quickly stopped himself. He had no right. Malcolm wasn't doing anything wrong, especially after Luke had given him the green light to pursue Hope. Luke put aside his personal feelings for her, but he had to wonder—what was Hope doing holding Mal's hand over a romantic dinner? She was involved with Noah Drake! Had she changed in this way, too? Or was it a matter of Malcolm being so smooth with the ladies?

In high school, Malcolm had been unpopular, but he'd shed that persona many, many years ago. By his early twenties, he'd grown taller and filled out considerably, thanks to a rigorous six-days-a-week exercise and weight-lifting regimen. Luke knew that with Malcolm's physical changes came plenty of female attention. With that attention had come confidence.

Call Malcolm a late bloomer, but over the years since Hope had left, he'd enjoyed his newfound popularity. Mal readily admitted that he'd earned his reputation for being a player. Although he'd had a few serious but short-lived relationships over the years, he'd never been sufficiently attracted to any woman emotionally to consider marriage. Why hadn't Luke thought of Malcolm's reputation before he'd given him the go-ahead?

Luke had to let it go because none of it was his business, he reminded himself. Besides, even as a teenager, Hope had always been strongly principled, and—until tonight—he'd seen no reason to reassess that trait. On the contrary, she'd demonstrated nothing but grace and dignity since she'd arrived, virtues that others—and he included himself—hadn't necessarily reciprocated. But regardless of what he was seeing, he trusted that Hope wouldn't do anything to compromise the relationship with her partner in Monterey. He found it hard to believe she'd be unfaithful. But then...what was she doing here with Mal, holding hands, the two of them looking so intimate?

Malcolm must have sensed Luke staring. Almost imperceptibly, he lifted his glass a little higher, toward Luke in a toast.

Having no intention of making a scene, Luke nodded at his friend and quickly followed the maître d' to his table.

Luke greeted Jim and slumped down in a chair, positioning himself with his back to Mal and Hope's table, but his appetite was gone. He noted the open bottle of wine on their table and thought a glass of the rich Malbec might be just what he needed.

Yeah, he'd told Malcolm to go ahead and take his chances with Hope, but only now did he realize that he'd never expected anything to come of it. He also hadn't appreciated what a direct hit to his heart it would be to see Hope with another man—not just in photographs, as he had with Drake. Part of the reason Luke had held back from pursuing Hope was out of respect for her relationship with that Drake character. Yet, there she was, sitting with Malcolm. If Hope was having a romantic dinner with anyone other than Drake, it should have been him!

Luke grumbled something to Jim in response to a question but went back to his fuming. He had more than a handful of reasons for not wanting a relationship with Hope, but none of them seemed to be much of a deterrent.

When Luke left the restaurant, with Hope still on his mind, he acted on impulse. He called her mobile, knowing she wouldn't answer, since she was still in the restaurant with Malcolm. He left her a voice mail. They might never be more than friends, but he'd have to accept that. He invited her to go riding with him at his ranch.

"Do you have the contract?" Harry asked as soon as Hope walked into his office the next morning. It might have been Saturday, but neither of them took weekends off.

Hope went to the coffee machine to pour herself a cup. "No," she said, with her back to Harry.

"No?"

She glanced at him. "He didn't sign it."

"But that was the purpose of the dinner."

"So we thought." Mug in hand, she walked back to Harry. "I think he'll sign. He wanted last night to be about 'our relationship.'"

"Excuse me?"

"Yeah, that was my reaction, too. He, um… wanted to make sure we can work together." Based on how the evening had progressed,

Hope suspected it was about a lot more than that, but she didn't think Harry needed to know that. Wasn't it just her luck that the first person in Canyon Creek who was prepared to be friendly with her wanted to be *too* friendly. And while she was on the topic of *friendly*, the voice mail Luke had left for her while she was having dinner with Malcolm had come out of the blue. Two invitations in one night, and she wasn't sure what to do with either one.

Even if she didn't still have feelings for Luke, she'd never get involved with Malcolm. Intellectually, she could rationalize that he'd grown into a great-looking guy with charisma, but he wasn't for her. She had loved Malcolm as she would a brother when they were teens. The way she felt about Noah Drake. But she couldn't look at Malcolm without thinking of Luke. The longer she stayed in Canyon Creek, the more it seemed her emotions were transporting her back in time, and her feelings for Luke, confused at first, were coming into clear focus. With Luke so serious and Malcolm so carefree, she thought Malcolm would be the easier one to love. Yet her heart was still drawn to Luke and she was beginning to suspect it always would be. And that was why she was going to accept his invitation. How could she not? She—

A sudden noise made her jump.

Harry was snapping his fingers in front of her face. "Are you back with us now?" He softened the words with a smile.

She took a sip of her coffee. "Sorry. I was just…" She was just what? Fantasizing about Luke? "I guess I'm tired. I'm not used to being out at night."

"No. But you're used to working into the late hours. A bit of a social life wouldn't hurt you."

That brought her musings full circle, back to Luke.

Harry skirted his desk and sat down, wrapping a hand around his own coffee mug. "So where did the two of you leave things last night?"

Hope contemplated Malcolm's offer to take her for a picnic at Stillhouse Hollow Lake, but she knew that wasn't what Harry meant. "He said he'd have his lawyer look at the contract. If everything's in order, he'll have it signed and in our hands by Monday. We can get ready to start construction. Malcolm *will* sign it. I'm sure of it." She was. Reasonably.

The executed contract was waiting for Hope when she arrived home on Monday afternoon, tucked between the front door and the screen. She understood why it was delivered to her house rather than Harry's local office when she opened the envelope. Along with the contract was a thank-you note and a reminder about the invitation for a trip to the lake. Assuring herself that everything was fine with the contract, she slipped it back in its envelope. As for the invitation, she was tempted but only if she could keep things on the level of friends. She wasn't interested in anything else from Malcolm, but the idea of a friend in Canyon Creek brought a longing she couldn't ignore.

Luke, on the other hand… She'd accept his invitation, and she was looking forward to seeing him.

HOPE ARRIVED AT Whispering Springs right on time. Luke had suggested she bring Einstein. She'd said she appreciated the offer, but he was simply too old to go on a long ride with them.

Luke stood in front of the barn doors as she climbed out of her Jeep. She waved and smiled. He watched with appreciation, mingled with a degree of discomfort, her long-legged, graceful stride as she came toward him.

She was in faded jeans, cowboy boots and a yellow shirt, and she wore her hair pulled back in a long braid. It didn't matter what she wore; she looked more beautiful every time he saw her. He reminded himself that today was all about making peace. There were a number of reasons they could never be more than friends, their fathers and her relationship with Drake at the top of his list. But…he could take this brief time and simply enjoy being with her.

She might have been living in California and probably hadn't ridden in a dozen years, but she still knew how to saddle a horse and was a natural at riding.

They rode, they talked, they laughed, and at times they silently enjoyed the peaceful scenery. Luke hadn't intended it, but they ended up at the pond on the Hawkins ranch. They dismounted and let their horses drink and graze while they sat on the large rock at the edge of the water. Luke tossed a pebble in the pond, and they watched the koi do their frenzied dance.

Luke sensed that Hope was in a pensive mood, and he gave her the time she needed.

He thought about their first kiss right here at this rock, a vivid memory etched indelibly in his mind, and it made him smile. His memories fast-forwarded to the day she'd told him she was leaving Canyon Creek for good, and he wondered for the millionth time if there was anything he could have said or done to change her mind. She'd chosen to make her life elsewhere and with someone other than him, and he had to accept that.

"It doesn't seem like a dozen years have passed," she said. She must have been reminiscing, too.

"No, it doesn't. Do you miss Monterey?" he asked.

"Oh, I miss the rain in summertime," she said with a smile. "I miss working with the animals at the shelter."

Odd that she hadn't said she missed Drake. He was thankful for her discretion, since that kind of remark would have soured his mood. "And what do you like most about being back?" he asked.

Laughter burst forth. "The lack of rain in the summer," she said with a grin. "The work that I'm doing here."

He laughed, too. "I suppose the grass is always greener on the other side," he said good-naturedly, but he couldn't help wondering if she'd missed him at all while she was gone and if there was any pleasure for her in seeing him again.

By the time they got back to his stables, Luke had decided he'd made a huge mistake. Having her as a friend was just not possible for him. Anything more was out of the question... He felt foolish when he stuck out his hand to shake goodbye, but he thought that would clarify where they stood with each other.

WITH THE FINANCING for Barkley Green at risk—jeopardizing not only the plans for expansion but its very existence—Hope was more determined than ever to complete the school and community center project on time. She had to send her monthly progress report to her father's lawyer, and she knew the schedule would show just how little slack she had.

Since Hope's house was on the outskirts of town, the Wi-Fi was erratic at best, and this morning it was nonexistent. It shouldn't have surprised her that the Wi-Fi was out the day her report was due. That was just the way things seemed to go for her. She packed up her laptop and, leaving Einstein at home, drove to the Canyon Creek Mocha Shoppe.

She set up her computer on a table by the window and sipped her coffee as she started to proofread the email she'd drafted. The benefit of her Wi-Fi being down was that she could get a really great cup of mochaccino, something that was well beyond the capabilities of the little coffee machine she'd brought back from her house in Monterey.

Hope was on the second-last paragraph, when a child's squeal, followed by the screeching of tires and a dog's high-pitched yelp, had her eyes darting to the window. Unable to see anything from her vantage point, she rushed out the door, leaving her laptop, handbag, everything, behind.

The barista, having heard the commotion as well, hurried over and, resting her hands on the back of Hope's chair, craned her neck to see outside. Whatever was going on, it was out of her line of vision. As she was about to walk away, Hope's laptop screen dimmed as it readied to hibernate, drawing her attention.

The barista glanced around quickly to confirm what she already knew; she was alone in the coffee shop. She ran her finger across the computer's touch pad to keep it from shutting down. With another surreptitious glance out the window, she got her reading glasses out of her pocket, perched them on her nose and bent forward to read Hope's email. "My, my, my," she breathed. Straightening, she tucked her glasses in her pocket again and scurried back to the service counter, reaching it just as the door swung open. She hurriedly picked up a dishcloth and started wiping the counter.

"What was that all about?" she asked Hope.

Hope pushed her hair back from her face. "Fortunately, nothing serious. It could've been, though. A little girl was walking her dog. The dog parked itself on its butt and wouldn't move. She kept pulling and the collar slipped right over the dog's head. The dog ran into the street, and the little girl followed. Thankfully, the driver of an approaching car had fast reflexes and good brakes, and he was able to stop in time." Hope exhaled. It could have been tragic.

"Would you like another coffee?" the barista asked.

Hope smiled. "No, thanks. I'll be leaving in a few minutes."

She settled back in her chair and finished the dregs of her coffee as she logged into her computer, read over her email and clicked Send. She was barely out the door when the barista dashed behind the counter again, picked up the phone and dialed. "Suzie? It's Karen. Guess who was just in here?...No. It was Hope Wilson...Well, you *will* care when I tell you what I learned..."

WITH CONSTRUCTION READY to start, Hope debated accepting Malcolm's repeated invitations to get together. She hadn't heard from Luke again since the day they'd gone riding. Frankly, she was frustrated by the ups and downs of their relationship.

She admitted she was lonely and, as Aunt Clarissa often pointed out, she needed some downtime, since she spent nearly every waking moment either on her project or the bookkeeping for Barkley Green. In the end, she decided to take Malcolm up on one of his offers. She felt another dinner would be the least date-like of the options he'd presented. She also insisted on driving herself rather than having him pick her up, again to keep it friendly rather than romantic.

To avoid running into people they'd know—and having them jump to the wrong conclusion—she chose a casual steak house on the outskirts of Austin and said she'd meet him there. Unsure of what to expect, Hope was tense when she first arrived, but Malcolm's relaxed attitude put her at ease. She was surprised at how quickly, and enjoyably, the evening passed, and before she knew it, they were leaving.

The restaurant had been busy when she got there, and she'd parked her Jeep in a far corner of the lot. Malcolm insisted on walking her to it.

"Thank you for dinner," she said as she reached into her handbag for her keys.

"My pleasure." He opened the door for her but effectively blocked her from climbing in. "We'll have to do it again, soon."

Hope saw the light in his eyes and sensed

what he was about to do, but not soon enough to prevent it. When he leaned in and placed his lips on hers, her eyes flew wide open. With the Jeep's door behind her and Malcolm in front, she couldn't escape. Her best line of defense was to press her lips together and hold her head as far back as she could.

It must have been very clear to Malcolm that she wasn't participating in the kiss. He stepped away.

She feared his anger but, with her wide-eyed look and tightly compressed lips, she must have looked comical, because his scowl faded and he burst into laughter. She blinked rapidly, trying to assess this turn of events.

Malcolm dropped his hands on her shoulders, rested his forehead against hers and struggled to contain his merriment. "That…" He chuckled again. "That was like…" At a loss for words, he paused.

Her lips twitched. "Like kissing your sister?" she suggested, because kissing a brother was exactly how it had felt for her. She couldn't help laughing, too.

Malcolm nodded with a smile. "That sums it up."

When he leaned in toward her again, Hope flinched, but this time he placed a kiss on her forehead and moved back to let her get into the Jeep. "Are we okay?" he asked.

"Yeah. Friends?" she asked in return.

"Friends," he confirmed.

SUZIE SAT ON a stool by two tables that had been pushed together at the Long Horn to accommodate their usual group and sipped her iced tea. "Honest, I'm not making this up. Karen saw it with her own eyes. She read the email Hope was working on at the Mocha Shoppe. Hope has to report to someone on how she's doing here. You know. How the school and community center complex is coming along."

Luella Grieves, the mayor's sister, took a long drink from her glass of Diet Coke. "And that's newsworthy because…? We've all heard from Carly that the only reason she's here is because there's a lot of money at stake for her."

Suzie shifted on her stool, leaned an elbow on the table. "If y'all would let me *finish*, you'd find out. The email was to some lawyer and it went on about an animal shelter in California. I looked it up on Google. Hope runs it with a guy called Noah Drake. Anyway, what Karen got from the email is that Hope only cares about the inheritance because of what it can do for the animal shelter, since they're having financial difficulties."

Joe removed the toothpick he'd been chewing on and guffawed. "Her father had to be worth a few million. That's a lot not to care about."

Suzie's laughter tinkled through the room. "Hold on to the table there, Joe, so you don't fall off your stool. Her father was worth a couple of *hundred* million when he died. This school and community center project will be maybe ten million, from what I heard."

Joe nearly spit up his beer, but managed to choke it down. "Seriously?"

"I wouldn't kid you about this."

"Then why is she living in that run-down house outside town?" Miranda asked.

"Who knows?" Suzie responded. "Maybe she just doesn't want to be in town, with the way we've been treating her."

"Couldn't blame her," Miranda added.

When no one else said anything, Suzie continued. "As much as it pains me to say this, I wonder if we've been wrong." She swept her gaze across her audience dramatically. "All of us. We figured she was living in the lap of luxury with her father's millions, but that's not the case. According to Karen, her email to this lawyer said she won't get any of her inheritance unless and until she finishes the project."

"Well, what do you know," Miranda murmured.

MALCOLM STRODE INTO the Long Horn Grill-house. He'd gone from one job site to another all day long in the hot, dry heat, and he was ready for a cold drink. He immediately noticed Luke at a back booth, but took a moment to greet Travis behind the counter, ask for a large iced tea, heavy on the ice, and flirt with the Collins sisters as they shared a banana split.

He then pulled up a chair and wedged himself in with the group around the two tables. "What's Luke doing back there by himself?"

"Don't ask us," Luella replied. "We invited him to join us, but he said he had something to work out."

"Huh" was Malcolm's response. "So, what's new with y'all?"

"Well, we've just been talking about what Karen—you know, at the coffee shop—learned today…" Suzie began.

Once Malcolm was caught up on the local gossip, or at least as caught up as he wanted to be, he asked Carly for another iced tea and went to join Luke. He dropped a hand on Luke's shoulder in greeting and sat down opposite his friend.

"You're done early today," Malcolm remarked.

"What? Yeah," Luke agreed distractedly.

"I had some meetings in town and thought I'd enjoy Travis's chef's cooking, rather than fend for myself at home."

"Makes sense." It occurred to Malcolm that this would be as good a time as any to clear the air about his strikeout with Hope. "I'm glad I ran into you. There's something I want to talk to you about."

"Sure. About what?"

"About Hope."

Luke's brows furrowed and he glared at Malcolm. "What about her?"

"Well, about us, really."

"I don't want to hear it," Luke cut in abruptly.

"But—"

"I said I don't want to hear it."

"But—"

Luke raised a hand. "Look, do me a favor."

Malcolm eyed him cautiously.

"Let's you and I *not* talk about Hope."

Malcolm was about to interject, explain that he just wanted Luke to know he'd been a fool to think of pursuing Hope, but Luke jumped in again.

"Ever. I don't ask you for much, but I'm asking this."

Malcolm shrugged. Whatever was bugging his friend, he figured it was better to leave the subject of Hope alone for the time being. If Luke was going to be that bullheaded about it, let him think what he wanted.

CHAPTER NINETEEN

HOPE STOOD JUST inside the hoarding on the construction site. She wore faded jeans, a white T-shirt and safety boots. She had a pair of rawhide work gloves stuck in her back pocket and a hard hat tucked under her arm. Her hair hung loose down her back. A camera was slung over her shoulder and she had a paper coffee cup in one hand.

She could hardly believe that nearly fifteen months had passed since they broke ground. The work had progressed well. Malcolm knew what he was doing. Thinking of Malcolm, she chuckled. She was glad he'd gotten the crazy notion of dating her out of his head, and they managed to settle into a comfortable, friendly relationship.

She faced the easement at the north end of the site, and her thoughts turned to Luke once more. The two of them had mostly managed to avoid each other since the day they went riding together, but that hadn't kept her mind from wandering to him, time and again.

Whenever seeing him had been unavoidable, there'd always been other people around, sparing them the need for conversation. If she'd felt his brooding eyes on her when she wasn't looking, she'd convinced herself it was her overactive imagination. She'd tried hard to keep her eyes off him.

The one time they couldn't escape acknowledging each other's presence since their horseback ride was months ago, when they'd walked the perimeter of Luke's property to inspect the restoration work along the easement. Perhaps because Harry and Malcolm were both with them, their interaction had been perfunctory and entirely business. And her heart had broken a little more. When Harry had told her someone in town had suggested that Luke had been smoothing the way for her with the town council, she'd laughed it off. Harry had said that Luke had intervened to get her the rezoning and building permits. He'd heard that Luke had even talked Malcolm into taking on the construction. She figured whoever told Harry that had been pulling his leg. And if it *was* true, the only purpose would've been to help her get the project finished as soon as possible and to be gone.

Hope turned her attention to the building again. She loved the construction site first thing in the morning, before the dust and noise and energy of all the activity consumed it. She'd fallen into the habit of showing up before anyone else. It gave her a chance to take it all in and assess the progress from one day to the next. She'd been documenting the construction through photographs from the beginning, planning to prepare a photo journal both as a keepsake for herself but also as a gift to the school board. This morning she'd arrived earlier than usual, wanting to capture some shots as the sun rose.

She'd stood in this very spot more mornings than she could count, watching the building take shape. She remembered how excited she'd been when the steel skeleton of the structure had first risen to reach for the sky. Even back then she could visualize the building as it would be. It was easy to imagine what it would look like with the cladding materials over the skeleton. The stone and wood, the glass windows and doors, over the steel posts and beams, the concrete foundation.

And now the cladding was in place and the stone glowed crimson orange with the sun's first wash of light. The sky was stained with an artist's watercolor palette of pinks and lavenders, intense behind the building and fading into pale blue above. She'd been rewarded for her early start with some great shots.

Hope loved the sense of accomplishment she got from watching the building take shape. And despite the aggressive time line, they were on schedule, thanks to Malcolm.

She took a sip of her coffee and brushed back some flyaway strands of hair. Her gaze skimmed the construction materials stockpiled on one side of the site and the small trailer, serving as an office, on the other side before resting on the building again.

They were in the home stretch.

However it had come about, she was doing something she enjoyed. The people of Canyon Creek might never forgive or accept her, but through what she was doing, she thought she might be able to absolve herself. And she was making some small measure of restitution on behalf of her father, as he'd wanted. The more time that passed, the more sympathetic she was to her father, and she truly did think of him as her father now. She wished fervently that her mother had been truthful with her, but it was hard to resent her for it. Hope had made her peace with what both her parents had done. She held no resentment.

Hearing the distant rumble of thunder, she

cast her eyes skyward. The forecast hadn't called for rain and it was a rare occurrence this time of the year.

There was barely a cloud in the sky. Before she could wonder where the thunder had come from, she realized the persistent sound wasn't thunder at all.

She stepped through the opening in the hoarding in time to see a beautiful sorrel horse charging toward her on the dirt road. It reared up in a cloud of dust as its rider reined him in. The large stallion danced and turned, as if intending to ride off again in the opposite direction. Then the rider brought the horse under control with no more than a squeeze of his knees and some soft words.

The rider was Luke.

He sat comfortably on the horse but his eyes darted to the building visible over the hoarding, down the lonely stretch of road—everywhere but at Hope.

She raised a hand to shield her eyes as she looked up at him. Running away and hiding would have been cowardly, so she offered a greeting instead.

He calmed the horse again and finally let his eyes light on her. "Morning. You're up early," he remarked.

An odd feeling churned in Hope's stomach at the sound of his voice and his now-steady gaze. There was something particularly appealing about Luke astride the handsome horse. She forced herself to remain outwardly composed. "Perhaps a little earlier than usual today, but I like coming out here in the morning. You're up early, too."

"It's my usual time to ride by."

She could see he wished the words back as soon as he'd said them.

"And it's the best time to get out on a horse and enjoy the beauty of the sunrise," he amended quickly as he leaned forward and stroked a hand along the gorgeous animal's neck.

For a moment, they both turned to the horizon, where the sun now infused the entire sky with brilliant color. Then Luke shifted his gaze toward his own property in the distance.

"I appreciate that you honored the covenant about the easement. The grass has all grown back pretty much as it was before."

It was more of a compliment or kind word than he'd offered her in some time. "I made a commitment to you," she said simply.

"Well, thanks. The construction seems to be coming along well," he added, nodding toward the building.

"Yes, it is. Malcolm's doing a great job." Hope smiled, lowering her hand. "It's hard to look at Malcolm now and imagine him the way he was in high school."

Luke hesitated—as if something displeased him—but then he chuckled. "Tell me about it! If I so much as pull out our yearbook, he threatens to take a swing at me. And I'm not sure I could best him anymore. It looks good," he repeated, nodding toward the building.

Hope's smile widened. They were having an actual conversation without awkwardness and without antagonizing each other. It felt familiar and good. Even with everything that had happened in the past, she didn't want this fragile truce to end. "Would you like to see the building?"

He glanced at the structure visible over the hoarding. "If it's no trouble." He slid off his horse and looped the reins around a fence post.

"He's beautiful. May I say hello to him?"

"Sure. Just watch your fingers…and toes. It wouldn't be beyond him to bite, or stomp on your foot if you're not careful."

Hope walked up to the stallion with unhurried steps. She held out her hand, palm up, fingers tightly together to let him get her scent. He whinnied, then tossed his head and snorted, but he didn't back away, try to rear or nibble her fingers—all good signs. She stepped slowly toward him and glided her hand along his neck, over his silky mane. Another whinny, a little more head-tossing, but he seemed to accept her.

Luke rested an arm on the top rung of a fence. "He likes you. He's generally not that friendly with strangers. I seem to have some temperamental horses."

"A little temperament can be overlooked when a horse is this handsome. Aren't you handsome?" she cooed to the horse. "What's his name?"

At the prolonged silence, Hope glanced at Luke.

"Uh...Sprite," he mumbled.

Hope's hand froze on the horse's muzzle and she stared at Luke. Sprite had been his nickname for her when they were teenagers.

Luke straightened and hooked his thumbs in his pockets. "I like the name. It suits him."

He seemed impatient, and she wished they could recapture the ease of a few moments ago. "Ready to go see the building?" she suggested as she stroked Sprite's nose a final time.

As Hope led Luke to the trailer, she was acutely aware of his presence behind her. She wasn't generally self-conscious, but right now she felt mindful of her every step. Pulling her keys out of her pocket, she unlocked the trailer door and held it open for Luke.

"What size shoes do you wear?" she asked, tossing her empty coffee cup in the wastebasket.

"Eleven."

She selected a pair of boots from a shelf, grabbed a hard hat and handed both to him.

Hope tried not to focus on the top of Luke's head as he sat down and bent over to change his boots. His hair was as thick and dark as it had been when they were young. She was shocked to realize she could remember the feel of it. She longed to touch it again.

When he straightened and his eyes met hers, she was afraid he could read her thoughts.

"Anything wrong?" he asked, rising.

"No. No... I just...remembered something." She pulled an elastic out of her pocket. With impatient motions, she tied her hair back in a ponytail and reached for her own hard hat. "Ready?"

Hope took him through the building, section by section, explaining what each area, each room, was for. She spoke with enthusiasm about the quality of the design, the ease of access and flow of the various spaces. She was glad their relaxed mood had been restored. He seemed to know quite a bit about how the construction had progressed, which made her wonder how often he rode by in the mornings. They finished the tour at the back of the building, just as the workmen were arriving. She pointed out to Luke the planned outdoor spaces—a grassy play area for the kids, three tennis courts, a baseball diamond, football field and a track around the perimeter.

Just as she had earlier when she'd stood by herself, she visualized everything as it would be when they were finished. Her voice rang with excitement and pride.

As she led Luke back to the construction trailer, she greeted some of the arriving workmen by name.

"It's going to be a special place," Luke said as he put his own boots back on. Hope felt pleasure bloom inside her. She walked him back to the street, back to Sprite.

"You're doing something important and meaningful here," he added, standing close to her. "I—" He was interrupted as a piece of equipment on the site backfired, causing Sprite to rear. Hope stumbled as she took a hasty step back. She might have fallen, if not for Luke's reaching out to steady her.

At his touch, warmth seeped through her, along her arms and up her spine, despite the sharp pain in her ankle. She tried to move away, but pain radiated up her leg when she tried to stand on her left foot. She groaned and quickly shifted her weight to her other leg. Her effort to avoid Luke's contact failed, as he tightened his grip with his right hand and wrapped his left around her waist. "Are you okay?"

No, she wasn't okay. But not in the way he meant. His face was so close to hers, she could smell the fresh, clean scent of his soap and feel the heat of his breath against her cheek. "Yes. I just need a minute."

"Let me help you back to the—"

"No. I'm fine." Or she would be, as soon as he let her go. She belatedly realized that she'd been rude to him—once again—when he was trying to help, reminiscent of when they'd first bumped into each other outside the pet store. She tested her ankle, putting a little weight on it, and thought she'd be able to manage. "I'm sorry. I just have to walk it off."

"Are you sure?" He was still holding on.

"Yeah. Really. See?" She backed away, out of his embrace, and tried not to wince at the ache.

As she turned, one of the workers stuck his head out of the opening. "Hope, we need you in the office."

"Is there a problem?"

"No, but you have to choose another tile for

the bathroom floors. The one you wanted has been discontinued."

"Okay. I'll be right there." She took another step back, grinding her teeth to keep from yelping at the pain in her ankle. "Thanks for stopping by," she managed to say.

"I appreciate the tour. You're doing a great job."

"It matters to me." *You matter,* she amended silently.

He released Sprite's reins and mounted him. He hesitated, as if he was going to say something else. Finally, he raised a hand and waved. "See you around."

Hope returned the wave and watched him ride off. She'd enjoyed discussing the project with him, just being with him. She felt they'd arrived at some kind of truce—and then she remembered the tingling sensation when he touched her. "Somehow I don't think this is going to make things easier for me," she murmured as she hobbled back to the construction trailer.

FORTUNATELY, HOPE'S ANKLE wasn't broken. She'd wrenched it and had to use a crutch for a couple of weeks. Considering how awkward it was to get around, she didn't spend as much time as she would've liked on the site. She took the opportunity to catch up on paperwork and to review the plans Noah had sent her for Barkley Green's expansion. She was excited about what they were planning to do there—add a veterinary hospital, a rehabilitation clinic, including a hydrotherapy pool, and expand the kennel/holding area to accommodate double the number of pens.

It was also an opportunity for her to spend time with Luke. They'd definitely reached a turning point the day they met at the construction site. He stopped by the next day to check up on her and brought her chocolate-coated almonds—which used to be and still was one of her favorite snacks. He offered to take Einstein for walks until her ankle had healed. Two days later, he brought her magazines and a book he thought she'd appreciate. Not only that, he fetched coffee and muffins for the entire crew at the job site one day. Once she was more mobile, they got into the habit of walking Einstein together.

Hope had been elated at first by how caring and considerate he was, but he remained painfully polite, and she suspected his solicitousness had to do with feeling responsible for her injury. When the attention persisted, she chose to accept his friendship if she couldn't have his love.

As the weeks passed, work on the school and community center neared completion. Other than Hope's monthly trips to Monterey, she was investing almost all her time and energy in making the complex a reality.

With the construction nearly complete, she was able to turn her attention to interior fit-up, furnishings and equipment. There was so much to be done, and her schedule just got tighter and tighter. Except for the time she spent with Luke, Hope kept mostly to herself, working harder than ever.

Her trips to Monterey were becoming less frequent, but that just made her feel guilty, as she could see the added strain her prolonged absences were putting on Noah.

Two months before the scheduled end of construction and less than three months before her allotted time ran out, she made another trip to Monterey. It was as much to help Noah as to recharge herself. The pressure and all the sleepless nights were taking their toll. She left Einstein in Harry's care as usual. It was early enough in the day when her flight landed that Noah took her directly to Barkley Green.

Hope was uncharacteristically quiet, and he searched her face as they knelt on opposite sides of a golden retriever–shepherd mix.

"You might want to reconsider coming home again before you're done," he suggested.

Hope raised her eyes to meet Noah's. "Why do you say that?"

"You look more worn-out than Bette," he said, indicating the dog. "And she's carrying a heavy load and ready to have her pups any time now."

Hope ran her hand gently along the dog's torso and distended belly. Satisfied that all was well with Bette, she offered some words of encouragement to the dog and then rose.

Noah stood, too, and they walked out of the enclosure, latching the door behind them. "From what you've told me, you're working yourself too hard, and your trips here aren't helping."

"But you can't handle all this on your own," she protested. "The deal was that I'd keep up my end here, as much as I could. And, frankly, I'm worried about you. You've done so much, including the plans for the expansion."

"We can make do, especially with Gillian working full-time now." He smiled when he said her name. "I'll try to find a volunteer, someone with basic accounting skills, to help with the books for the next little while."

"I can't let you take all of that on, too, on top of how much more you're already doing."

He shrugged. “We’re nearly there. It’s not for much longer.” They continued through the holding area and paused to look into a cage. Its resident was a coyote with his right rear leg splinted and bandaged.

“How’s Wiley?” Hope asked.

“He seems to be healing nicely. We should be ready to release him soon. That’ll free up a cage. We need them badly.”

“We won’t have to worry about that when our expansion plans are in place.”

They moved to the next cage. “You’re feeling confident that you’ll make the deadline?” he asked.

“I am. The further along we get with the construction, the better I feel. We don’t have a lot of time to spare, but I’m hoping we won’t need it.”

“That’s good,” he said in a subdued voice.

Hope stopped and turned to him. Her touch on his elbow made him pause, too. “Has Reeves been blustering about decreasing our line of credit again?”

Noah thrust his hands in the pockets of his khakis and stared into the kennel occupied by two miniature schnauzers. “He’s done more than that.”

Hope tightened her hold on his arm. “What do you mean?”

"He's given us six months' notice. Then he intends to reduce our line of credit by a third."

"When did this happen?" she asked angrily.

"Last week."

"And you didn't consider it important enough to tell me?"

Noah pulled a couple of dog biscuits out of his pocket and bent down to offer one to each of the schnauzers. "Telling you wouldn't have changed anything, and you've got enough to worry about. I know how tight your schedule is and…and if you don't get your inheritance, I'm not sure how we'll come up with the cash since we're pretty well maxed out on the line of credit right now."

Hope shook her head slowly. "Reeves knows how close we are to satisfying the condition. Okay, his lawyers might not have wanted to take a risk on a conditional agreement, but *come on*. He could've waited to see how we did."

They started walking again. "I made that argument to him."

"And?"

"He said he took that into consideration. He said if you get your inheritance, we won't need the line of credit anyway. And if you don't…"

"He wants the bank's money back," she finished for him. "Malcolm really is doing an incredible job. Barring any unforeseen circumstances, we'll be okay," she assured him and wished she felt as confident as she sounded.

CHAPTER TWENTY

As Hope drove into Canyon Creek, just arriving back from Monterey, she immediately sensed there was something wrong. People were rushing about, having hurried conversations or motioning to each other across Center Street.

Curious, she parked her vehicle and hopped out. She caught snippets, but not enough to figure out what was happening. Whatever it was had people in a state bordering on panic. She finally halted a woman rushing past. "What's going on?"

The woman motioned toward the east. "It's a brush fire, and it's spreading fast. There's a meeting in front of the town hall to find out how bad it is and what we can do." She pulled her arm free and continued down the sidewalk at a rapid pace.

Hope turned toward the east and saw the portentous low-hanging cloud. Why hadn't she noticed that from the plane? She answered her own question. Because she'd been reviewing construction reports that Harry had sent her. When she inhaled, she thought she could smell the acrid odor of smoke, carried on the strong east wind.

How could she have missed it when she drove in from the airport? Wrong direction for her line of sight, she suspected.

She'd never experienced a brush fire when she lived in Canyon Creek, but she'd heard plenty about the devastation they could cause. Especially during the summer, with the low levels of rainfall and the arid heat drying everything out. She knew even concrete foundations had to be watered to keep them from cracking when it got this hot. That meant dry brush could catch fire with the slightest careless spark or, in extreme cases, simply from the heat of the sun.

Hope had seen the effects of fires in the canyons of California, and she could only imagine the destruction they would cause here, if left unchecked. From what the woman had said, with the strong prevailing wind, the fire was headed in the direction of Canyon Creek. Toward their homes, ranches and livestock. She thought momentarily of her project and what it would mean if the fire damaged it. There was no margin for repairs or rebuilding. But she'd worry about that later. Hers was just one building in town, and the people and animals came first. If the fire reached them, it could be catastrophic.

Hope jumped back in her Jeep, made a quick U-turn and drove to her house.

Harry had stayed at her place while she was gone. He would've left for his Northcliffe office by now; he'd mentioned that he had an important presentation for a potential new client today. When Hope let herself in the front door, Einstein greeted her anxiously. Hope knew animals sensed changes in weather patterns and impending disaster. Not surprisingly, Einstein was restless, his agitation evident.

"I know, Einstein. Yes, I know something's very wrong." She felt conflicted; she wanted—needed—to help. But what about Einstein? How could she go and, at the same time, make sure he was safe?

Einstein whimpered, his ears plastered to his head as he leaned against her leg. She scratched his ear and checked her watch. She'd have to impose on Harry again, if she could reach him. Surely he'd be finished with his meeting by now.

She picked up the phone, punched in his number and tapped her fingers on the table while she waited. When her call went to voice mail, she left a message, appealing to him to come and get Einstein as soon as he could. She asked him to take the dog home and to text her once he had Einstein.

"Let's get you packed up, Einstein. You're going on a trip with Harry." Or at least she hoped so. Now that she was with him, the dog seemed to have put his worries aside. He pranced around, tail wagging furiously, and barked excitedly.

When Hope had packed all the things Einstein would need for a few days, she rushed to her closet and pulled out an old pair of jeans and a short-sleeved shirt. Changing quickly, she slid her feet into a thick pair of socks and her work boots. In the bathroom, she braided her hair and slathered on some sunscreen.

She bent over to hug Einstein. "You be good for Harry, okay? He should be here in a couple of hours."

If things went worse than expected and Harry was detained, Hope would come back for Einstein and take him to safety herself. She was counting on that not being necessary, but she wouldn't put the dog in jeopardy. No matter what. Still, she'd feel much better when she heard from Harry that he had Einstein and that they were safely on their way out of town.

She hugged the dog once more and hurried out the door. She checked to make sure Harry had replaced the spare key he used when he stayed at her place; as usual, it was under the flowerpot.

She ran to her Jeep, then made her way downtown.

Vehicles were parked haphazardly near the town hall, and more were coming and going. Groups of people congregated around two long tables. Hope parked her Jeep and ran toward the crowd. She saw Suzie hurrying away from one of the tables. They weren't friends, but that wasn't her concern at this point. She just wanted to be pointed in the right direction. "Suzie!" she called out as she ran up to intercept her. Suzie slowed but didn't stop until Hope blocked her path. Not unexpectedly under the circumstances, Suzie seemed out of sorts, disconcerted.

"How can I help? What can I do?" Hope asked.

A range of emotions crossed Suzie's face, but her expression eventually settled on gratitude. "The fire is headed straight for my parents' ranch. All help is appreciated. The people behind that table—" She pointed to the one on the left. "They can use you to organize supplies."

"And the other table?"

"That's for people wanting to help closer to the front. Assist with evacuation efforts and related activities. Listen, I have to go help my folks." Her voice quavered. "If they can't stop the fire from spreading, my folks might lose everything they've worked for their entire lives."

Suzie moved away, but stopped, turned and took a step back. She placed a hand on Hope's shoulder. There were tears shimmering in her eyes. "Hope, thanks. You don't owe us anything. Not after how we've treated you. That you're here, wanting to help, means a lot. So, thanks." Suzie squeezed Hope's shoulder, then rushed off.

Hope hesitated a moment, then hurried over to the table on the right. She knew that volunteers without specific training weren't allowed to help at the front; the front was for the trained firefighters. But there was a lot volunteers could do a little further ahead that wouldn't put them at risk of injury. She wanted to do what she could.

Brush fires had been a source of worry when she was growing up in Canyon Creek, and although she'd never seen one herself, she remembered as a child hearing about fires threatening nearby communities. California was also prone to wildfires.

She knew that volunteers made all the difference in the fight against fires. There just weren't enough trained professional personnel to do the job alone, especially since government funding had been cut back over the years.

As she drove to the location she'd been instructed to, she could see the fire on the horizon. It was still at a distance, but she'd been told it was advancing rapidly. Was it her imagination that she already could feel the heat? With her window open, she thought she could hear it greedily devouring the brush as it advanced.

She knew a brush fire was just another name for a wildfire, because in their area it was the low-lying, dry brush that fed it. Whatever name it was given, the danger lay in its extensive size, the speed at which it could propagate and its unpredictability. With the right conditions, it could jump roads, riverbeds and even the man-made fire breaks intended to thwart its spread.

From what Hope had surmised, they were lucky that this one was still relatively small and the winds driving it were moderate. That meant the firefighters had a better chance of stopping it before it reached Canyon Creek.

As she got closer to the front, she saw the staging area for the various fire departments called in to help. She noticed vehicles and equipment with the name National Interagency Fire Center emblazoned on them.

Looking to the east, she could see a number of small planes. In town, Hope had heard that Texas Forest Services was using their planes to battle the fire. From the haze beneath them, it was clear that they were actively spraying fire-suppressants. They kept circling in the distance, much like vultures swooping over carcasses in the desert. Despite the heat that caused beads of sweat to form on her forehead and along her spine, the thought made her shiver.

She parked her Jeep in the area she was directed to by a flagman. Then she was pointed to the volunteer coordinator, a tall, gangly man with a clipboard.

When she reached him, he quickly explained to her and a handful of other volunteers that the firefighters would try to squelch the fire but, if necessary, they were ready to try a controlled burn. That meant burning off strips of brush and other low-lying vegetation to consume the flammable material feeding the fire, causing it to starve or burn out.

He explained that they were fortunate; the direction from which the fire was coming had only low ground cover to burn, so it wouldn't be as big or move as rapidly as if there were more combustible materials. With a lot of fuel, brush fires could travel up to fifteen miles per hour. That meant it could've been on them in no time, and there wouldn't have been much they could do to prepare.

Hope took some comfort in knowing, from her years in California, that most wildfires could be extinguished before they grew out of control. The statistics were in their favor. One of the firefighters said that about 99 percent of the more than ten thousand wildfires in the States each year were contained before the damage was significant. On the downside, the ones that got out of hand caused extensive harm. He'd added that wildfires in North America destroyed more than thirteen million acres per year.

Fighting the fires could be deadly, too. Whenever she heard about a wildfire in the news, invariably firefighters had suffered injuries and sometimes lost their lives. A wildfire's burning front could shift unexpectedly with the slightest change in wind or ground conditions. Intense heat and smoke could also disorient the firefighters. Hope assumed that the dangers of the job were the reason aerial suppression was used whenever possible.

Command personnel required that anyone

involved in fighting the fire, or assisting those who did, have regular periods of rest and refreshment, including plenty of water. As important as it was to dole out food and drink to those fighting the fire, that wasn't what she wanted to do.

As part of her orientation, the organizers explained to Hope that the fire was shaped like a teardrop. The wide, rounded end was the front of the fire, the pointed part of the drop what they called the *propagation axis*. The more fuel the fire consumed, the wider the front and the fatter the teardrop, the greater the path of destruction. No wonder they were focused on cutting off the fuel supply.

The volunteer coordinator asked everyone if they had any areas of specialization for consideration for assignments. He decided that Hope could assist with the evacuation of livestock and domestic animals from the ranches closest to the front. Even though her veterinary expertise was mostly with small domestics, she'd also be working with local veterinarians to aid injured and infirm animals.

Hope drove herself and a couple of other volunteers to one of the westerly ranches. She was barely out of her Jeep when she heard it. The shrieking of the animals, driven by fear or pain. It tore at her. She wanted to hide from it—cover her ears and close her eyes—but she ignored it and sprang into action. She focused determinedly on what needed to be done. She had no sense of time. Her muscles ached from the exertion. Her throat was parched. She felt the slap of heat, received some minor burns. From cinders—not from the brush fire but from the intentional, controlled burn to keep it from reaching the ranches—and from the ropes they used to evacuate the animals.

She breathed a sigh of relief when her phone signaled that she'd received a text message. It was Harry informing her that he had Einstein and they were on their way out of Canyon Creek. Harry said he was sorry he couldn't help with the fire, but he had asthma. He told her what he'd heard from the media reports, and she shared what she'd gleaned from some of the residents in town. It didn't look good. The winds had picked up and the fire was moving faster than expected. It had already scorched thousands of acres of land at the last estimate and was now less than a hundred miles from Canyon Creek.

Hope labored resolutely alongside the other volunteers. Her face was sooty, her clothes and hair drenched from sweat and her hands raw and chafed. Her muscles were beyond sore and her head pounded, but she didn't—*wouldn't*—stop, because neither would the fire.

When the news came that the front of the fire was nearing Suzie's parents' Walbridge Acres Ranch and there was a call for volunteers to help with the evacuation of livestock, Hope was one of the first in line. Walbridge Acres was in the grouping of ranches closest to the fire, but Hope knew that Luke's ranch was part of the next grouping, if the direction of the fire remained unchanged.

Hope rode to Walbridge Acres in the back of a pickup with a half-dozen men. Her experience with animals came in handy once again, and she was assigned a crew of three to help round up the horses and cattle in the field. The pungent smell of smoke rode on the gleefully swirling winds and was a sinister harbinger of the fire ruthlessly heading their way.

She had trouble breathing in the hot, stifling air.

The animals were frenzied and difficult to herd, but the volunteers persisted, and all the animals they could find had been evacuated by the time Command ordered them to pull back because it was no longer safe to stay there.

Although not unexpected, when the evacuation order came to clear Walbridge Acres Ranch, the dejection of those present was palpable. Yes, they had been working on vacating the ranch, but it had been precautionary. Now it was essential. If they were pulling out, it was highly probable that the fire was near enough and strong enough that the ranch would be lost.

They were told that those who were still able to should move on to the neighboring ranches, the next ones threatened by the fire. Those ranches needed to prepare for evacuation, as well.

Of the five ranches to which volunteers had been dispatched, she was assigned to Whispering Springs—Luke's ranch. She understood that if Whispering Springs was at risk, so was her project, located on its southwestern tip.

If her project suffered any significant damage, she would miss her schedule. No question. She wondered fleetingly if an "act of God" would qualify for an extension under the terms of her father's will. But she couldn't think about that now, when lives and livelihoods were at stake.

As the afternoon faded into evening, Hope could smell the smoke, see in the distance the whirling masses of ash and debris in the air. She'd heard the warnings that the dense, dark cloud more than likely contained toxic gases such as carbon monoxide, sulfur dioxide and formaldehyde. To limit exposure, the crews at the front were rotated on a regular basis, even though they all used respirators. It was disheartening to see a crew brought back, covered in grime, drained of energy, heads hanging, as they felt powerless against the onslaught of the spreading fire.

Hope knew that the location of the command post had been shifted a couple of times already to ensure it remained out of the path of the fire. Protective clothing and equipment were being flown in from all available sources, but there didn't seem to be enough to go around for the all firefighters and volunteers.

Hope lugged and dragged and stocked and tended. Her lungs were raw, her muscles screamed, but she kept at it without faltering.

Hope was hauling some bags of feed to the vehicles waiting at Whispering Springs when she ran into Luke, loading his dogs into a truck. She almost didn't recognize him. Her heart lurched when she did and saw that he was coated in soot and dirt and blood. She could see blistering on his forearm. The burn looked nasty and in need of treatment.

Their eyes met. Hope didn't know how he'd sustained the injuries; the fire hadn't reached this far yet and hopefully wouldn't. Instinctively, she placed a hand on his uninjured arm. "What happened?"

Luke glanced down at himself, as if he'd suddenly realized it was his appearance that had put the look of distress in her eyes. "I was on the front, fighting the fire, when we got the call that the wind had shifted, picked up intensity on its way to Canyon Creek. I came back to do what I can here."

"You were fighting the fire?"

"Yeah. I've been trained as a smoke jumper." Someone called him. He shouted out a reply. "I've got to go."

Her hand still on his arm, she acted on impulse, rose up on her tiptoes and brushed her lips across his soot-covered cheek. "Let me know if there's anything I can do."

Luke looked at her long and hard. "You're doing it. I'm grateful for your help."

Their exchange had taken no more than half a minute, but for Hope time was suspended. In the months she'd been back in Canyon Creek, she'd visited Luke's ranch on several occasions. Now that it was threatened, she gazed around her, absorbing what he'd built.

It was a strange sensation—like a movie playing in fast forward, people everywhere rushing, men shouting and animals screaming, superimposed on a striking image of the ranch itself. The sun was still bright over the horizon—unobscured in the west by smoke and ash—the sky overhead a clear and brilliant china blue. In that moment, she could see the beauty of the place. The two-story brick house, the barns and paddocks, everything clean and orderly and well maintained. The colors and textures, vibrant and crisp, in stark contrast to the menacing gray sky to the east.

She saw Luke by the barn working to calm an agitated stallion, Sprite, the same one he'd ridden to her construction site. Sprite reared, snorting loudly, his neck extended, but Luke had a good hold on him. They cleared the barn and Luke led Sprite to a waiting transport vehicle.

Then she saw the ranch hand behind him, struggling to get a terrified mare out of the barn. Hope could see the whites of her eyes. The animal's nostrils flared, her ears were pinned back and her coat glistened with nervous perspiration.

Hope sensed it coming before it happened. The mare reared and twisted to the right, pulling hard on the reins, unbalancing the ranch hand. He fell over and rolled just in time to avoid her hooves as her forelegs pounded the dry earth. He hit a post hard and appeared to be momentarily dazed. The mare reared once more.

Hope dropped the bag of cornmeal she'd been carrying and sprinted to the barn. The mare missed the young man again, but was rearing for a third time, perilously close to him, as Hope reached them. She lunged for the reins just as the mare was at the pinnacle of her upward trajectory. The force of what must have been eleven hundred pounds of horse rearing and straining against the reins made it feel as if her arms were being torn out of their sockets, but she hung on tight and threw all her weight into it. She was able to turn the mare's head a fraction. The horse's body naturally followed as she dropped back down to the ground, her forelegs barely missing the head and torso of the ranch hand.

Hope knew what could have happened if the horse's hooves had come down on the young man, no more than a kid, really. She held tight to the reins, even though the pain in her left shoulder caused her vision to blur and a clammy sweat to break out across her body.

With soothing words and steady hands she led the mare to the spot where they were gathering livestock for transport. Luke was suddenly beside her. She didn't know where he'd come from, but he'd obviously been running, since he was out of breath. He cupped her face with his hands, dropped a kiss on her brow, then drew her close and cradled her head against his chest. "Thank you," he whispered, his voice hoarse. "Thank you for what you just did." Then the moment was gone, and they each went back to the tasks that needed doing.

It was nearing midnight when a palpable change took place. There was an energy that was at odds with the fatigue of the volunteers. It took only a few minutes for the news to reach Hope.

The fire was out.

They'd managed to extinguish it, and most of the ranches had been spared. What damage there was seemed to be primarily heat- and smoke-related.

There was a cheer of sorts—lacking intensity because of everyone's weariness—but it was a cry of relief and triumph all the same. Many of the volunteers accepted the offer of spare beds and hay in the barns, as they were too physically depleted and emotionally drained to make the drive home or to wherever they'd left their own vehicles. Food and refreshments were available for those who wanted it, but most people just craved a couple of hours' sleep and then their own showers and beds.

But Hope stayed on to help the livestock.

There were reported injuries, blessedly few people, but many animals. She wasn't a veterinarian, but her years of working at Barkley Green had provided her with enough knowledge and skill to dispense first aid and some basic life-saving medical care. If animals were hurt and suffering, and she could do something about it, her work wasn't finished. When she'd done all she could, and since her Jeep was still at Walbridge Acres, she got a ride with one of the ranch hands going home.

What they saw when they reached Suzie's parents' ranch devastated them. Hope realized it could have been far worse, but—unlike most of the other ranches—theirs hadn't fared well. Whether from flame or heat or a combination of both, the destruction was substantial. She was dropped off in front of a barn, where a handful of fatigued, soot-covered workmen were gathered. As she slid out of the truck, she could smell the strong coffee being dispensed. To the right of the barn, she saw a horse with an injured foreleg. She felt the familiar tightening around her heart, the nausea in her belly, whenever she saw an injured animal—a reaction she'd never been able to shake, despite more than a decade of working with them.

The total exhaustion that had threatened to pull her under vanished and she jogged, favoring her left leg, over to the horse. She cleaned and bandaged the cut on her foreleg, probably the result of kicking through her stall in panic.

Hope checked on a barn cat's litter of kittens, moved into the ranch house bathroom, with wet towels shoved under the door to keep the smoke from getting in. They were safe and mewling to be fed. She calmed the mother enough to be able to tend to her kittens.

And, heart-wrenchingly, she assisted the veterinarian with putting down a calf when it was obvious his injuries were too severe to be treated, and he was in excruciating pain. Hope's hands were competent and efficient as she soothed the baby, but tears were coursing down her cheeks, tracking bright in the filth smeared across her face.

CHAPTER TWENTY-ONE

THE SUN WAS rising above the horizon, streaking the sky with colors not unlike those of the ravenous fire. It seemed that everything that could be done had been done, at least for the present.

Hope had worked through the night without rest. The adrenaline pumping through her system had been so powerful she'd hardly slowed in all that time. Having tended to the last of the livestock in need at the Walbridge ranch, she wiped her forearm across her brow, smudging the sweat and dirt. She stumbled over to the table in front of the barn with a slight limp, surprised that her left knee was sore and not certain how it had happened. She helped herself to a cup of coffee—black, as they had long since run out of cream and milk—and drank deeply, feeling the immediate kick of caffeine. A large barrel filled with water, with an adjacent table holding bars of soap and towels, was her next stop. She scooped clean water in a bucket, set it on the table and rinsed her hands and arms, then started to scrub her face.

"Hope?" a familiar voice called.

She dried herself with a towel and glanced up at Suzie—who looked as dirty and unkempt as Hope felt. Suzie's skin was spattered with dirt and tears, her usually impeccable blond hair a matted, muddy brown mess. Hope squared her aching shoulders and braced herself, unsure of what to expect.

Suzie turned her head to cough into her elbow. Her voice was raw from smoke and fatigue when she spoke. "I…I want to thank you for coming. I know you've been working with everyone from the start. You didn't need to come back here to help. Certainly not *here* after the way I've acted." There were tears in her eyes.

"We all did the best we could, Suzie. Whatever's between us is nothing compared to what could've happened here." Hope shrugged and realized belatedly that the simple gesture made her back and shoulder throb. She was about to turn back to the bucket to finish cleaning up, but Suzie prevented her.

"I just wanted to say…thank you." Her voice cracked. "And that I'm sorry for everything I've said and done. I hope you can forgive me." She wiped at her tears as she spoke.

Hope reached for Suzie's arm in a conciliatory gesture, baffled at the other woman's reaction, attributing it to a combination of weariness and pent-up emotion. "Hey, it's okay. Why don't you get some rest?"

"I…I can't. It's…it's my father. He's in the hospital. He…he was trying to get the animals out of the barn, and part of the roof collapsed. A beam hit him on the head…" Suzie sobbed.

Hope hesitated only a moment before enfolding Suzie in her arms. "I hadn't heard. Is he going to be okay?"

"I…I don't know… Mom took him to the hospital, but she forgot her mobile. I haven't been able to get hold of her, and the hospital's lines are all tied up. There's so much confusion everywhere."

"Okay. Let's do this." Hope stepped back. "Get yourself cleaned up a bit, and I'll take you to the hospital. You can be with your mom, find out about your father's condition. How's that?"

Suzie continued to cry. "I can't thank you enough."

"YOU SOUND…DIFFERENT somehow," Noah observed as he and Hope chatted on the telephone later that afternoon.

Hope laughed, rubbed Einstein's head, Harry

just having dropped him off. "Does exhaustion count?"

"I heard about what happened. The brush fire and all. Was your project affected?"

"There's some damage, mostly smoke- and heat-related." She didn't go into detail, since she didn't want to worry him.

"Let me know if you want me to come out, or if there's anything I can do."

"Thanks, but we'll work it out." She prayed that was true and changed the subject. "There *is* something I wanted to talk to you about, though. An idea that occurred to me while I was helping with the animals during and after the fire."

"You were *there*? *During* the fire? And helping out when those people have done nothing but throw obstacles in your way?"

Noah sounded indignant, and Hope had to smile at the way he automatically championed her. "Yeah. I was here and, yes, I helped out. You would've done the same thing. Now listen to me. Not only did the domesticated animals and livestock need tending, but so did a variety of wildlife." Hope shuddered. "It was horrible, Noah. You can't imagine. And we couldn't help all the injured animals.

"But," she went on, "it made me think. There's nothing like Barkley Green here. Not within a hundred-mile radius. I checked. But there sure is a need."

"What are you saying?"

"I'd like to set up a shelter here. Think of it as Barkley Green Two."

"You're planning on staying in Canyon Creek? I was afraid of that."

Hope couldn't deny that it had occurred to her, but there was no way she could stay in Canyon Creek. She'd more or less lived like a recluse for the better part of two years, and that wasn't something she could continue. "No. I'm not planning to stay. But I *am* considering setting up a shelter and hiring someone to run it. If…when—" she corrected herself "—when I get my inheritance, I'll be able to afford the funding for two shelters." The fatigue was gone, and she could tell that her voice had gained vigor. "Would you do it with me?"

There was a pause. "It sounds…interesting," he finally conceded. "As long as you come back here. We're a team. I can't do this on my own, as wonderful as Gillian's been. I need you back here, especially if…when—" he corrected himself, too "—when we do the expansion."

"But you'll think about it?"

"Yeah, I will."

After the call, Hope sat with Einstein on

her front porch and mulled over the idea. She really wanted to establish a shelter in Canyon Creek. Her father had wanted to make amends by building the school and community center. Whether the people of Canyon Creek liked her or not, she had an opportunity to atone on her own behalf—and do something she was passionate about—by establishing an animal shelter. The more she thought about it, the more fervent she became.

She'd need to find a site. They could use the same design they'd come up with for Barkley Green. They could make it better, since it would be new construction rather than a renovation and expansion. She and Noah had put a lot of thought into what they needed in Monterey. It would work just as well right here in Canyon Creek. Sure, Canyon Creek was a much smaller town than Monterey, but as she'd told Noah, there wasn't a facility like it in nearly a hundred miles, so the area they'd serve would be much larger, justifying a similar-sized building.

She realized she hadn't been entirely truthful with Noah—or herself. More and more, it wasn't just about the shelter but about staying in Canyon Creek. If only… Her thoughts turned to Luke again. If only she could find a way to make things right with him.

She smiled, the emotion bittersweet. Yeah,

she still loved Luke. If she hadn't known it before, it was driven home when she'd seen him hurt at his ranch, during the fire.

She'd reconciled herself to her newly acknowledged feelings. She also understood that those feelings weren't shared by Luke. Regardless, she was happy that they could at least be friends. No one in Canyon Creek mattered more to her than Luke.

Considering where her thoughts had strayed, it didn't surprise her when she saw Luke's silver pickup truck turn into her driveway.

She rose from the glider and with Einstein at her side went to greet him. "Hi," she said as he climbed out of his truck. "What brings you here?"

Luke bent down to scratch Einstein behind the ears, then reached back into his truck. "This," he said. Pulling out an enormous bouquet of bright flowers, he handed them to her.

"They're beautiful!" Hope exclaimed, burying her nose in the blooms. "What's this for?"

"For you." Luke smiled. "It's a very small token of my appreciation."

"For?"

"For everything you did during and in the aftermath of the fire."

Hope sniffed the flowers again. "It was the least I could do, but thank you."

She motioned to the patio and the glider. “Why don’t you sit down? I’ll put these in water and get us some iced tea.”

“I don’t want to impose.”

“No imposition.” She hesitated. “Since you’re here, there’s something I’d like to get your opinion on anyway.”

She emerged from the house a short while later, smiling as she noticed Einstein’s head on Luke’s lap.

Luke glanced up when he heard the screen door slam and rose to help her with the pitcher and glasses. She passed him his drink as they sat back down. He rested the ankle of one leg over the opposite knee and draped his arm behind her back, stroking her bare shoulder with his thumb.

She loved that he could do that now. Touch her casually and with affection. It might not have been the passionate kiss she would’ve liked, but it was friendly and comfortable.

Hope took a sip of her tea, then outlined her plan for a shelter in Canyon Creek.

“It’s a terrific idea!” Luke said enthusiastically.

“You wouldn’t happen to have another vacant parcel of land available, would you?”

“Sadly, no. Nothing that would work for a shelter.” He toyed with the ends of her hair as he thought for a moment. “You’d want something outside town, wouldn’t you? Easier to accommodate wildlife and you’d have fewer noise complaints.”

Hope nodded. “Yes. That makes sense.”

“The town owns vacant land. They might have an appropriate piece they could sell you.”

Hope rolled her eyes. “That’s not going to happen.”

“Why?”

She wiped at the condensation on the outside of her glass. “Because of how people feel about me.”

“It might’ve been like that when you first arrived, but not now. Especially after the fire.”

“People have been more tolerant, even friendlier,” she admitted. She thought of Suzie, of how they were becoming friends—and most important, her relationship with Luke—and smiled. “You included. But Mayor Grieves isn’t one of those people. It was hard enough to get the required approvals for the school and community center. Do you really think he’d want to sell me a parcel of land for another project? He’ll be happy to see me finish up and get out of town.”

“A lot of time has passed since then. People value what you’re doing. I also know they appreciate everything you did during the fire.

Their feelings are changing," he said. "I can talk to Tim, if you like."

For a moment Hope wondered if the rumors Harry had heard—about Luke's having smoothed the way with the mayor—were true, but she doubted it, based on the state of their relationship at the time. People might have been nicer recently, but that wasn't the same as acceptance or, in most cases, true friendship. "I appreciate the offer, Luke, but I need to think it through some more."

"Okay." He lowered his arm and placed his hand over hers. "If I can help, let me know."

That simple touch caused such a longing in her, she turned her hand over and closed her fingers around his. Feeling the warmth of his palm against hers only intensified her yearning. Before she was even aware of what she was doing, she leaned in and placed her lips on Luke's. There was a moment of complete bliss, as she felt his mouth respond to hers. Then he sprang up. Staring at her, he took a couple of steps back.

"Luke?" She couldn't keep the hurt and uncertainty from her voice.

"I'm sorry." He backed up to the edge of the porch, bumped into the railing. "I just remembered I have something to do." He rushed down the steps and to his truck.

Hope looked around to make sure no one was walking by. What had she been thinking? Well, she'd managed to put to rest any doubts she might've had about Luke being interested in her in *that* way.

Maybe it was a bad idea all around to think about a shelter in Canyon Creek…to think about anything beyond the completion of the current project.

The sooner she finished, the sooner she could be back in Monterey, where she belonged. The sooner she could carry on with her life, solitary as it was.

"THIS IS WONDERFUL!" Hope exclaimed as she, Malcolm and Harry walked around the building and then into the auditorium.

Harry wandered off to inspect some detail, leaving her with Malcolm.

Malcolm laid a hand on her shoulder. "If it's so wonderful, why do you look so unhappy?"

She turned away. "I don't know."

He turned her toward him again. "Sure you do. You just don't want to say."

She raised both eyebrows.

"Talk to me," Malcolm urged.

"It's…everything. I'm running out of time here. I have to go back to Monterey. I have responsibilities there, made a commitment to my partner, and I love the work we do."

"But that's not all of it."

"No." Hope hesitated. She weighed the pros and cons of taking Malcolm into her confidence and finally decided she needed someone to talk to. "I don't understand Luke."

Malcolm's rich, spontaneous laugh echoed through the empty auditorium, causing Harry to look in their direction. "I don't either. But that, in itself, is not a cause for unhappiness."

Hope shook her head. "No. But I really thought we still…had something. I thought he still had feelings for me."

"Do you have feelings for him?"

"I'd think that was obvious, otherwise why would I be talking about this?"

"All right." He nudged her shoulder gently and they walked toward the auditorium door. "Admitting it is an important step. So what's the problem?"

"I just don't understand what sets him off. I know it must've been hard for him to lose his father, but every time my father or his comes up in conversation, he either shuts down or gets angry. I don't know why he has so much resentment about how his father died."

"But you do know," Malcolm said.

"I know it was a car crash."

Malcolm halted and turned her toward him again. "You realize it's more complicated than that."

The confusion must have shown in her eyes. "What do you mean?"

Now it was Malcolm's turn to look confused. "You and I are the only ones who know."

"Know *what*?"

Malcolm stared at her as if she'd lost her mind.

"What?" she repeated.

"You know. He poured it all out to you in his emails and letters. It was only when you ignored his pleas that he filled me in."

Hope opened her mouth but no words came. She remembered Priscilla telling her that Luke had sounded distraught when he'd called; he'd said he really needed to talk to her. Had it been about more than her leaving? She frowned, shook her head. "I don't know anything about what happened," she finally said.

"But—"

"I never opened his letters or read his emails," she admitted.

"You're not serious." Malcolm looked horrified.

"Yes, I am." The words came out on a whisper. "What don't I know?"

"It's not up to me to tell you. It's—"

Hope clutched his arm. "You need to tell me. I *have* to know."

Malcolm cast his eyes skyward. "All right. You remember that Luke's dad left the family after your father closed the plant."

Hope nodded.

"He took one job after another, but couldn't hold on to any of them. He started drinking, which only made matters worse. Luke and Travis stayed in touch with him, but Luke was the only one who recognized his father's downward spiral. Travis was too young, and you know how Luke's always been his protector? Well, he shielded him from that, too, as much as he could."

All Hope could do was nod.

"Luke received a disjointed, garbled letter from his father one day," Malcolm went on. "It was obvious he'd been drinking when he wrote it." Malcolm's laughter held no humor. "But then, when *hadn't* he been drinking by that point? Anyway, Luke detected something different in that letter. Something very dark. He left the same day to drive to Fort Worth, hoping to find his father. By the time he got there, it was too late. His dad had wrapped his car around a concrete embankment. It was a single-vehicle accident and Luke will never know if it was an accident or intentional."

"I don't understand..." She blinked at the tears that clouded her vision. "It's very sad and I'm sorry I didn't know. But what does that have to do with me?"

Malcolm paused. When he finally spoke, his voice was subdued. "Two things, really. First, the letter Luke received made it clear that his father held your father responsible for all his troubles, even after the passage of so many years." He gave her time to absorb the blow. "Secondly, Luke drove to Fort Worth with the hope of saving his father. Whatever it took, he planned to convince him to come home. He was too late."

Malcolm paused again, and there was sorrow in his eyes. "The one person...the only person who could have consoled him...was you."

Malcolm's words echoed in her mind. She rubbed a hand over her mouth. "I'm so sorry. I don't know what to say."

"You don't have to say anything, but this might help you understand why Luke feels about your father the way he does and why he may harbor some...resentment. He believes it was your father's actions—the closing of the plant—that not only drove his father away, but precipitated his drinking and ultimately led to his death."

With her hand still over her mouth, Hope held back a sob. "I'm sorry," she repeated, before she ran to her car.

Hope drove straight to Whispering Springs. There was a terrible ache in her heart. Part of her wanted to reject what Malcolm had told her, but she knew he wouldn't lie. Ronnie was the first person she saw when she arrived at Luke's ranch. She asked him where she could find Luke, and he directed her to the barn.

She found him inside baling hay.

"Luke," she called, out of breath from emotion as much as the exertion of running. He tossed the hay on his pitchfork into a stall and turned. One look at her and he stuck the fork in a bale and hurried over.

"What's wrong?"

"I'm sorry. I'm s-o-o-o sorry," she choked out, with tears in her eyes and her voice.

He led her to a bale of hay, eased her down on it, but didn't ask what she was talking about. It appeared he didn't have to. "Who told you?"

Hope shook her head. "That's not important. What's important is I had no idea. I'm so sorry," she repeated. She clasped his hands in hers, but he seemed to have withdrawn.

"But you knew…"

She shook her head again, tears streaming down her face.

"No, I didn't. I…I didn't read any of your letters or emails," she sobbed. Covering her face with her hands, she continued to weep softly. When she felt Luke's arm encircle her, she nestled her head against his shoulder and wound her arms around him, holding tight. It felt comforting to be in his arms, even under these circumstances.

When she'd quieted, he spoke softly into her ear. "I imagine you can appreciate my feelings about your father now. I couldn't understand how you could defend him to me. Because I believed you knew what had happened."

With a palm on his chest, Hope gently pushed him back and looked into his eyes. "Honestly, I didn't know. If I had, I wouldn't have said the things I did."

"I'm not sure why you'd defend him regardless. You never did when we were kids, and he certainly didn't do you or your mother any favors."

Hope hadn't confided to anyone what her father had revealed to her on his deathbed. Only Noah, Priscilla, Morris and Clarissa knew that she'd seen him before he died, but they weren't aware of what he'd divulged. Hope hadn't even shared it with Clarissa, not wanting to taint the memory of her mother in her eyes.

But now it all came out. All the feelings she'd kept inside about her father, her mother and her paternity. Luke continued to hold her long after the story was told and her tears were spent.

Finally, he dropped a kiss on her forehead, and it was his turn to apologize.

CHAPTER TWENTY-TWO

"WHAT DO YOU mean we're not going to make our deadline?" Hope cried.

"I didn't say we *won't* make it. I said it's a risk," Harry clarified.

"I don't understand. There's always been a risk, but I thought we were on schedule."

"It's the damage from the fire. I know I said it wasn't going to be an issue when we first assessed what needed to be done. However, I didn't factor in the demand for tradesmen here in Canyon Creek, with everyone trying to rebuild."

"We have a contract with Malcolm's company and it includes all the trades. They've made commitments to us for the completion date. We just need to replace some drywall, check some electrical work. How can that be a problem?"

"It might not sound like a lot. Malcolm's still committed, but no one's available for the extra work. All the trades are working at full capacity right now."

"Can't we offer them more money?"

"That's what everyone else is doing. Offering premiums."

Hope slumped into a chair. How was it possible that they'd come this far, were only a matter of weeks from completion, and yet meeting her deadline was now in jeopardy?

With the threat to her schedule, the project required all her attention, and she tried to put the idea of an animal shelter in Canyon Creek out of her mind. It wasn't as easy keeping Luke out of her thoughts.

She valued the friendship she and Luke were developing. Whenever she started to wonder if there could be anything more between them, remembering his rejection of her impulsive kiss brought her back to reality.

Still, it was eye-opening to discover that they had more common interests now than they had as kids, chief among them their shared love of animals and concern for their well-being.

Hope had oddly conflicting feelings about the passing of the days. She wanted to be done with the complex, know that she'd finished it in the required time and thereby satisfied her father's will.

On the other hand, each day took her closer

to the time she'd have to leave Canyon Creek. And the thought of that depressed her. Even if she and Noah decided to go ahead with the animal shelter in Canyon Creek—a big *if*, given the way she was feeling—she doubted she'd stay to see it built.

There was no point prolonging the inevitable, hoping for something she could never have. Canyon Creek was no longer her home. Despite the fire, despite her part in the livestock rescues, she would never be one of these people again. And Luke would never be hers—not in the sense she longed for.

With just weeks remaining of her allotted two years, Hope was feeling progressively more unsettled, more on edge.

She called Aunt Clarissa, hoping that talking things through with her would help her put things in balance. Unable to reach Clarissa, Hope left a message. After disconnecting, she realized her message probably sounded quite panicky. She decided to go into town to run some errands in an attempt to occupy her mind.

Clarissa called back while Hope was in the Canyon Creek General Store. What she'd suspected about the tone of her message was confirmed when Clarissa's first words were "Are you okay?"

Hope moved to a quiet corner. "Yes. No. I don't know." Her eyes filled with tears. "Oh, Aunt Clarissa, I don't know what to do," she almost wailed.

"Calm down, sweetie, and tell me what's going on."

"You were right. You were right all those years ago."

Clarissa's confusion and concern were evident in her voice. "About what?"

Hope brushed at her tears and huddled in the corner. "I…I shouldn't have put on that charade when I left. I was such a stupid, foolish kid."

"You weren't stupid. You were just scared."

Hope tried to collect herself.

"Tell me what brought this on and how I can help."

"That's just it! You *tried* to help. You told me to tell everyone the truth when Mom passed away and my father made me move. But I didn't listen." She realized she sounded like a teen again. "Everything I said was so far from the truth, and that's all people remember."

"Don't be too hard on yourself. You did what you thought was best at the time. You were just trying to cope with everything, your grief and fear. You'd lost your mother. That was huge. No one could blame you for how you reacted."

"Maybe at the time, but it doesn't help me now. I never thought I'd have to come back, but I *am* here. Knowing I'll be leaving again soon, all I want to do is stay." She hiccupped, searched her bag for a tissue and blew her nose.

"Then why don't you? At least for a while. See how it goes once your project is finished."

That got Hope sniffling again. She turned in a half circle and faced the corner behind the shelves. "That's what I want, but I can't. I want people here to accept me for who I am, to *like* me. That's not going to happen. And that's not the worst of it. Oh, Aunt Clarissa, I *love* Luke. I love him. But...but he doesn't feel that way about me anymore." She remembered how humiliating it had been when he'd rebuffed her kiss. "Oh, he's being nice to me now. He's the nicest to me of anyone here, but he just doesn't have the same feelings for me that I have for him." At a rustling sound behind her, Hope spun around and stared directly into the eyes of Luella Grieves, the mayor's sister and busybody owner of the general store.

Mortified, Hope could only imagine what Luella had "accidentally" overheard. Next to Suzie, Luella was the biggest gossip in Canyon Creek. Wouldn't it be great if Hope's little meltdown got back to the mayor, which she suspected wouldn't take much time once she left the store. Or worse, to Luke.

Hope turned back to the corner and continued in a hushed voice. "Aunt Clarissa, I'll be okay. Honestly. I need to go. There's someone here. I appreciate you talking to me about this, but I'll be fine."

Forgetting all about the purchase she needed to make, Hope stuffed her phone back in her bag, said a hurried goodbye to Luella and headed out to her Jeep.

"HOPE SAVED MY LIFE," Ronnie Miller declared to the group gathered around two tables at the Long Horn Grillhouse.

"You're dramatizing things," Miranda stated.

"No. That darn mare—usually gentle as a lamb—was spooked big-time. She reared up, yanking the reins right out of my hands, and I lost my footing. The mare would've stomped on my face, if it wasn't for Hope. She—"

"C'mon, Ronnie," Luella interjected. "You're exaggerating."

"No." Ronnie was adamant. "It's the truth."

Luke, who'd entered the Long Horn a while earlier, overheard the conversation as he walked over to the group. He laid a hand on Ronnie's shoulder. "The kid's absolutely right. I saw it. I was trying to get Sprite to settle. I'd just tied him off, when I saw Ronnie go down. I ran over, but I wouldn't have reached him in time." He squeezed Ronnie's shoulder reassuringly.

"Is it true she got hurt doing it?" Miranda asked.

"Yeah. The mare's hoof grazed her knee. Fortunately, she didn't break it. But Hope was beat when she left Whispering Springs," Luke added, with a mix of guilt and gratitude.

"Hey, Suz," Luella said as Suzie joined their table.

"Hi, y'all." Suzie took a chair one of the guys pulled over for her, then took a swig of another guy's beer. "And that wasn't the end of it."

All eyes turned to her. "After Hope left Luke's ranch, she came back to Walbridge Acres."

"She did?" That was the first Luke had heard of it.

"Yeah. She came to help us with the animals."

"She could barely stand when she left Whispering Springs," Luke said, "and she was limping because of her injury."

Suzie tilted her head. "You wouldn't have known it from the way she worked at my folks' place. She must've been with us for at least five hours. She saved more than a few of our livestock. Then she drove me to the hospital so I could be with my mom and dad." Suzie glanced down. "And, boy, do I feel bad about how I've treated her since she's been back."

"You're not the only one," Miranda admitted. A chorus of general agreement followed.

Luke felt his own culpability where Hope was concerned; it was something he'd been struggling with more and more since they'd resolved most of what had been holding him back. If not for her relationship with Drake... but he forced that aside. He was grateful for what Hope had done for him and for so many others. "Think about what she'd come here to do in the first place. Forget the source of the funding. She's building that school and community center. She's given up two years of her life to do something good for us, and what thanks have we given her?"

"We certainly haven't made it easy," Miranda said.

"No, we haven't," Luke agreed. "I sure haven't done her any favors." And he realized he hadn't properly thanked her for everything she'd done during the fire. A bouquet of flowers just wasn't enough. They'd grown closer since the fire, and more so after her revelations about her father. With all those misunderstandings straightened out, Luke knew that if not for her relationship with Drake, he would've told Hope how he felt about her. It didn't make things easier for him that his feelings for her continued to grow.

"Before we kick ourselves too much," Joe chimed in, "let's not forget how she left us when we were in high school. She couldn't care less about us. Wanted to be like her father. What should we believe now?"

Luella made a gesture of slapping her forehead. "How could I not have told you this? I told Tim but forgot to tell y'all." She paused dramatically, enjoying the attention. "I heard Hope talking to someone on the phone. Everything she said to us back then was a lie. She was a young girl, hurt and grieving, and she didn't want to be pitied. Apparently, she didn't want to leave, but her father made her."

"And let me remind you again," Karen, the barista from the coffee shop, piped up. "The reason the money's important to her is because of the animal shelter in Monterey."

Meaningful glances were exchanged. Luke felt an overpowering, all-consuming feeling for Hope and realized with a jolt that it was love. For the first time, he wondered if he should try to win her love from Drake. She and Drake had been together for so long, he wondered if he would have a chance. And what about Malcolm? He had no idea where that had gone and, frankly, had blocked it out of his mind. But if he didn't at least try, how could he live with himself after she was gone again? A sobering thought, but he suspected there would be no one else for him.

As if remembering something else, Luella focused her attention on Luke and in a quieter voice said, "Luke, you really should have a chat with Hope. You know, about the two of you."

"So," Ronnie, Luke's ranch hand, broke in. "Will she make it? Do you think she'll get the project done in time to make her deadline?"

"I can't say for sure." Luke voiced what he'd been worried about since the fire. No one—especially not Hope—knew that since construction had begun, he'd made it his morning routine to ride by the site to check on progress. It was why he'd run into her at the site when she'd shown up at sunrise that one morning. "She's doing her best, but with the damage from the fire on top of everything else she's had to contend with, she'll be cutting it close."

"She'll make it." Everyone looked at Malcolm as he strode over to join the group. He slapped Luke on the back, pulled up a chair and crowded in between Suzie and her neighbor on the right, soliciting a not-so-polite complaint. "Forget it, Joe. You don't have a chance with our lovely Suz," he said as he swung an arm behind Suzie's back. Glancing at Luke, he continued. "She'll make it because I'm going to ensure that she does. But as you said, the damage from the fire has set us back. I'm going to have to add an extra shift—in the evenings—to see that we don't miss the deadline. And I'm going to absorb the cost."

His words were followed by whistles and cheers.

"But that's going to cut into your profit margin," Karen noted.

Malcolm shrugged. "So be it."

Carly placed a beer in front of Malcolm and handed Suzie a glass of wine.

Malcolm took a sip. "The real problem won't be the cost but finding people to do the work. Everyone's putting in long hours right now, and there still aren't enough people for all the jobs."

"I could help out," Luke said. "After I finish at the ranch." He swept an inquiring look around the table. "Anyone else interested in pitching in?"

Suzie was the first to agree. "If there's anything I can do, count me in."

"Me, too," Ronnie said. "I worked in construction in Chicago for a while."

One by one, everyone around the table offered to assist. Luke nudged Malcolm. "Well, it looks like you have your evening shift crew, and you won't be out of pocket for the expense."

Luke and Malcolm lingered after the others had dispersed.

"It's a good thing you're doing for Hope," Luke commented.

"It's the least I can do. She deserves it. She's a good person."

"Yeah, she is." Luke appreciated that Mal hadn't discussed his relationship with Hope since that time he'd nearly bitten his head off over it. But now Luke realized that he'd have to get over whatever relationship Malcolm and Hope had, if he wanted to stay friends with both of them. "So, uh, how are you and Hope doing?" he asked in an attempt to broach the subject and wondered if that Drake guy was still in the picture.

"Great! She's an absolute dream as a client. Knows exactly what she wants and how she wants it. I wish all my clients were that clear and decisive."

Luke nodded. "That's...nice. But, you know, how's the relationship going?"

"We work well together."

"I mean on a personal level."

Malcolm's confusion was obvious. "What?"

"You and Hope."

Several heartbeats passed. "You think we're *seeing* each other?" Malcolm managed to get out, but just barely, he was laughing so hard.

Luke glowered. "You mean you're not?"

"No-o-o." The word was drawn out and Malcolm was still laughing. "What made you think that?"

"For one thing, you asked my permission, if you remember. And second, I saw the two of you together not long after, having dinner at Mendocino's."

"Are you kidding? That had to be over a year ago. I tried to tell you, but you wouldn't let me. I figured you could believe what you wanted if you were going to be bullheaded."

"But...I thought you were interested in her."

"I thought so, too." Malcolm hesitated.

"Go ahead. Say what you're thinking."

"Well, I went as far as trying to kiss her. Now, before you take a swing at me, she wasn't having any of it. Also, we both found it rather... awkward. Sort of like kissing a sibling. After the shock wore off, we laughed about it."

Luke remembered when Hope had kissed him on her front porch not that long ago. How good it had felt. There hadn't been anything sisterly about it. And he'd wanted to prolong the kiss, until first Malcolm and then Drake had popped into his mind. After that, he couldn't follow through with the kiss. Whether Hope was seeing one of them or both of them…he couldn't do it. He wasn't like that.

"Well, if you're not dating her, what about that Drake character?"

"No idea. You'd have to ask her."

CHAPTER TWENTY-THREE

HOPE TOOK A slow turn around the large gymnasium that would be shared by the school and community center. The floor had all the necessary markings in bold colors over pale oak that gleamed with the diamond-hard varnish. The high ceiling was open, revealing the steel webbing of the structure from which the bright overhead lights were suspended. Various pieces of equipment, including a climbing wall, basketball hoops and gymnastics apparatus, were in place and ready for use.

Hope ran her hands along the smooth surface of the ballet barre. She could see in her mind's eye little girls in pink leotards and frilly tutus giggling as they used it, the strains of "The Nutcracker Suite" accompanying them.

"Well? What do you think?" Harry prompted.

Hope did one more slow turn and grinned. "It's fantastic! I can't believe we're almost done!"

"We are. The school portion's already complete, and the furniture will be coming in next week. For the community center, as you know, we only have some interior finishes to worry about and the bathrooms. There should be no problem getting all of that done next week."

Hope whooped and hugged Harry. "We did it! We really did it!"

"It looks that way. With the work you and the school board have been doing to get the building ready, and the town hiring all the needed staff for the community center, everything should be in place by the time the facility's ready to open!"

"Thanks, but I did very little. Just alerted them to the timing and they did the rest."

"What we need now is the occupancy permit."

"Oh, oh. Should I be worried about *another* obstacle?"

"You'd know better than me, but I doubt it. Do you really think the town wouldn't provide an occupancy permit at this point?"

"I just don't want to set my expectations too high, only to be disappointed. How long do you suppose it'll take us to get the permit?"

"Shouldn't be more than a week or two."

Hope didn't need to check her calendar. She had the dates indelibly etched in her mind. Using the longer time frame Harry suggested, she had only two weeks of contingency to meet her deadline. Cutting the time frame so close, she'd made sure she had everything in writing from the lawyer. Her job would be done when the complex was *ready* for occupancy. It didn't actually have to be occupied and in operation. That was the school board's and town's responsibility. But the occupancy permit had to be issued, meaning that the building *could* be utilized for its intended purpose.

Although she'd been able to get the rezoning and building permits, she knew Town Council could still block her from opening the school and community center by not granting the final permit. Hope moved away from Harry, under the pretense of inspecting various sections of the gymnasium. She reminded herself not to worry about things that hadn't happened. So far, everything had worked out. Surely, at this stage, they wouldn't block her. Then again, she'd gotten this far by hoping for the best and planning for the worst, always having contingency plans in place.

If she didn't obtain the occupancy permit in the allotted two-year time frame, all her efforts would have been wasted.

Now that the building was essentially complete, she was hearing the excited chatter from people when she went into town. A few of them had approached her and thanked her personally. There was no question that they were becoming appreciative and anxious to have it operating in time for the new school year.

But it had become common knowledge that she had a deadline and that it was looming. If Council chose to, they could spite her by holding up the occupancy permit for the remaining weeks and issuing it *after* her allotted time had passed. That way, they'd have their facility, but she wouldn't receive her inheritance. Yes, she was getting along with many of the residents, but she'd never felt that the mayor had warmed up to her. He continued to take every opportunity he could to remind the town about her father's betrayals. And hers... Maybe not in so many words, but it was there. She glided a hand along the top of the floor-hockey net. With a sigh, she turned and walked back to where Harry was standing, talking on his cell.

There wasn't much she could do at this point, since she'd tried her best to rebuild relationships and earn people's trust. If they wanted to hurt her—to get payback—this was the perfect opportunity.

Harry disconnected the call just as Hope reached him. "I've got the paperwork started for the occupancy permit. We should be able to submit it tomorrow. But that look on your face concerns me. Do we need to talk about one of *those things* again?"

Hope found she could smile, even laugh. "No. There's nothing new here. Just the same old stuff," she said with a shrug. "It's just that everything's so perfect. You really have done an excellent job and—"

"We," he interjected. "*We've* done an excellent job."

"Okay, but now that we're so close, now that we're at the finish line, I can't help worrying that something might still go wrong. That the mayor will block the permit. After all our work, I might not meet the deadline."

Harry glanced at Hope as they walked out of the gymnasium. "Let's think positive."

HOPE HAD TAKEN Noah's advice, and in the past couple of months, she'd put off returning to California. There was no real need. Noah had been managing well in her absence, especially with Gillian's help. And it had been a great opportunity for Gillian to prove herself. Besides, Noah and Gillian's relationship was evolving, so Noah had less free time.

The day Hope had blurted out to Clarissa how much she wanted to stay in Canyon Creek but couldn't had been a closure of sorts for her.

She knew she couldn't stay and had begun to plan what she'd do when she returned to Monterey. She'd oversee the development and construction of their expansion. She thought again about how much she'd love to open a shelter in Canyon Creek. If only she *could* stay. Be welcomed. But she knew that would be a stretch. Grudging acceptance, even some tenuous friendships, didn't constitute real welcome. And even if it did, would she be able to live in Canyon Creek, see Luke on a regular basis—especially now that they were friends—with no possibility of ever having more from him? She didn't believe there'd be a second chance. She told herself she should be thankful for his friendship.

But the more time she'd spent with him, the deeper her feelings became. Somewhere along the way, she'd surpassed what she now saw as immature emotion in her youth. Luke wasn't cantankerous or mean, as she'd suspected for a while. He'd just been hurt far more deeply than she'd realized. Under the circumstances, she couldn't blame him. He needed to adjust, too. He'd been as uncomfortable about her returning as she was about being back.

A week passed, and there was no word from the town about the occupancy permit. Malcolm and his crew had cleared the job site, all the hoarding had been dismantled and the landscaping was almost complete. There was only an occasional construction worker at the complex now to address deficiencies. Hope's days were filled with making sure all the fixtures, furnishings and equipment arrived and were properly positioned or installed. Although it wasn't required, she used some of the funds she'd set aside for contingencies to stock both the school and the community center with supplies, such as schoolbooks, papers, towels.

With the work complete, there was no reason to go into town. When she wasn't at the project site, she confined herself to her house.

It had been nearly two weeks since they'd submitted the application for the occupancy permit, and they still hadn't heard anything. Harry had checked a couple of times, but couldn't get an update. Hope worried that she was running out of time. She took Einstein for long walks, trying to absorb as much of Canyon Creek as she could before leaving again—with or without her inheritance. As for the little house she'd come to love… She started the process of packing up the things she'd take back to Monterey.

She was trying to retrieve a dog toy from under her bed when her phone rang. Jerking up, she banged her head on the bed rail. All of a sudden she knew why they showed cartoon characters with little stars circling their heads. She crawled out from under the bed and answered her phone.

"Do you want the good news or the bad news?" Harry asked.

"Not again! I'd rather not have any bad news at all, but let's start with the good."

"Okay. There's movement on the occupancy permit."

She felt a knot forming on her head, but she'd worry about that later. "Movement? Is that good?"

"Well, that leads us to the bad news."

Hope's nerves were frayed. The throbbing at the back of her head wasn't helping. "Harry, please don't play games with me now. Just tell me what's going on."

"Okay. Apparently, the application has gone through the review. The various authorities visited the site today. It was very short notice. I tried calling you, but there was no answer."

She must have been out walking with Einstein.

"Anyway, all seems to be in order."

"Why is that bad news? Are we getting the permit?"

"I don't know."

"What do you mean you don't know?" Her voice was shrill.

"They've called a special meeting of council. It's scheduled for Wednesday at ten."

"Is that usual? Isn't it supposed to be like it was for the building permit? They approve it and we get a piece of paper?"

"Yeah. Yeah, that's the way it should be. Frankly, I've never heard of this before, but that's how it is. And you need to be there."

"You're kidding! Why?"

"No, I'm not kidding, and I have no idea why."

By the time Hope hung up the phone, her head was pounding, thanks to the hard hit she'd endured and the disconcerting information Harry had shared.

She pulled a small pack of frozen peas out of the freezer and plunked down on the sofa. Holding the bag to her head, she grimaced at the pain and the cold. Einstein ambled over and stretched out at her feet, asleep and snoring in no time.

What was going on? Why did Council have to meet and why did they want her there? This couldn't be good news.

Two years of her life spent on this project, and her inheritance and all her plans for the shelter depended on a dozen people—the Canyon Creek Town Council.

CHAPTER TWENTY-FOUR

HOPE FINISHED PACKING and kept to herself the next two days. Luke was the one exception. He'd continued to be supportive. He promised her that he'd be there for the council meeting.

On Wednesday, she met Harry outside the town offices. She looked around anxiously.

"What's up?" Harry asked.

"Luke said he'd be here, but I don't see him anywhere."

"Maybe he's already inside."

She craned her neck. "No. I don't think so. He said he'd meet me outside. I don't see Malcolm either. He said he'd be here, too." The absence of the two men added to her agitation. Why weren't they here? Did they know something she didn't?

Glancing around, expecting to see either Luke or Malcolm, she followed Harry inside, and her heart sank.

If her purpose for being here was to receive the decision on her occupancy permit, the council chamber being packed was *not* a good sign.

Even with the progress she'd made, she was afraid that everyone had turned out to see her defeat. All of Canyon Creek's residents seemed to have crowded into the chamber to witness her humiliation. She knew that Council would vote with the mayor. She'd learned that the hard way. He was the driving force behind Council, and she knew where she stood with him. That would explain why Luke and Malcolm hadn't shown up. The two people she'd come to trust didn't want to see her beaten.

If she was leaving in a couple of weeks anyway, maybe sooner if there was no hope of getting the occupancy permit in time, why worry about Luke and Malcolm.

Even friendship obviously had its limits with Luke. She tried to put him out of her mind as she and Harry made their way through the chamber.

Her future, and that of her animal shelter in Monterey and the one she'd been planning for Canyon Creek—everything was in the hands of the mayor, Council and, indirectly, the people of Canyon Creek.

The cacophony fell to a dull hum as she moved through the room. People whispered to each other as she passed them. She felt a cold sweat break out on her forehead. She wanted to avoid all eye contact, but that would make her look like a victim. She'd refused to be a victim at seventeen. She refused to be a victim again today, and she prayed for a better outcome. She kept her spine straight, held her head high and met everyone's stares.

She followed Harry to a couple of reserved seats at the front. Now she could feel the stares burning into her back.

Once they were seated, the mayor thumped his gavel and a hush fell over the chamber.

The time had come.

Hope was certain that this was it. Her two-week contingency wouldn't matter, since the decision announced today would hold. If they wanted her to have the occupancy permit, they would simply have granted it. This would be their version of a public flogging. All her time and effort would have been for nothing.

Harry nudged her. She must've been mumbling as he hushed her and pointed to the mayor, who'd risen and was standing at the lectern.

"We have only one agenda item before us today," he began. "This is an unusual item for Council to be deliberating in the manner that we are. Normally it's a straightforward procedural matter. However, this particular case has generated a great deal of interest and speculation. As such, we've taken the unprecedented step of bringing the occupancy permit application for the new school and community center to a public meeting."

Hope clenched her hands, nails digging into her palms. The prickling sensation on the back of her neck intensified, signaling that more eyes were trained on her than on the mayor. When he paused briefly, she could hear the murmurs but couldn't decipher the comments.

The mayor reminded the assembled crowd of the project's history, its benefits and the economic stimulus it had already created through the construction work.

Listening to what the mayor was saying, taking it at face value, Hope would have thought he supported the project, but he had a peculiar little smirk on his face every time he looked at her. She wished it was over, whichever way it went.

As the mayor continued, his voice became a buzzing in her ears. When he got to Council's decision, she thought she'd misheard. "What did he say?" she asked Harry.

Harry whispered back. "They're granting it! Shh. Shh. Listen! He's not done yet."

"What? *Really?*"

"Yes. Really."

She'd expected to be excited or at least relieved, but she just felt numb.

The mayor focused all his attention on Hope. "So, the purpose of today's proceedings, and the reason it's a bit unorthodox, isn't merely to advise you that we've granted your permit. Perhaps more importantly, it's to thank you for your hard work and to congratulate you on the results. I'd appreciate you joining me up here for this."

Hope looked at Harry with disbelief.

He grinned at her and clasped her elbow none too gently. "Go on! Get up there. Everyone's waiting for you."

She grabbed his hand. "Will you come with me?" she asked in an insistent whisper.

"No." He laughed. "*Absolutely* not. This is for you."

Hope's legs were shaking as she rose. When she reached the podium, turned and glanced around the room, it confirmed that all eyes *were*, in fact, on her.

"Now for the final order of the day, I would like to offer you two things. First, on behalf of myself, my family, our council and let's say the entire town, a heartfelt apology for how we've treated you. We made it hard for you, despite the fact that you were here to do something so important and meaningful for us. But you persisted, and through your perseverance, you presented us with the most important gift this town has received in its entire history."

Hope gaped at him, speechless.

"And in recognition of that, the second thing I would like to give you..." He reached under the lectern and pulled out a rectangular red velvet box. He opened the lid and held it out to her. "It is my great honor to present you with a key to our town. To *your* town."

He'd barely gotten the words out when every person in the chamber rose to clap as the mayor handed Hope not only the permit but the ceremonial key.

Hope was trying to take it all in. She truly had the occupancy permit in her trembling hands. The school and community center could now open. She'd met the condition of her father's will with just two weeks to spare.

As she stepped down from the podium, people came over to shake her hand, congratulate her, thank her. Hope accepted it all with as much dignity as she could muster, then made her way back to Harry.

She stopped abruptly when Luke stepped into her path. His smile nearly melted her heart.

He cradled her cheek in the palm of his hand. "You did it," he whispered softly.

When he took her hand in his, she worried that her legs would finally buckle. With her emotions so much on edge, she knew she was overreacting to his presence and the simple gestures of friendship. But it felt so good to have him there, touching her.

She'd have to accept his friendship for what it was. She'd be saying goodbye to him in a matter of days.

"Congratulations," he added and placed a gentle kiss on her temple, then brushed his lips across hers.

She stared at him, and he continued to smile at her warmly.

"Ah… I still can't believe it. But you weren't here…"

"I'm sorry about that, but I got delayed. You'll understand why very soon." He took her elbow and guided her toward the doorway, where Harry waited.

Luke turned to him. "Can you meet us at the site?"

Harry nodded, and Luke led Hope to his own truck.

"What's going on?" she asked once he was in the driver's seat.

"You'll see."

She wanted to question him, but let it go. "Do you know where Malcolm is?" she asked instead. "He was supposed to be here this morning, in case Council had questions about the construction, but I didn't see him."

Luke smiled as they pulled out of the parking lot. "He's meeting us at the site. Do you want a coffee?"

She shook her head.

"I do. I'm going to grab us a couple of coffees. Then we'll go," he said as he headed for the Tim Hortons at the far end of town.

"But what if we'd needed him?" Hope persisted, as they waited in the surprisingly long line of cars at the drive-through.

Luke reached over and took her hand in his again. "You didn't. We knew you wouldn't." Their conversation was put on hold while Luke accepted his order through the window. He handed Hope a coffee cup and a bag containing a couple of muffins.

"How? Oh..." She finally understood. "You and Malcolm knew we'd get the permit? How long have you known?"

"A week or so."

"Why didn't you *tell* me? I've been a nervous wreck, worrying about it."

He flashed her another heart-stopping grin. "It would've spoiled the surprise," he said as he rounded the curve in the road, approaching the complex.

"What sur—" The question died on her lips

as the building came into view. There were cars parked bumper to bumper along both sides of the road. The ample parking lot was full to capacity, too.

Luke pulled into the drive and stopped his truck just inside the property line. People were gathered at the base of the wide steps leading up to the main entrance. There was a smaller group at the top of the steps—the mayor, a few council members, the school board trustee and the newly hired general manager of the center. She also saw Malcolm, Harry with Einstein and—to Hope's considerable delight and surprise—Aunt Clarissa and Noah. Gathered at the foot of the steps, she recognized many of the people who'd been in the council chamber. She even saw Gillian, with her bright red hair and beaming face. The whole coffee run must have been a ruse to allow people to get from the town hall to the site before she and Luke arrived.

A wide red ribbon with a huge bow was secured to the columns on either side of the landing. There was a table farther back, laden with refreshments. The reporter for the local newspaper was there, with a camera around his neck.

Hope turned to Luke. "What's all this?"

"I'd think it's self-evident." He ran a hand

along her arm. "When Malcolm and I learned that the permit was going through, we decided it was cause for celebration. What better way to celebrate the completion of your project than with a formal ribbon cutting?"

They reached the landing where the members of the ribbon-cutting party were clustered. Clarissa, Noah and Malcolm each embraced her in turn, while the mayor and others shook her hand enthusiastically. Finally, with a muttered "the heck with it," the mayor also took Hope briefly in his arms.

Greetings dispensed with, the mayor stepped up to a microphone just behind the big red bow. While he made some introductory comments, summarizing what he'd already said in council chambers, Hope leaned in to Noah and murmured, "Don't take this the wrong way. I'm thrilled that you're here, but how did you know? How did you get here?"

Noah motioned toward Luke. "Do you really have to ask? He arranged it for me, Clarissa and Gillian. Paid the airfare for Gillian and me and wouldn't take no for an answer. Oddest thing, though. Did you know he thought we were a couple?"

"You and Gillian?"

Noah laughed. "No. *You and me.*"

Hope's shocked eyes met Noah's. "Why would he have thought that?"

"You got me. But when he called to say he figured you'd want me to be here for this, I asked if I could bring Gillian. It threw him. After I explained who Gillian is to me, and assured him that, no, you and I weren't an item and never had been, he laughed for probably ten minutes. Then he thanked me. Profusely."

Hope felt faint and slipped her arm through Noah's to steady herself. She glanced over at Luke. He stood beside Malcolm, a half grin on his face as he listened to the mayor. She felt the now-familiar warmth and excitement that seemed to fill her when she was with Luke. "Huh" was all she said in response.

When Luke turned his head toward her, the look he sent her made Hope's breath catch. She tried to focus on what the mayor was saying, but she had a difficult time concentrating. There was just so much swirling around in her brain, so much emotion churning in her belly.

It was hard to believe everything that was happening. And for Luke to be so considerate as to have Aunt Clarissa and Noah both present—how could she not love him? Her smile wavered. How could she bear to leave him?

And why had Luke assumed that she and Noah were together when she'd never implied anything of the sort? Was it possible that all this time he'd kept his distance from her because he assumed she was seeing Noah?

Noah nudged her gently. "Hey, pay attention. The mayor just called you up to the microphone."

"Oh, gosh. Thanks," she murmured. With mixed emotions, she moved to where the mayor stood, Luke and Malcolm flanking him.

She swallowed hard as she took the final step. She still felt the joy, but as she looked into Luke's amber-colored eyes, his lion eyes, so warm and encouraging, she wanted to cry. Yeah, they'd stay in touch when she returned to California, maybe get together every once in a while, but she wanted so much more with Luke. How was she going to be able to carry on with her life, be happy without him?

Somehow she managed to force those thoughts aside as she faced the crowd. Today was about accomplishment, about a celebration she'd worked hard to deserve. She'd satisfied the condition in her father's will, yes, but it turned out to be so much more than that for her. She'd rediscovered her hometown and all her friends and acquaintances. She'd learned that love could be enduring—for her father and for her. She still loved Luke and always would.

Hope realized, too, that she would forever

think of Canyon Creek as home, in concept if not in reality. And then another thought occurred to her as she scanned the familiar faces, all smiling and encouraging. Maybe, just maybe…it *would* be possible for her to stay. She was starting to establish relationships all over again. Her gaze landed on Suzie, grinning and clapping. Who would've thought Suzie would be her friend?

And now that her inheritance was assured and with Noah's help, she could set up the second Barkley Green animal shelter. Noah could manage the one in Monterey without her now that they could afford to hire staff, and she'd run the new one. Her enthusiasm grew the more she thought about it. She glanced at Luke, holding a large pair of ceremonial scissors.

The only sad part was that her love for Luke was unrequited. He'd given no indication that he felt anything for her but friendship. Would she be able to live with that? He'd helped her immeasurably. Someone had let it slip a few weeks ago—confirmed it, really—that Luke had been responsible for assembling all the volunteers for the evening shift to finish the complex on time. Without that shift, she knew she would've missed her deadline. The rumors that he'd helped her in other ways were probably true, as well.

Yes, Luke had become an exceptional friend, but she'd come to accept that he had no desire to be anything more. The embarrassment of having kissed him, only to be so obviously rejected, still stung. But maybe...could his belief that she'd been seeing Noah have had anything to do with it? No, she was simply rationalizing, because if that was what he thought, why hadn't he just asked? Hope stepped behind the bold red ribbon and accepted the scissors from Luke.

A cheer rose from the crowd and everyone was looking up and behind her. She turned to look, too. She stared at the lettering on the front of the building, which had just been exposed when a large tarp was pulled back. Unbeknownst to her, the facility had been named the Jock Wilson Center. The applause was almost deafening. To think of her father receiving this honor brought tears of joy to her eyes.

She swept her gaze across the people gathered at the bottom of the steps. The whole town must have been there, and they all seemed to be *happy* for her. In addition to Suzie, she could see Travis, Luella, Joe, Ronnie, Miranda, Joanna, Carly and others, all wreathed in smiles.

"And now for the ribbon cutting!" the mayor announced.

With the mayor on one side of her and Luke on the other, she raised the scissors and cut the ribbon right in the middle. Almost in slow motion, blown by the gentle breeze, the two ends of the ribbon unfurled and fluttered to the ground. The applause and cheers reached a crescendo, and the reporter continued to snap photos.

Despite all the noise, Hope heard a clattering as she lowered the scissors. She shot a quick glance at the blades, wondering if she'd somehow broken them, but they seemed to be intact.

Something shiny, what looked like a small cube, had tumbled to the ground, still attached to one end of the ribbon. Flustered, she glanced up at Luke. He was still grinning—a foolish, schoolboy grin—and he gestured toward the little box. A gleam in his eyes compelled her to pick it up.

She bent down to retrieve a small, metallic box and untied it from the red ribbon. Confused, she stepped back with the box in her hand.

Everyone was silent.

"Open it. It's for you," Luke said quietly.

With a final, puzzled look at him, Hope raised the lid of the box.

In the silence, her loud gasp was carried across the crowd and reverberated back at her from the concrete walls.

Nestled inside the small box was a diamond ring. Hope gazed around in bewilderment, fearing someone was playing a cruel joke on her. Then her eyes rested on Luke again.

Luke sank down on one knee in front of Hope. Taking her chilled hand in his warm one, he began, "Hope, you've received thanks today from our mayor and from many of those gathered here. I want to add my own words of appreciation, as well. I echo everything you've already heard, about your dedication, commitment and perseverance in creating something so wonderful for this town. Something that will benefit us all. But my thanks are much more personal. Thank you for showing me again that I could find fulfillment in a relationship." His voice softened. Now he was speaking solely to her. "I love you, Hope. Thank you for bringing love back into my life."

More cheers erupted, but others hushed the noisemakers as it was evident that Luke wasn't finished.

The grin remained on his face. "Hope, you've given so much of yourself to this town already.

I thought you were lost to me, even after we sorted out our…issues. I tried—tried *really hard*—to live with it." Luke looked over at Noah. "How foolishly I longed for you, thinking you belonged to someone else, until Noah set me straight about your relationship with him.

"Would you stay in Canyon Creek? Build a life with me here? Most importantly, would you do me the honor of marrying me? Of spending the rest of your life with me?"

In the silence that ensued, Hope exclaimed, "Yes—oh, yes!"

Luke slipped the ring on her finger. Ignoring all the excitement around them, he swept her into his arms and kissed her.

After giving Luke and Hope a few minutes, the mayor moved up to the microphone again and got everyone's attention. "I have one final duty here today," he announced. "Hope, might I have you come and join me again, please?"

Her head spinning, she flicked a glance at Luke, but he just shrugged. The mayor smiled at her warmly as she approached him. "Although your engagement is a bit of a surprise—to me, anyway—it seems opportune to make what I'm about to give you an early wedding present. Following the tragic fire, Luke mentioned to me your idea for an animal shelter in Canyon Creek. At Luke's urging, I spoke with Mr. Noah Drake a week ago and again last night when we were finalizing the plans for our event today." He nodded at Noah. "Mr. Drake was kind enough to share with me some of the specifics concerning the animal shelter you want to establish. After what you did for so many of us, helping with our livestock and pets affected by the fire, we've witnessed first-hand your dedication and skill. The fire also drove home the need for the type of facility you and Mr. Drake operate in Monterey." Now he grinned at her. "And with your upcoming nuptials, I think it's safe to assume you won't be returning to California. So you'll need something to do here."

Hope looked at Luke. She really *was* going to be able to stay in Canyon Creek. For good! Smiling, Luke bent toward her and whispered in her ear, "I love you."

The mayor turned to one of the other council members, who handed him a large manila envelope with the town's crest stamped on the front. "So...as a wedding gift..." He winked at Luke. "On behalf of Council and the citizens of Canyon Creek, I hereby grant you the deed to a parcel of town land just off Bluebonnet Drive, for the purpose of establishing an animal shelter." With a flourish, the mayor passed her the envelope.

Hope clapped a hand over her mouth. She glanced at Clarissa, then at Noah. They were both applauding, along with everyone else. She gave the mayor a quick, spontaneous hug and whispered her thanks in his ear. She embraced Clarissa and Noah next, tears glistening in her eyes.

Finally, she turned back to Luke and threw her arms around him. He lifted her off her feet again and, to the delight of their audience, spun her around while he kissed her once more. "I love you, Hope, with all my heart, and I've never stopped loving you."

"I..." She couldn't believe all this was happening to her, that she wasn't imagining it. "I love you, too, Luke, and always have."

Holding Luke's hand tightly, Hope thought about the journey that had brought her here, about everything that had been between her and Luke through all the years. The losses and sorrows, the distance and misunderstandings. Yet, through it all, they'd been moving inexorably to this point. There was a reason neither of them had ever had another serious relationship. She thought of her father and knew that everlasting love would have a happier ending for her than it had for him.

People might have scoffed that she and Luke were only kids when they first fell in love, discounting the strength of those feelings. There was no question that what they shared now was stronger, deeper. But that first love *had* endured, through all the twists and turns, through the obstacles and the heartaches, as true love was meant to do.

Luke slipped an arm around her.

In the warmth of his embrace, Hope said a silent thanks to her father for setting her on the final part of this journey. If he hadn't wanted her to make amends on his behalf, she wouldn't have returned to Canyon Creek. Without him, the townspeople wouldn't have learned the truth about her.

And she wouldn't have learned the most precious lesson of all—the truth about love.

* * * * *